INSPECTOR
AND THE SE

Freeman Wills Crofts (1879–1957), the son of an army doctor who died before he was born, was raised in Northern Ireland and became a civil engineer on the railways. His first book, *The Cask*, written in 1919 during a long illness, was published in the summer of 1920, immediately establishing him as a new master of detective fiction. Regularly outselling Agatha Christie, it was with his fifth book that Crofts introduced his iconic Scotland Yard detective, Inspector Joseph French, who would feature in no less than thirty books over the next three decades. He was a founder member of the Detection Club and was elected a Fellow of the Royal Society of Arts in 1939. Continually praised for his ingenious plotting and meticulous attention to detail—including the intricacies of railway timetables—Crofts was once dubbed 'The King of Detective Story Writers' and described by Raymond Chandler as 'the soundest builder of them all'.

Also in this series

Inspector French's Greatest Case
Inspector French and the Cheyne Mystery
Inspector French and the Starvel Hollow Tragedy
Inspector French and the Sea Mystery
Inspector French and the Box Office Murders
Inspector French and Sir John Magill's Last Journey

By the same author

The Cask
The Ponson Case
The Pit-Prop Syndicate
The Groote Park Murder
Six Against the Yard*
The Anatomy of Murder*

*with other Detection Club authors

FREEMAN WILLS CROFTS

Inspector French and the Sea Mystery

COLLINS
CRIME
CLUB

COLLINS CRIME CLUB
An imprint of HarperCollins*Publishers*
1 London Bridge Street
London SE1 9GF
www.harpercollins.co.uk

This paperback edition 2017

First published in Great Britain
by Wm Collins Sons & Co. Ltd 1928

A catalogue record for this book is
available from the British Library

ISBN 978-0-00-819067-5

Set in Sabon Lt Std by Palimpsest Book Production Limited, Falkirk, Stirlingshire

Printed by RR Donnelley at Glasgow, UK

CONTENTS

1

Mr Morgan Meets Tragedy

The Burry Inlet, on the south coast of Wales, looks its best from the sea. At least so thought Mr Morgan, as he sat in the sternsheets of his boat, a fishing line between his fingers, while his son, Evan, pulled lazily over the still water.

In truth the prospect on this pleasant autumn evening would have pleased a man less biased by pride of fatherland than Mr Morgan. The Inlet at full tide forms a wide sheet of water, penetrating in an easterly direction some ten miles into the land, with the county of Carmarthen to the north and the Gower Peninsula to the south. The shores are flat, but rounded hills rise inland which merge to form an undulating horizon of high ground. Here and there along the coast are sand-dunes, whose greys and yellows show up in contrast to the green of the grasslands and the woods beyond.

To the south-east, over by Salthouse Point and Penclawdd, Mr Morgan could see every detail of house and sand-dune, tree and meadow, lit up with a shining radiance, but the north-west hills behind Burry Port were black and solid against a setting sun. Immediately north lay Llanelly, with its dingy coloured buildings, its numberless chimneys, and the masts and funnels of the steamers in its harbour.

It was a perfect evening in late September, the close of a perfect day. Not a cloud appeared in the sky, and scarcely a ripple stirred the surface of the sea. The air was warm and balmy, and all nature seemed drowsing in languorous content. Save for the muffled noise of the Llanelly mills, borne over the water, and the slow, rhythmic creak of the oars, no sound disturbed the sleepy quiet.

Mr Morgan was a small, clean-shaven man in a worn and baggy Norfolk suit, which was the bane of Mrs Morgan's existence, but in which the soul of her lord and master delighted as an emblem of freedom from the servitude of the office. He leaned back in the sternsheets, gazing out dreamily on the broad sweep of the Inlet and the lengthening shadows ashore. At times his eyes and thoughts turned to his son, Evan, the fourteen-year-old boy who was rowing. A good boy, thought Mr Morgan, and big for his age. Though he had been away at school for nearly three years he was still his father's best pal. As Mr Morgan thought of the relations between some of his friends and their sons, he felt a wave of profound thankfulness sweep over him.

Presently the boy stopped rowing.

'Say, Dad, we've not had our usual luck today,' he remarked, glancing disgustedly at the two tiny mackerel which represented their afternoon's sport.

Mr Morgan roused himself.

'No, old man, those aren't much to boast about. And I'm afraid we shall have to go in now. The tide's beginning to run, and I expect we could both do with a bit of supper. Let's change places and you have a go at the lines while I pull in.'

To anyone attempting navigation in the Burry Inlet the tides are a factor of the first importance. With a rise and fall at top springs of something like twenty-five feet, the placid estuary of high water becomes a little later a place of fierce currents and swirling eddies. The Inlet is shallow also. At low tide by far the greater portion of its area is uncovered, and this, by confining the rushing waters to narrow channels, still further increases their speed. As the tide falls the great Llanrhidian Sands appear, stretching out northwards from the Gower Peninsula, while an estuary nearly four miles wide contracts to a river racing between mud banks five hundred yards apart.

Mr Morgan took the paddles, and heading the boat for the northern coast, began to pull slowly shorewards. He was the manager of a large tinplate works at Burry Port and lived on the outskirts of the little town. Usually a hard worker, he had taken advantage of a slack afternoon to make a last fishing excursion with his son before the latter's return to school. The two had left Burry Port on a flowing tide and had drifted up the Inlet to above Llanelly. Now the tide was ebbing, and they were being carried swiftly down again. Mr Morgan reckoned that by the time they were opposite Burry Port they should be far enough inshore to make the harbour.

Gradually the long line of the Llanelly houses and chimneys slipped by. Evan had clambered aft and at intervals he felt with the hand of an expert the weighted lines which were trailing astern. He frowned as he glanced again at the two mackerel. He had had a good many fishing trips with his father during the holidays and never before had they had such a miserable catch. How he wished he could have a couple of good bites before they had to give up!

The thought had scarcely passed through his mind when the line he was holding tightened suddenly and began to run out through his fingers. At the same moment the next line, which was made fast round the after thwart, also grew taut, strained for a second, then with a jerk slackened and lay dead. Evan leaped to his feet and screamed out in excitement:

'Hold, Daddy, hold! Backwater, quick! I've got something big!'

The line continued to run out until Mr Morgan, by rowing against the tide, brought the boat relatively to a standstill. Then the line stopped as if anchored to something below, twitching indeed from the current, but not giving the thrilling chucks and snatches for which the boy was hoping.

'Oh, blow!' he cried disgustedly. 'It's not a fish. We've got a stone or some seaweed. See, this one caught it too.'

He dropped the line he was holding and pulled in the other. Its hooks were missing.

'See,' he repeated. 'What did I tell you? We shall probably lose the hooks of this one too. It's caught fast.'

'Steady, old man. Take the oars and let me feel it.'

Mr Morgan moved into the stern and pulled the resisting line, but without effect.

'Rather curious, this,' he said. 'All this stretch is sand. I once saw it uncovered at very low springs. Keep rowing till I feel round the thing with the grappling, and see if I can find out what it is.'

Evan passed the small three-pronged anchor aft and his father let it down beside the line. Soon it touched bottom.

'About three and a half fathoms: say twenty feet,' Mr Morgan remarked. 'Keep her steady while I feel about.'

He raised the grappling and, moving it a few inches to one

side, lowered it again. Four times it went down to the same depth; on the fifth trial it stopped three feet short.

'By Jove!' he exclaimed, 'there's something there right enough.' He danced the grappling up and down. 'And it's certainly not seaweed. Treasure trove, Evan, eh?'

'Try round a bit and see how big it is,' Evan suggested, now thoroughly interested.

Mr Morgan 'tried round.' Had he been by himself he would have dismissed the incident with a muttered imprecation at the loss of his hooks. But for the sake of the boy he wished to make it as much of an adventure as possible.

'Curious,' he therefore commented again. 'I'm afraid we shall not be able to save our hooks. But let's take bearings so that we may be able to ask about it ashore.' He looked round. 'See, there's a good nor'-west bearing: that signal post on the railway is just in line with the west gable of the large white house on the hill. See it? Now for a cross bearing. Suppose we take that tall mill chimney; the tallest of that bunch. It's just in line with the pier head beacon. What about those?'

'Fine, I think. What can the thing be, dad?'

'I don't know. Perhaps something drifted in from a wreck. We'll ask Coastguard Manners. Now I'll pull in the grappling and then the line, and if the hooks go I can't help it.'

The little anchor had been lying on the bottom while they talked. Mr Morgan now seized the rope and began to pull. But he had not drawn in more than two feet when it tightened and remained immovable.

'By Jove, the grappling's caught now,' he exclaimed. 'A nuisance, that. We don't want to lose our grappling.'

'Let's pull up. Perhaps it will come clear.'

Evan put down the oars and joined his father in the stern.

Both pulled steadily with all their strength. For a time nothing happened, then suddenly the rope began to yield. It did not come away clear, but gave slowly, as if the object to which it was attached was lifting also.

'By Jove!' Mr Morgan exclaimed again. 'We shall get our hooks after all. The whole thing's coming up.'

Slowly the rope came in foot by foot. The object, whatever it was, was heavy, and it was all they could do to raise it. Mr Morgan pulled in sudden heaves, while Evan took a turn with the line round a thwart, so as to hold the weight while his father rested.

At last the end of the rope was reached and the shank of the grappling appeared. Then dimly beneath the surface Mr Morgan was able to see the object hooked. It was a large wooden packing case or crate.

Round the sides were cross pieces, holding the sheeting boards in place. Two of the sharp flukes of the grappling had caught beneath one of these, and, of course, the greater the pull on them, the more firmly they became fixed.

To raise the crate while submerged and displacing its own volume of water had been just possible. To lift it aboard was out of the question. For a time the two considered the problem of getting it ashore, then Mr Morgan said:

'I'll tell you what we'll do. We'll make the rope fast and row in with the crate hanging to our stern. Then we'll beach it on the lifeboat slip and when the tide falls it will be left high and dry. We can examine it then and get our hooks.'

Evan approving of the plan, they proceeded to carry it out. They made the rope fast round the after thwart, then taking the oars, pulled slowly in shore. As they drew nearer the current lessened, until off Burry Port they were in almost still water. Slowly they glided past a line of sandhills which

6

presently gave place first to houses and works and then to a great deposit of copper slag like a stream of lava which had overflowed into the sea. Finally rounding the east mole, they entered Burry Port harbour.

Having manœuvred the boat over the lifeboat slip, they cast off the rope and the crate settled down in five feet of water. Then with a bight of the rope, they made the boat fast.

'Now for that supper,' Mr Morgan suggested. 'By the time we've had it our treasure trove will be high and dry, and we can come down and see what it is.'

An hour later father and son were retracing their steps to the harbour. Mr Morgan looked business-like with a hammer, a cold chisel, and a large electric torch. It was still a lovely evening, but in a few minutes it would be dark.

As Mr Morgan had foretold, the crate was high and dry, and they examined it with interest in the light of the torch. It was a strongly made wooden box about three feet by two by two. All round at top and bottom were strengthening cross pieces, and it was beneath the upper of these that the two flukes of the grappling had caught.

'Well and truly hooked,' Mr Morgan remarked. 'We must have drifted across the thing, and when we pulled up the grappling it slid up the side till it caught the cross piece. It's a good job for us, for now we shall get our grappling and our hooks as well.'

Evan fidgeted impatiently.

'Don't mind about them, Dad; we can unfasten them later. Open the box. I want to see what's in it.'

Mr Morgan put his cold chisel to the joint of the lid and began to hammer.

'Strictly speaking, we shouldn't do this,' he declared as he

7

worked. 'We should have handed the thing over to Manners. It's a job for the coastguards. However, here goes!'

The crate was strongly made, and though Mr Morgan was a good amateur carpenter, it took him several minutes to open it. But at last one of the top boards was prized up. Instantly both became conscious of a heavy, nauseating smell.

'A case of South American meat or something gone west,' Mr Morgan commented. 'I don't know that I'm so keen on going on with this job. Perhaps we can see what it is without opening it up further.'

Holding his breath, he put his eye to the slit and shone in a beam from the electric torch. Then with a sharp intaking of the breath, he rose.

'It's a disgusting smell,' he said in rather shaky tones. 'Let's go round and ask Manners to finish the job.'

'Let me look in, Dad.'

'Right, old man. But come round with me first to see Manners.'

With some difficulty Mr Morgan drew his son away. He was feeling sick and shaken. For beneath that well-fitting lid and sticking up out of the water which still remained in the crate, was a gruesome and terrible object—the bent head and crouching body of a man dressed in under clothes only and in an advanced state of decomposition!

It was all Mr Morgan could do to crush down the horror which possessed him and to pretend to the boy that nothing was amiss. Evan must not be allowed to see that ghastly sight! It would haunt his young mind for weeks. Mr Morgan led the way round the harbour, across the dock gates and towards the road leading to the town.

'But aren't we going to Manners?' Evan queried, hanging back.

'Not tonight, if you don't mind, old chap. That smell has made me rather sick. We can go down in the morning. The tide should be right after breakfast.'

Evan demurred, suggesting that he alone should interview the coastguard. But he was what Mr Morgan called 'biddable,' and when his father showed that he was in earnest he allowed the subject to drop.

In due course they reached home. Discreet suggestion having resulted in Evan's settling down with his meccano, Mr Morgan felt himself at liberty. He explained casually that he wanted to drop into the club for an hour, and left the house. In ten minutes he was at the police station.

'I've made a discovery this evening, sergeant, which, I'm afraid, points to something pretty seriously wrong,' he explained, and he told the officer in charge about the hooking of the crate. 'I didn't want my son to see the body—he's rather young for that sort of thing—so we went home without my saying anything about it. But I've come back now to report to you. I suppose you, and not Manners, will deal with it?'

Sergeant Nield bore a good reputation in Burry Port as an efficient and obliging officer, as well as a man of some reading and culture. He listened to Mr Morgan's recital with close attention and quietly took charge.

'Manners would deal with it at first, Mr Morgan,' he answered, 'but he would hand over to us when he saw what the object was. I think we'll call for him on the way down, and that will put the thing in order. Can you come down now, sir?'

'Certainly, that's what I intended.'

'Then we'll get away at once. Just let me get my bicycle lamp.' He turned to a constable. 'Williams, you and Smith get another light and take the handcart down to the lifeboat slip. Watson, take charge in my absence. Now, Mr Morgan, if you are ready.'

It was quite dark as the two men turned towards the harbour. Later there would be a quarter moon, but it had not yet risen. The night was calm and fine, but a little sharpness was creeping into the air. Except for the occasional rush of a motor passing on the road and sounds of shunting from the docks, everything was very still.

'Just where did you say you found the crate, Mr Morgan?' the sergeant asked.

'Off Llanelly; off the sea end of the breakwater and on the far side of the channel.'

'The Gower side? Far from the channel?'

'The Gower side, yes. But not far from the channel; I should say just on the very edge.'

'You didn't mark the place?'

'Not with a buoy. I hadn't one, and if I had I should not have thought it worthwhile. But I took bearings. I could find the place within a few feet.'

'I suppose you've no idea as to how the crate might have got there?'

'Not the slightest. I have been wondering that ever since I learned what was in it. What do you think?'

'I don't know, sir, unless it has been dropped off a steamer or been washed into the Inlet from some wreck. We'll get it to the station and examine it, and maybe we shall find where it came from. If you wait here a second I'll get hold of Manners.'

They had reached the coastguard's house, and the sergeant ran up to the door. In a few seconds he returned with a stout, elderly man who gave Mr Morgan a civil good evening.

'It's your job, of course, Tom,' the sergeant was saying, 'but it'll be ours so soon that we may as well go down together. Perhaps, sir, you'll tell Manners about how you found the crate and brought it in?'

By the time Mr Morgan had finished his story for the second time they had reached the boatslip. The sergeant and Manners peeped into the crate in turn.

'Yes, sir, it's just what you said,' the former remarked. 'It's a man by the look of him and he's been dead some time. I think we'll have the whole affair up to the station before we open any more at it. What do you say, Tom?'

'Right you are, sergeant, I'll go with you. I shall 'ave to put in a report about the thing, but I can get my information at the station as well as 'ere. You'll be coming along, Mr Morgan?'

'If you please, sir,' the sergeant interjected, 'I have to get a statement from you too.'

'Of course I'll go,' Mr Morgan assured them. 'I'll see the thing through now.'

The constables having arrived with the handcart, it was wheeled down the slip, and all five men got round the crate and with some difficulty lifted it on.

'By Jove!' Mr Morgan exclaimed. 'That's some weight. Surely there must be something more than a body in it?'

'It's certainly heavy, but it's a very solid crate. We shall see when we get it to the station.'

With a good deal of pushing and shoving the handcart was got up the slip and the little party moved off along the mole and across the sidings to the town. On reaching the police station the crate was wheeled into a small courtyard in the rear and Nield invited the others into his office.

'On second thoughts, Mr Morgan,' he explained, 'I'll not

11

unpack the crate until I have reported to the superintendent and get hold of a doctor. Meantime, sir, I'd be glad to get your statement in writing.'

For the third time Mr Morgan told his story. The sergeant took it down, read over what he had written, and got the other to sign it.

'That will do, sir, for tonight. You will, of course, be required at the inquest tomorrow or next day.'

'I'll be there all right.'

'Then about your son, sir? Has he anything to say that might be of use?'

Mr Morgan looked distressed.

'Nothing, sergeant, more than I can tell you myself. I hope you won't have to call the boy. He's going back to school tomorrow.'

'That's all right: he'll not be wanted. And now, sir, I shouldn't say more about the affair than you can help. Just keep the discovery of the body quiet and content yourself with the story of finding the crate.'

Mr Morgan promised, and the sergeant wished him goodnight.

His visitor gone, Sergeant Nield handed a carbon of the statement to Manners, promising to let him know how the affair progressed. The coastguard being got rid of in his turn, Nield telephoned the news to Superintendent Griffiths at Llanelly. The superintendent was suitably impressed and in his turn rang up Major Lloyd, the chief constable at Llandilo. Finally the latter gave instructions for Nield to arrange a meeting at the police station for nine o'clock on the following morning. Both the superintendent and the chief constable would motor over, and the local police doctor was to be in attendance. The body would then be removed from the crate and the necessary examination made. Meanwhile nothing was to be touched.

Glad to be relieved from the sole responsibility, the sergeant made his arrangements, and at the hour named a little group entered the courtyard of the police station. In addition to the chief constable and superintendent, the sergeant and two of the latter's men, there were present two doctors—Dr Crowth, the local police surgeon, and Dr Wilbraham, a friend of Major Lloyd's, whom the latter had brought with him.

After some preliminary remarks the terrible business of getting the remains from the crate was undertaken. Such work would have been distressing at all times, but in the present case two facts made it almost unbearable. In the first place the man had been dead for a considerable time, estimated by the doctors as from five to six weeks, and in the second his face had been appallingly maltreated. Indeed it might be said to be non-existent, so brutally had it been battered in. All the features were destroyed and only an awful pulp remained.

However, the work had to be done, and presently the body was lying on a table which had been placed for the purpose in an outhouse. It was dressed in underclothes only—shirt, vest, drawers, and socks. The suit, collar, tie, and shoes had been removed. An examination showed that none of the garments bore initials.

Nor were there any helpful marks on the crate. There were tacks where a label had been attached, but the label had been torn off. A round steel bar of three or four stones weight had also been put in, evidently to ensure the crate sinking.

The most careful examination revealed no clue to the man's identity. Who he was and why he had been murdered were as insoluble problems as how the crate came to be where it was found.

For over an hour the little party discussed the matter, and then the chief constable came to a decision.

'I don't believe it's a local case,' he announced. 'That crate must in some way have come from a ship: I don't see how it could have been got there from the shore. And if it's not a local case I think we'll consider it not our business. We'll call in Scotland Yard. Let them have the trouble of it. I'll ring up the Home Office now and we'll have a man here this evening. Tomorrow will be time enough for the inquest and the C.I.D. man will be here and can ask what questions he likes.'

Thus it came to pass that Inspector Joseph French on that same afternoon travelled westwards by the 1.55 p.m. luncheon car express from Paddington.

2

Inspector French Gets Busy

Dusk was already falling when a short, rather stout man with keen blue eyes from which a twinkle never seemed far removed, alighted from the London train at Burry Port and made his way to Sergeant Nield, who was standing near the exit, scrutinising the departing travellers.

'My name is French,' the stranger announced: 'Inspector French of the C.I.D. I think you are expecting me?'

'That's right, sir. We had a 'phone from headquarters that you were coming on this train. We've been having trouble, as you've heard.'

'I don't often take a trip like this without finding trouble at the end of it. We're like yourself, sergeant; we have to go out to look for it. But we don't often have to look for it in such fine country as this. I've enjoyed my journey.'

'The country's right enough if you're fond of coal,' Nield rejoined with some bitterness. 'But now, Mr French, what would you like to do? I expect you'd rather get fixed up at an hotel and have some dinner before anything else? I think the Bush Arms is the most comfortable.'

'I had tea a little while ago. If it's the same to you, sergeant, I'd rather see what I can before the light goes. I'll give my bag to the porter, and he can fix me up a room. Then I hope you'll come back and dine with me and we can have a talk over our common trouble.'

The sergeant accepted with alacrity. He had felt somewhat aggrieved at the calling in of a stranger from London, believing it to be a reflection on his own ability to handle the case. But this cheery, good-humoured-looking man was very different from the type of person he was expecting. This inspector did not at all appear to have come down to put the local men in their places and show them what fools they were. Rather he seemed to consider Nield an honoured colleague in a difficult job.

But though the sergeant did not know it, this was French's way. He was an enthusiastic believer in the theory that with ninety-nine persons out of a hundred you can lead better than you can drive. He therefore made it an essential of his method to be pleasant and friendly to those with whom he came in contact, and many a time he had found that it had brought the very hint that he required from persons who at first had given him only glum looks and tight lips.

'I should like to see the body and the crate, and if possible have a walk round the place,' French went on. 'Then I shall understand more clearly what you have to tell me. Is the inquest over?'

'No, it is fixed for eleven o'clock tomorrow. The chief constable thought you would like to be present.'

'Very kind of him: I should. I gathered that the man had been dead for some time?'

'Between five and six weeks, the doctors said. Two doctors saw the body, our local man, Dr Crowth, and a friend of the chief constable's, Dr Wilbraham. They were agreed about the time.'

'Did they say the cause of death?'

'No, they didn't, but there can't be much doubt about that. The whole face and head is battered in. It's not a nice sight, I can tell you.'

'I don't expect so. Your report said that the crate was found by a fisherman?'

'An amateur fisherman, yes,' and Nield repeated Mr Morgan's story.

'That's just the lucky way things happen, isn't it!' French exclaimed. 'A man commits a crime and he takes all kinds of precautions to hide it, and then some utterly unexpected coincidence happens—who could have foreseen a fisherman hooking the crate—and he is down and out. Lucky for us and for society too. But I've seen it again and again. I've seen things happen that a writer couldn't put into a book, because nobody would believe them possible, and I'm sure so have you. There's nothing in this world stranger than the truth.'

The sergeant agreed, but without enthusiasm. In his experience it was the ordinary and obvious thing that happened. He didn't believe in coincidences. After all it wasn't such a coincidence that a fisherman who lowered a line on the site of the crate should catch his hooks in it. The crate was in the area over which this man fished. There was nothing wonderful about it.

But a further discussion of the point was prevented by their arrival at the police station. They passed to the out-house containing the body, and French forthwith began his examination.

The remains were those of a man slightly over medium

height, of fairly strong build, and who had seemingly been in good health before death. The face had been terribly mishandled. It was battered in until the features were entirely obliterated. The ears even were torn and bruised and shapeless. The skull was evidently broken at the forehead, so, as the sergeant had said, there was here an injury amply sufficient to account for death. It was evident also that a post-mortem had been made. Altogether French had seldom seen so horrible a spectacle.

But his professional instincts were gratified by a discovery which he hoped might assist in the identification of the remains. On the back of the left arm near the shoulder was a small birthmark of a distinctive triangular shape. Of this he made a dimensioned sketch, having first carefully examined it and assured himself it was genuine.

But beyond these general observations he did not spend much time over the body. Having noted that the fingers were too much decomposed to enable prints to be taken, he turned his attention to the clothes, believing that all the further available information as to the remains would be contained in the medical report.

Minutely he examined the underclothes, noting their size and quality and pattern, searching for laundry marks or initials, or for mendings or darns. But except that the toe of the left sock had been darned with wool of too light a shade, there was nothing to distinguish the garments from others of the same kind. Though he did not expect to get help from the clothes, French in his systematic way entered a detailed description of them in his note-book. Then he turned to the crate.

It measured two feet three inches by two feet four, and was three feet long. Made of spruce an inch thick, it was strongly put together and clamped with iron corner pieces. The boards were tongued and grooved, and French thought that under ordinary conditions it should be water-tight. He examined its whole surface, but here again he had no luck. Though there were a few bloodstains inside, no label or brand or identifying mark showed anywhere. Moreover, there was nothing in its shape or size to call for comment. The murderer might have obtained it from a hundred sources, and French did not see any way in which it could be traced.

That it had been labelled at one time was evident. The heads of eight tacks formed a parallelogram which clearly represented the position of a card. It also appeared to have borne attachments of some heavier type, as there were seven nail-holes of about an eighth of an inch in diameter at each of two opposite corners. Whatever these fittings were they had been removed and the nails withdrawn.

'How long would you say this had been in the water?' French asked, running his fingers over the sodden wood.

'I asked Manners, our coastguard, that question,' the sergeant answered. 'He said not very long. You see, there are no shells nor seaweed attaching to it. He thought about the time the doctors mentioned, say between five and six weeks.'

The bar was a bit of old two-inch shafting, some fourteen inches long, and was much rusted from its immersion. It had evidently been put in as a weight to ensure the sinking of the crate. Unfortunately it offered no better clue to the sender than the crate itself.

French added these points to his notes and again addressed the sergeant.

'Have you a good photographer in the town?'

'Why, yes, pretty good.'

'Then I wish you'd send for him. I want some photographs

of the body, and they had better be done first thing in the morning.'

When the photographer had arrived and had received his instructions French went on: 'That, sergeant, seems to be all we can do now. It's too dark to walk round tonight. Suppose we get along to the hotel and see about that dinner?'

During a leisurely meal in the private room French had engaged they conversed on general topics, but later, over a couple of cigars, they resumed their discussion of the tragedy. The sergeant repeated in detail all that he knew of the matter, but he was able neither to suggest clues upon which to work, nor yet to form a theory as to what had really happened.

'It's only just nine o'clock,' French said, when the subject showed signs of exhaustion. 'I think I'll go round and have a word with this Mr Morgan, and then perhaps we could see the doctor—Crowth, you said his name was? Will you come along?'

Mr Morgan, evidently thrilled by his visitor's identity, repeated his story still another time. French had brought from London a large scale Ordnance map of the district, and on it he got Mr Morgan to mark the bearings he had taken, and so located the place the crate had lain. This was all the fresh information French could obtain, and soon he and Nield wished the manager goodnight and went on to the doctor's.

Dr Crowth was a bluff, middle-aged man with a hearty manner and a kindly expression. He was off-hand in his greeting, and plunged at once into his subject.

'Yes,' he said in answer to French's question, 'we held a post-mortem, Dr Wilbraham and I, and we found the cause of death. Those injuries to the face and forehead were all inflicted after death. They were sufficient to cause death, but they did not do so. The cause of death was a heavy blow on the back of the head with some soft, yielding instrument. The skull was fractured, but the skin, though contused, was unbroken. Something like a sandbag was probably used. The man was struck first and killed, and then his features were destroyed, with some heavy implement such as a hammer.'

'That's suggestive, isn't it?' French commented.

'You mean that the features were obliterated after death to conceal the man's identity?'

'No, I didn't mean that, though of course it is true. What I meant was that the man was murdered in some place where blood would have been noticed, had it fallen. He was killed, not with a sharp-edged instrument, though one was available, but with a blunt one, lest bleeding should have ensued. Then when death had occurred the sharp-edged instrument was used and the face disfigured. I am right about the bleeding, am I not?'

'Oh, yes. A dead body does not bleed, or at least not much. But I do not say that you could inflict all those injuries without leaving some bloodstains.'

'No doubt, but still I think my deduction holds. There were traces of blood in the crate, but only slight. What age was the man, do you think, doctor?'

'Impossible to say exactly, but probably middle-aged: thirty-five to fifty-five.'

'Any physical peculiarities?'

'I had better show you my report. It will give you all I know. In fact, you can keep this copy.'

French ran his eyes over the document, noting the points which might be valuable. The body was that of a middle-aged man five feet ten inches high, fairly broad and well built, and weighing thirteen stone. The injuries to the head and

21

face, were such that recognition from the features would be impossible. There was only one physical peculiarity which might assist identification, a small triangular birthmark on the back of the left arm.

The report then gave technical details of the injuries and the condition the body was in when found, with the conclusion that death had probably occurred some thirty-five to forty days earlier. French smiled ruefully when he had finished reading.

'There's not overmuch to go on, is there?' he remarked. 'I suppose nothing further is likely to come out at the inquest?'

'Unless someone that we don't know of comes forward with information, nothing,' the sergeant answered. 'We have made all the inquiries, that we could think of.'

'As far as I am concerned,' Dr Crowth declared, 'I don't see that you have anything to go on at all. I shouldn't care for your job, Inspector. How on earth will you start trying to clear up this puzzle? To me it seems absolutely insoluble.'

'Cases do seem so at first,' French returned, 'but it's wonderful how light gradually comes. It is almost impossible to commit a murder without leaving a clue, and if you think it over long enough you usually get it. But this, I admit, is a pretty tough proposition.'

'Have you ever heard of anything like it before?'

'So far it rather reminds me of a case investigated several years ago by my old friend Inspector Burnley—he's retired now. A cask was sent from France to London which was found to contain the body of a young married Frenchwoman, and it turned out that her unfaithful husband had murdered her. He had in his study at the time a cask in which a group of statuary which he had just purchased had arrived, and he disposed of the body by packing it in the cask and sending it to England. It might well be that the same thing had happened in this case: that the murderer had purchased something which had arrived in this crate and that he had used the latter to get rid of the body. And, as you can see, doctor, that at once suggests a line of inquiry. What firm uses crates of this kind to despatch their goods and to whom were such crates sent recently? This is the sort of inquiry which gets us our results.'

'That is very interesting. All the same, I'm glad it's your job and not mine. I remember reading of that case you mention. The papers were absolutely full of it at the time. I thought it an extraordinary affair, almost like a novel.'

'No doubt, but there is this difference between a novel and real life. In a novel the episodes are selected and the reader is told those which are interesting and which get results. In real life we try perhaps ten or twenty lines which lead nowhere before we strike the lucky one. And in each line we make perhaps hundreds of inquiries, whereas the novel describes one. It's like any other job, you get results by pegging away. But it is interesting on the whole, and it has its compensations. Well, doctor, I mustn't keep you talking all night. I shall see you at the inquest tomorrow.'

French's gloomy prognostications were justified next day when the proceedings in the little courthouse came to an end. Nothing that was not already known came out, and the coroner adjourned the inquiry for three weeks to enable the police to conclude their investigations.

What those investigations were to consist of was the problem which confronted French when after lunch he sat down in the deserted smoking-room of the little hotel to think matters out.

In the first place there was the body. What lines of inquiry did the body suggest?

One obviously. Some five or six weeks previously a fairly tall, well-built man of middle-age had disappeared. He might merely have vanished without explanation, or more probably, circumstances had been arranged to account for his absence. In the first case information should be easily obtainable. But the second alternative was a different proposition. If the disappearance had been cleverly screened it might prove exceedingly difficult to locate. At all events, inquiries on the matter must represent the first step.

It was clearly impossible to trace any of the clothes, with the possible exception of the sock. But even from the sock French did not think he would learn anything. It was of a standard pattern, and the darning of socks with wool of not quite the right shade was too common to be remembered. At the same time he noted it as a possible line of research.

Next he turned his attention to the crate, and at once two points struck him.

Could he trace the firm who had made the crate? Of this he was doubtful: it was not sufficiently distinctive. There must be thousands of similar packing cases in existence, and to check up all of them would be out of the question. Besides, it might not have been supplied by a firm. The murderer might have had it specially made, or even have made it himself. Here again, however, French could but try.

The second point was: How had the crate got to the bottom of the Burry Inlet? This was a question that he must solve, and he turned all his energies towards it.

There were here two possibilities. Either the crate had been thrown into the water and had sunk at the place where it was found, or it had gone in elsewhere and been driven forward by the action of the sea. He considered these ideas in turn.

To have sunk at the place it was thrown in postulated a ship or boat passing over the site. From the map, steamers approaching or leaving Llanelly must go close to the place, and might cross it. But French saw that there were grave difficulties in the theory that the crate had been dropped overboard from a steamer. It was evident that the whole object of the crate was to dispose of the body secretly. The crate, however, could not have been secretly thrown from a steamer. Whether it were let go by hand or by a winch, several men would know about it. Indeed news of so unusual an operation would almost certainly spread to the whole crew, and if the crate were afterwards found, someone of the hands would be sure to give the thing away. Further, if the crate were being got rid of from a steamer it would have been done far out in deep water and not at the entrance to a port.

For these reasons French thought that the ship might be ruled out, and he turned his attention to the idea of a row-boat.

But here a similar objection presented itself. The crate was too big and heavy to be dropped from a small boat. French tried to visualise the operation. The crate could only be placed across the stern: in any other position it would capsize the boat. Then it would have to be pushed off. This could not be done by one man: he doubted whether it could be done by two. But even if it could, these two added to the weight of the crate would certainly cause disaster. He did not believe the operation possible without a large boat and at least three men, and he felt sure the secret would not have been entrusted to so many.

It seemed to him then that the crate could not have been thrown in where it was found. How else could it have got there?

He thought of Mr Morgan's suggestion of a wreck from which it might have been washed up into the Inlet, but according to the sergeant, there had been no wreck. Besides, the crate was undamaged outside, and it was impossible that it could have been torn out through the broken side of a ship or washed overboard without leaving some traces.

French lit a fresh pipe and began to pace the deserted smoking room. He was exasperated because he saw that his reasoning must be faulty. All that he had done was to prove that the crate could not have reached the place where it was found.

For some minutes he couldn't see the snag, then it occurred to him that he had been assuming too much. He had taken it for granted that the crate had sunk immediately on falling into the water. The weights of the crate itself, the body, and the bar of steel had made him think so. But was he correct? Would the air the crate contained not give it buoyancy for a time, until at least some water had leaked in?

If so, the fact would have a considerable bearing on his problem. If the crate had been floated to the place he was halfway to a solution.

Suddenly the possible significance of the fourteen holes occurred to him. He had supposed they were nail-holes, but now he began to think differently. Suppose they were placed there to admit the water—slowly, so that the crate should float for a time and then sink? Their position was suggestive; they were at diagonally opposite corners of the crate. That meant that at least one set must be under water, no matter in what position the crate was floating. It also meant that the other set provided a vent for the escape of the displaced air.

The more French thought over the idea, the more probable it seemed. The crate had been thrown into the sea, most likely from the shore and when the tide was ebbing, and it had floated out into the Inlet. By the time it had reached the position in which it was found, enough water had leaked in to sink it.

He wondered if any confirmatory evidence of the theory were available. Then an idea struck him, and walking to the police station, he asked for Sergeant Nield.

'I want you, sergeant, to give me a bit of help,' he began. 'First, I want the weights of the crate and the bar of iron. Can you get them for me?'

'Certainly. We've nothing here that would weigh them, but I'll send them to the railway station. You'll have the weights in half an hour.'

'Good man! Now there is one other thing. Can you borrow a Molesworth for me?'

'A Molesworth?'

'A *Molesworth's Pocket Book of Engineering Formulæ*. You'll get it from any engineer or architect.'

'Yes, I think I can manage that. Anything else?'

'No, sergeant, that's all, except that before you send away the crate I want to measure those nail holes.'

French took a pencil from his pocket and sharpened it to a long thin evenly rounded point. This he pushed into the nail holes, marking how far it went in. Then with a pocket rule he measured the diameter of the pencil, the length of the sharpened portion, and the distance the latter had entered. From these dimensions a simple calculation told him that the holes were all slightly under one-sixth of an inch in diameter.

The sergeant was an energetic man, and before the half hour was up he had produced the required weights and the engineer's pocket book. French, returning to the hotel, sat down with the Molesworth and a few sheets of paper, and began with some misgivings to bury himself in engineering calculations.

First he added the weights of the crate, the body and the steel bar: they came to 29 stone or 406 lbs. Then he found that the volume of the crate was just a trifle over 15 cubic feet. This latter multiplied by the weight of a cubic foot of sea-water—64 lbs.—gave a total of 985 lbs. as the weight of water the crate would displace if completely submerged. But if the weight of the crate was 406 lbs., and the weight of the water it displaced was 985 lbs., it followed that not only would it float, but it would float with a very considerable buoyancy, represented by the difference between these two, or 579 lbs. The first part of his theory was therefore tenable.

But the moment the crate was thrown into the sea, water would begin to run in through the lower holes. French wondered if he could calculate how long it would take to sink.

He was himself rather out of his depth among the unfamiliar figures and formulæ given on the subject. The problem was, how long would it take 579 lbs. of water to run through seven one-sixth inch holes? This, he found, depended on the head, which he could only guess at approximately one foot. He worked for a considerable time, and at last came to the conclusion that it would take slightly over an hour. But that his calculations were correct he would not like to have sworn.

At all events these results were extremely promising, and gave him at least a tentative working theory.

But if the crate had floated from the coast to where it was found, the question immediately arose: At what point had it been thrown in?

Here was a question which could only be answered with the help of local knowledge. French thought that a discussion with the coastguard might suggest ideas. Accordingly he left the hotel and turned towards the harbour with the intention of looking up Manners.

3

Experimental Detection

Tom Manners was hoeing in his little garden when French hailed him. He was not a native, but the course of a long career had led him from Shoreditch, via the Royal Navy, to Burry Port. In person he was small, stout, and elderly, but his movements were still alert and his eyes shone with intelligence.

'I want to have another chat with you about this affair,' said French, who had already heard the other's statement. 'Just walk down to the end of the pier with me while we talk.'

They strolled down past the stumpy lighthouse to where they could get a view of the Inlet.

Again it was a perfect afternoon. The sun, pouring down through a slight haze, put as much warmth as was possible into the somewhat drab colours of the landscape, the steel of the water, the varying browns of the mud and sand, the dingy greys and slate of the town, the greens of the grass and trees on the hills beyond. Some four miles away to the right was the long line of Llanelly, with its chimneys sticking up irregularly like the teeth of a rather badly damaged comb. Fifty-three chimneys, French counted, and he was sure he had not seen anything like all the town contained. Beyond Llanelly the coastline showed as a blur in the haze, but opposite, across the Inlet, lay the great yellow stretch of the Llanrhidian Sands, rising through grey-green dunes to the high ground of the Gower Peninsula.

'Let us sit down,' French suggested, when he had assimilated the view. 'I have come to the conclusion that the crate must have been thrown into the sea at some point along the shore and floated out to where it was found. It would float, I estimate, for about an hour, when enough water would have got in to sink it. Now what I want to know is, where, along the coast, might the crate have been thrown in, so as to reach in an hour the place at which it was found?'

Manners nodded, but did not reply. French unrolled his map and went on: 'Here is a map of the district, and this is the point at which the crate was found. Let us take the places in turn. If it had been thrown in here at Burry Port, would it have got there in time?'

'It ain't just so easy to say,' Manners declared slowly. 'It might, if the tide was flowing, and then again it mightn't. It might 'ave started 'ere or from Pembrey—that's 'alf a mile over there to the west.'

This was not encouraging, but French tried again.

'Very well,' he said. 'Now what about Llanelly?'

Llanelly, it appeared, was also a doubtful proposition.

'It's like this 'ere, Mr French,' Manners explained. 'It's all according to 'ow the tide 'appens to be running. If the tide was flowing and that there crate was dropped in at Llanelly, it would go farther up the Inlet than wot you show on the

31

chart. An' if the tide was ebbing it would go farther down. But if the tide was on the turn it might go up or down and then come back to the place. You see wot I mean?'

French saw it and he sighed as he saw also that it meant that there was practically no part of the adjacent shores from which the crate might not have come. Then it occurred to him that both his question and Manners' reply had been based on a misconception.

The murderer's object was to get rid of the crate. Would he, therefore, choose a rising or half tide which might drift it back inshore? Surely not; he would select one which would take it as far as possible out to sea. French felt that only ebb tides need be considered. He turned again to Manners.

'I suppose a good ebb develops some strong currents in these channels?'

'You may say so, Mr French. An average of five knots you may reckon on. A deal faster than you could walk.'

'Five knots an hour?'

'No, sir; five knots. It's like this 'ere. A knot ain't a distance: it's a speed. If I say five knots I means five sea miles an hour.'

'A sea mile is longer than an ordinary one?'

'That's right. It varies in different places, but you may take it as 6080 feet 'ere.'

French made a short calculation.

'That is about five and three-quarter English miles per hour,' he remarked, as he scaled this distance up the Inlet from the position of the crate. And then his interest quickened suddenly.

A little over five miles from the point at which the crate had sunk the estuary narrowed to less than a quarter of a mile in width. At this point it was crossed by two bridges, carrying respectively the main road and the railway between

Swansea and Llanelly. Had the crate been thrown from one of these?

French saw at once that no more suitable place for the purpose could be found. Objects pushed in from the bank would tend to hug the shore and to be caught in backwaters or eddies. Moreover, even if they escaped such traps they would not travel at anything like the maximum speed of the current. But from a bridge they could be dropped into the middle of the stream, where the flow was quickest.

'What about the bridge up at Loughor?' he asked. 'If the crate was dropped off that on an ebb tide, do you think it would get down all right?'

Manners was impressed by the suggestion. Given a good ebb, about an hour should carry the crate to where it was found. French rose with sudden energy.

'Let's go and see the place. How soon can we get there?'

By a stroke of luck a train was approaching as they entered the station, and twenty minutes later they reached their destination.

Loughor proved to be a straggling village situated on the left bank of the estuary where the latter made a right-angled bend towards the north. The two bridges ran side by side, and a couple of hundred yards apart. That carrying the road was a fine wide structure of ferro-concrete, fairly new and leading directly into the village. The railway bridge was lower down stream, considerably older and supported on timber piles. Both were about three hundred yards long, and built with short spans and many piers. The tide was out, and the usual wide mud banks were exposed on either shore.

Directly French saw the spot he felt that here indeed was what he sought. On a dark night it would have been easy to drop the crate from the road bridge in absolute secrecy.

Nor, as far as he could see from the map, was there any other place from which it could have been done.

He had assumed that the criminal would select an ebb tide for his attempt in order to ensure the crate being carried as far as possible out to sea. For the same reason French believed he would choose the time of its most rapid run. That time must also be in the dead of night to minimise the risk of discovery from passing road traffic. From 2 to 4 a.m. would probably best meet the conditions, as the chances were a thousand to one that the road would then be deserted.

French wondered if he could get anything from these considerations. He turned to Manners.

'I suppose it takes a bit of time to get up a good run in an estuary like this? How soon after high water would you say the current was running at full speed under the bridge?'

'From one to two hours, more or less.'

One to two hours previous to the period 2 to 4 a.m. meant between midnight and 3 a.m.

'Now, Mr Manners, can you tell me whether high water fell between twelve and three on any night about five or six weeks ago?'

Manners once more produced his tide table.

'Five or six weeks ago,' he repeated slowly. 'That would be between the 16th and the 23rd of August.' He ran his stubby finger up the pages, then read out: '"21st, Sunday, 0.5—" that's five minutes past midnight, you understand. "22nd, Monday, 1.23 a.m.; 23rd, Tuesday, 2.55. a.m." 'Ow would that suit you, sir?'

'All right, I think,' French answered, as he noted the three dates. 'Any of those top springs?'

'No, sir, you don't get 'igh water of springs at night. 'Bout

34

six or seven o'clock it runs. Those dates wot I gave you are about dead neaps.'

'But there is still a strong flow at neaps?'

'Oh, bless you, yes. Not so strong as at springs o' course, but plenty strong enough.'

All this seemed satisfactory to French, and he felt a growing conviction that the small hours of the 21st, 22nd, or 23rd of August had witnessed the launch of the crate. But this was mere theory, and theory is popularly admitted to be worth only one-sixteenth of the value of practice. Could he not arrive at something more definite?

Suddenly he thought he saw his way.

'You say it was neap tides on those three dates in August? What rise and fall does that represent?'

''Bout eighteen feet.'

'How soon shall we have that again?'

'Not for nearly a week we shan't. Say next Monday.'

'I can't wait for that. What's the rise tomorrow?'

'Twenty-one foot eleven.'

'And what hour is high water?'

'Eight o'clock in the morning.'

'That'll have to do. Look, here is a bus labelled "Llanelly." Let us get aboard.'

At the police station they found not only the superintendent, but Chief Constable Lloyd.

'Glad to see you together, gentlemen,' French greeted them. 'I've been going into the matter of tides and currents in the Inlet with Mr Manners here, and now I want your help in trying an experiment. Manners informs me that about six weeks ago, the time at which the doctors believe our man was murdered, it was high water in the dead period of the night. Tomorrow, Thursday, it will be high water at 8. a.m. The maximum run out to sea, Manners says, will begin between one and two hours later, say at 9.30 a.m. Now, gentlemen, I want to load the crate with a weight equal to that of the body and throw it into the estuary from the Loughor bridge at 9.30 tomorrow morning. Will you help me?'

While French had been speaking the three men had stared uncomprehendingly, but as he reached his peroration something like admiration showed on their faces.

'Well, I'm blessed,' the superintendent said slowly, while Major Lloyd gave the suggestion his instant approval.

'Glad you agree, gentlemen,' said French. 'Now, if we're to be ready, we shall want a few things arranged. First we'll have to put stones in the crate to equal the weight of the body. Then we'll want a carpenter to repair the top where Mr Morgan broke it. He'll have to make it water-tight with pitch or putty or something. I don't want it to take any water through the cracks. A lorry will also be needed to carry the crate to the bridge, and three or four men to lift it over the parapet.'

'Very good,' the chief constable answered. 'Nield can arrange all that. Advise him, will you, Superintendent. But you'd better see him yourself, Inspector, and make sure he forgets nothing. Anything else?'

'Yes, sir. We don't want to lose the crate. We shall want a rope round it and a boat in attendance.'

'You can fix that up, Manners, can't you?'

'Certainly, sir. I'll see to it.'

'Good. I'll come down to watch the experiment. Shall we say 9.30 a.m. at the bridge?'

At nine o'clock next morning two vehicles left the Burry Port police station. The first was a lorry and on it stood the crate, repaired and loaded with the necessary weight of

36

shingle, due allowance having been made for the fact that the wood was now waterlogged. Behind followed a car containing French, Nield, and three constables in plain clothes.

The weather was ideal for their purpose. The fine spell had lasted and the sun shone with a summery warmth and brilliance. Not a breath of wind dulled the shining surface of the Inlet, now calm and placid at the turn of the tide. Inland the hills showed sharp against the clear blue of the sky. Out beyond the Gower Peninsula was a steamer going up to Swansea or Cardiff.

The chief constable and Superintendent Griffiths were waiting for them at Loughor. Already the tide was running swiftly, swirling and eddying round the piles of the bridge. Moored to the bank at the east end was a broad-beamed boat with Manners in the sternsheets and two oarsmen amidships.

'Good heavens, they'll never row against that current!' French exclaimed, aghast at the rushing flood.

'They're not going to try,' Nield declared. 'This is what I've arranged with Manners. He has an extra long painter fixed to his boat. We'll get the end up on the bridge and tie it to the Crate. Then we'll throw crate and rope over together, and Manners can pull the slack of the rope into the boat and float down beside the crate.'

'Right. Let me get into the boat first and then carry on.'

French scrambled down the stone pitching of the bank and with some difficulty got aboard. The rope had been passed up to the bridge and was now worked across till the boat was nearly in mid-stream. Even with the help of the oarsmen it was all those above could do to hold on. Then the crate appeared rising slowly on to the parapet. Presently it turned over and fell, the rope being thrown clear at the same time.

The crate entered the water with a mighty splash, drenching the boat with spray and disappearing momentarily beneath the surface. Then it came up again, and bobbing about like some ungainly animal, began to move quickly downstream. The boatmen rowed after it, while Manners hurriedly pulled in the slack of the rope.

After the first few plunges the crate settled down on what might be called an even keel, floating placidly down the estuary. They were rapidly approaching the railway bridge, the roar of the water through the piles being already audible. The passage was not without danger, and the oarsmen worked hard to keep the boat clear of the piles and to ensure its passing through the same opening as the crate. Then with a rush they were through and floating in the calm water beyond.

French enjoyed that unconventional trip down the Inlet. Apart from the interest of the quest, the glorious weather and the charming scenery made it a delightful excursion. Borne on by the current they first hugged the salt marshes of the northern shore, then heading out towards mid-channel, they passed the post on Careg-ddu and rounded the point at the Llanelly rifle range. They kept inside the long training bank or breakwater, and passing the entrance to Llanelly harbour, stood out towards the open sea. From the water the high lands north and south looked rugged and picturesque, and even the dingy buildings of the town became idealised and seemed to fit their setting. French took frequent bearings so as to be able to plot their course on the map.

The crate had been settling down steadily, and now only about two inches of freeboard showed, every tiny wavelet washing over it. The rope had been carefully coiled so as to run out easily when the time came. Presently the crate was entirely awash, and the air escaping through the upper holes bubbled as the little surges covered them. Then it was below the surface, showing like a phantom under the waves. At last, just one hour and seven minutes after they had left the bridge, it slowly vanished from sight, and the rope began to run out.

'That will do,' French said as soon as he had taken bearings. 'That's all I want. We may haul it up and get ashore.'

They followed the example set by Mr Morgan, and pulling up the crate until the top was showing beneath the surface, made the rope fast to the after thwart and pulled for the Burry Port harbour. There they beached their burden, the sergeant undertaking to salve it when the tide fell.

French, delighted with the result of his experiment, hurried to the hotel and plotted their course on his map. And then he was more delighted still. The crate had passed within fifty yards of its previous resting place.

It was true it had gone nearly half a mile farther, but that was to be expected and was attributable to the greater fall of the tide.

That the crate had been thrown from the Loughor bridge on the night of the 21st, 22nd, or 23rd of August French had now no doubt. The first problem of the investigation had therefore been solved, and he congratulated himself on having made so brilliant a start in his new case.

But as was usual in criminal investigations, the solution of one problem merely led to another: how had the crate been transported to the bridge?

There were three possibilities: by means of a handcart, a horse cart, or a motor lorry. All, however, had the serious objection that it would take at least three men to lift the crate over the parapet. Murders, of course, were sometimes the work of gangs, but much more frequently they were carried out by individuals, and French would have preferred a theory which involved only one man. However, there was nothing for it but to follow the theory which he had.

As far as he could see the only factor differentiating between the three vehicles was that of radius of operation. If a hand-cart had been used the body must have been brought from Loughor, Bynea, or some other place in the immediate vicinity. The same remarks applied to a horse vehicle, though to a lesser extent. With a motor the distance travelled might have been almost anything.

French did not believe that the body could have come from anywhere near by. Had anyone disappeared or left the neighbourhood under suspicious circumstances the police would have known about it. The motor lorry was therefore the more likely of the three.

He began to see the outlines of an inquiry stretching out before him. Had anyone seen a motor, loaded with something which might have been the crate, in any part of the surrounding country on the night of the 21st, 22nd, or 23rd of August?

Going to the police station, French rang up the chief constable, reported the result of the experiment, and asked him to see that his question was circulated, not only among the Carmarthenshire police, but also among those of adjoining counties. Then, thinking he had not done so badly for one day, he returned to the hotel for lunch.

A good deal of the afternoon he employed in speculating as to what he should do if there were no answer to his circular, but next morning he was delighted to find that his labour had not been in vain. Sergeant Nield appeared to say that there had just been a message from the police at Neath, saying that a lorry answering to the description had been seen on the evening of Monday, 22nd August. It was fitted with a breakdown crane and carried a large package covered with a tarpaulin which might easily have been the crate. A constable had seen it about eight at night standing in a lane some two miles north of the town. The driver was working at the engine, which he said had been giving trouble.

'That's a bit of good news, sergeant,' French said heartily. 'How can I get to this Neath quickest?'

'Direct train via Swansea. It's on the main line to London.'

'Right. Look up the trains, will you, while I get ready.'

French had little doubt that he was on a hot scent. He had not thought of a portable crane, but now he saw that nothing more suitable for the purpose could be obtained. There were, he knew, cranes—auto-cranes, he believed they were called—which were fixed on lorries and used for towing disabled cars. In certain types the jibs could be raised or lowered under load. With the jib down a load could be picked up from the ground behind the lorry. The jib could then be raised to its highest position and if the load was right up at the pulley it would clear the tail end of the lorry. When the load was lowered it would come down on the lorry. And all this could be done by one man.

As French closed his eyes he seemed to see the reverse process being carried out; a crane-lorry arriving on the Loughor bridge, stopping, backing at right angles to the road until its tail was up against the parapet—the road was wide enough to allow of it; the driver getting down, taking a tarpaulin off a crate, swinging the crate up to the pulley of his crane, lowering the jib until the crate swung suspended over the rushing flood beneath, then striking out some type of slip shackle which allowed the crate to fall clear. It was all not only possible but easy, and French had not the slightest doubt that it had been done.

A couple of hours later he was seated in the police station at Neath, listening to Constable David Jenkins's story.

It seemed that about eight o'clock on the night of Monday, the 22nd of August, Jenkins was walking along a lane leading through a small spinney some two miles north of the town when he came on a lorry drawn in close to one side. It was fitted with a crane such as is used for motor breakdowns, and behind the crane was an object covered with a tarpaulin. This object was rectangular shaped and about the size of the crate. There had been engine trouble which the driver was trying to make good. Jenkins paused and wished the man goodnight and they talked for a few minutes. The man was slightly over middle height and rather stout, and was dressed as a lorryman—a working man evidently. He had reddish hair, a high colour, and glasses, and Jenkins felt sure he would know him again. The man explained that he was going from Swansea to Merthyr Tydfil, and had got out of his way in trying to take a short cut. Then his engine had broken down and he was thus kept very late. But he had now found the defect and would be able to get on in a few minutes. Jenkins had stayed chatting, and in five minutes the man had said: 'There, that's got it,' and had closed up the bonnet and moved off.

'Coming from Swansea, was he?' French said. 'Does that lane lead from Swansea?'

'Oh, yes, it leads from Swansea all right, but it doesn't lead to Merthyr Tydfil.'

'Where does it lead to?'

'More like to Pontardawe.'

That was all right. French was delighted with the way

news was coming in. That the constable had seen his man he did not doubt.

At the time, Jenkins went on, it had struck him as curious that a breakdown lorry should be used for transporting goods. But on reading French's circular he had seen that here was a plant which would lift the goods over the parapet of a bridge. And when he remembered that the tarpaulin covered object was about the size given, he felt he ought to report the occurrence.

'Quite right, constable,' French said heartily. 'I am sure your superiors will not overlook your action.'

French's next step was clear. A crane-lorry should not be difficult to trace. He would go back to Swansea and put the necessary inquiries in train.

4

A Change of Venue

On reaching Swansea, French looked up Superintendent Howells at the police station.

'Glad to see you, Mr French,' the superintendent greeted him. 'I've known your name for a considerable time, and since I heard you were down over this job I've been hoping we should meet. That Neath report any good to you?'

'I think so,' French answered. 'It sounds promising at all events. On the strength of it I've come in to ask for your help.'

'That's all right. What do you want us to do?'

'I want to trace the lorry your man saw out at Neath. I've got his description of it, and I must say that seeing he suspected nothing at the time he observed it pretty closely. A smart man, superintendent.'

'I'm glad you think so, Inspector. Right, I'll put through a call to all stations immediately.'

'Splendid. And can you ask Superintendent Griffiths at Llanelly to advise the Carmarthen men also?'

The necessary circular, drafted, the two chatted for some

minutes until French excused himself on the ground that since he was at Swansea he might as well have a look round the town.

'There's not much to see in it, Mr French,' Howells rejoined, 'but Mumbles is worth visiting I should advise you to take a bus there and walk round the Head and back by Langland. If you're fond of a bit of good coast you'll enjoy it. You'll have plenty of time before we get any replies. Sorry I can't go with you, but I'm full up here.'

French went out, and after a stroll through some of the principal streets got on board a bus for Mumbles. There he took the walk Superintendent Howells had recommended. He enjoyed every minute of it. As he left the houses behind and the road began to rise up the side of the cliff he felt he was having one of the compensations of a country case. He walked up through the long rock cutting until at the top the wide expanse of the Bristol Channel came into view with the islands and lighthouse off the Head in the foreground. There was some wind and the deep blue of the sea was flecked with white. He stood and watched three outward-bound steamers pitching gently in the swell, the smoke from their stacks trailing away east. Then he took the footpath round the cliffs, rising high round Rams Tor and dropping again to Langland Bay, from which another road led across the neck of the peninsula back into Mumbles. It was getting on towards five when he returned to the police station.

'You've come at the right time, Inspector,' Superintendent Howells greeted him. 'I've just had two pieces of news. Your lorry was seen twice. About five o'clock on Monday evening, 22nd August, the evening in question, it was seen by one of our men passing through Morriston. Morriston is a town some two miles north of Swansea; indeed it is really a suburb.

The lorry came from the Swansea direction and turned east at Morriston towards Neath. It was then carrying the tarpaulin covered object.'

'Then it started from Swansea?'

'Looks like it. And it looks as if it finished up at Swansea also. It was seen again on the following morning. About ten o'clock a patrol saw a breakdown lorry coming towards Swansea along the Pontardulais road. It corresponded with the description in every respect except that it was carrying the tarpaulin only.'

'By Jove! Superintendent, that's good. It won't be long till we run it to earth. I take it there are not many breakdown lorries in Swansea.'

'Give you a list in half an hour.' He touched a bell. 'Here, Thomas, start in and ring up all the local garages and find out how many have repair lorries—you know what I mean, fitted with cranes. And see here. You needn't worry about any with fixed jibs: only those that can be raised and lowered. Got that?'

The constable saluted smartly and withdrew. Howells turned to French and was beginning a remark when his desk telephone rang.

'Yes. Superintendent Howells speaking . . . Yes . . . Gorseinon . . . Yes . . . What time was that? . . . Very good, I've got you.' He rang off. 'There's another, Mr French. I think you're all right this time. At half-past twelve that same Monday night a patrol found your lorry in another lane, also hidden by trees. It was a mile or so east of a little place called Gorseinon: that's about five miles north-east of Loughor. It was standing in the lane and the driver was working at his engine. Our men stopped and spoke, and the driver said he had been on a job out beyond Llandilo and

46

was returning to Swansea. The description matches and the crate was then on the lorry.'

'Fine!' French exclaimed. 'That settles it. He was evidently going round killing time until it was late enough to throw in the crate. Could we fix his course from all those places you mentioned?'

'Pretty nearly, I think. Here is a map of the district. He seems to have just made a circle from Swansea to Loughor via Morriston, Neath, Pontardaw, and Gorseinon: say twenty-five miles altogether. Goodness knows how he returned, but it may have been through Bynea and Pontardulais. We may take it he made another detour anyhow.'

'He made a blunder going with the lorry in that open way,' French said grimly.

'I don't see what else he could have done. But I bet he wasn't worrying much about being seen. He was banking on the crate not being found.'

'You're right, and on odds he was justified. It was by a pretty thin chance that it was discovered. I was saying that to Nield: how the one unlikely chance that a man overlooks or discounts is the one that gets him.'

'That's a fact, Inspector, and it's lucky for us it is so. I remember once when—'

But French was not destined to hear the superintendent's reminiscence. The telephone bell once again rang stridently.

'Got it in one,' Howells observed, after listening to the message. 'There is only one lorry in Swansea fitted with a movable crane, and it is owned by Messrs Llewellyn of Fisher Street. Moreover, it was hired about four o'clock on the afternoon of that Monday, 22nd August, and returned next morning. Will you see them now? If so I'll come along and show you the place.'

They soon reached Fisher Street, where there was a large garage bearing the name: 'The Stepney Motor Car Co.' The superintendent, entering, asked for Mr Llewellyn.

The proprietor looked thrilled when he learned French's business.

'By Jove! you don't say that that crate was carried on my lorry!' he exclaimed. 'I read about its discovery and a dam' good tale it made. How did you find out so much?'

'I've not proved anything,' French replied. 'The whole thing is pure suspicion. But you may lead me to certainty. I'd be obliged if you would tell me what took place.'

'Surely; I'll tell you all I can, but it won't be much.' He opened a day-book and ran down the items. 'The 22nd of August,' he went on. 'Yes, here it is. We hired out the lorry on that date. But it was ordered beforehand. We got a letter several days before from London from one of the big hotels, signed Stewart, asking if we had a breakdown lorry for hire, and if so, at what rate. It particularised one with a movable jib which would pick up a load from the ground and set it on the lorry table. The machine would be wanted on the afternoon of the 22nd for one day only. If we agreed, the writer's man would call for it about four on that afternoon and would return it before midday on the 23rd. As the writer was a stranger he would be willing to deposit whatever sum we thought fair as a guarantee. The lorry was wanted to pick up a special machine which the writer was expecting by sea from London, and carry it to his place in Brecknock, where it was to be lowered on to a foundation. As it was part of an invention he was perfecting, he didn't want any strangers about. He made it a condition therefore that his man would drive.

'It wasn't a very usual request, but it seemed reasonable enough, and of course it was none of my business what he wanted the machine for. At first I wasn't very keen on letting it go, but I thought if he would pay a deposit of £300 and £5 for the hire, I should be safely covered. It was only a Ford ton truck with the crane added. I wrote him the conditions and he replied agreeing to the figure and asking that the lorry should be ready at the hour mentioned.

'At the time stated a man came in and said he had been sent for the machine by his employer, Mr Stewart. He produced the three hundred pounds, and I gave him a receipt. Then he drove away.

'Next day, about ten-thirty, he came back and said he had got done earlier than he expected. I had the lorry examined, and when I found it was all right I paid him back £295. He returned me my receipt, and went out, and that was all about it.'

'It's a pleasure to get a clear statement like that, Mr Llewellyn,' French said, with his friendly smile, 'and it's surprising how seldom one does get it. There are just one or two further points I should like information on. Have you got those letters from the London hotel?'

'No, I'm afraid they're destroyed. They were kept until the transaction was finished and then burned.'

'But you have the address?'

'Mr John F. Stewart, St Pancras Hotel, London.'

'You might give me the dates of the correspondence.'

This also the owner was able to do, and French added them to his notes.

'Can you describe the hand they were written in?'

'They were typewritten.'

'Purple or black ribbon?'

Mr Llwellyn hesitated.

'Black, I think, but I couldn't be sure.'

'Now about the driver. Could you describe him?'

'He was a middling tall man, middling stout also. His hair was red and his complexion fresh, and he wore glasses.'

'His dress?'

'I could hardly describe it. He was dressed like a well-to-do labourer or a small jobbing contractor or something of that sort. He was untidy, and I remember thinking that he wanted a shave pretty badly. I took him for a gardener or general man about a country place.'

'You couldn't guess where he had come from by his accent?'

'No, I couldn't tell. He wasn't a local, but that's all I could say.'

'The same man came back next day?'

'Yes.'

'Had you any conversation with him on either occasion?'

'No, except that he explained about lowering the machine on to the foundation, same as in the letter.'

This seemed to French to be all he could get and after some further talk he and the superintendent took their leave.

'He's loaded up the crate here in Swansea at all events,' French observed when they were in the street. 'That seems to postulate docks and stations. I wonder if I can trespass still further on your good nature, Superintendent?'

'Of course, I'll send men round first thing tomorrow. It's too late tonight; all the places would be shut.'

'Thanks. Then I'll turn up early in the morning.'

At the nearest telegraph office French sent a message to the Yard to have inquiries made at the St Pancras Hotel as to the mysterious Mr John F. Stewart. Then, tired from his exertions, he returned to his hotel at Burry Port.

Early next morning he was back in Swansea. It was decided that with a constable who knew the docks, he, French, was to apply at the various steamship offices, while other men were to try the railway stations and road transport agencies. If these failed, the local firms and manufacturers who usually sent out their products in crates were to be called on. French did not believe that the search would be protracted.

This view speedily proved correct. He, had visited only three offices when a constable arrived with a message. News of the crate had been obtained at the Morriston Road Goods Station.

Fifteen minutes later French reached the place. He was met at the gate by Sergeant Jefferies, who had made the discovery.

'I asked in the goods office first, sir,' the sergeant explained, 'but they didn't remember anything there. Then I came out to the yard and began inquiring from the porters. At the fifth shot I found a man who remembered loading the crate. I didn't question him further, but sent you word.'

'That was right, sergeant. We shall soon get what we want. This the man?'

'Yes, sir.'

French turned to a thick-set man in the uniform of a goods porter who was standing expectantly by.

'Good day,' he said pleasantly. 'I want to know what you can tell me about that crate that was loaded up on a crane lorry about six weeks ago.'

'I can't tell you nothing about it except that I helped for to get it loaded up,' the porter answered. 'I was trucking here when Mr Evans came up: he's one, o' the clerks, you understand. Well, he came up and handed me a weighbill and sez: "Get out that crate," he sez, "an' get it loaded up on this lorry," he sez. So I calls two or three o' the boys to give me a hand and we gets it loaded up. An' that's all I knows about it.'

'That's all right. Now just take me along to Mr Evans, will you?'

The man led the way across the yard to the office. Mr Evans was only a junior, but this fact did not prevent French from treating him with his usual courtesy. He explained that the youth had it in his power to give him valuable help for which he would be very grateful. The result was that Evans instantly became his eager ally, willing to take any trouble to find out what was required.

The youth remembered the details of the case. It appeared that shortly after four o'clock one afternoon, some five or six weeks previously, a man called for a crate. He was of rather above medium height and build, with reddish hair and a high colour and wore glasses. He sounded to Evans like a Londoner: at all events he was not a native. Evans had looked up the waybills and had found that a package had been invoiced to someone of the name given. The crate answered the man's description and was carriage paid and addressed 'To be called for.' Evans had therefore no hesitation in letting him have it. Unfortunately he could not remember the stranger's name, but he would search for it through the old waybills.

He vanished for a few minutes, then returned with a bulky volume which he set down triumphantly before French.

'There you are,' he exclaimed, pointing to an item. '"Mr James S. Stephenson, Great Western Railway Goods Station, Morriston Road, Swansea. To be called for." "Stephenson" was the name. I remember it now.'

This was good enough as far as it went, but Evans' next answer was the one that really mattered.

'Who was the sender?' French asked, with thinly veiled eagerness.

'"The Vida Office Equipment Manufacturing Co., Ltd., Ashburton, South Devon,"' read Evans.

The name seemed dimly familiar to French, but he could not remember where he had heard it. Evans went on to say that the crate was invoiced from Ashburton on Tuesday, 16th August, and had reached Swansea on Saturday, 20th. Carriage had been paid by the Vida Company, and the whole transaction had been conducted in a perfectly ordinary and regular way.

French left the goods office, and at the nearest telephone call office rang up the police station in Ashburton. After a considerable delay he got through. Would the sergeant inquire for him whether the Vida Company had sent out a crate on the 16th August last, addressed to the Morriston Road Goods Station, Swansea, to be called for, and if so, what was in this crate and who had ordered it.

For nearly three hours he hung about the police station before being recalled to the telephone. The Ashburton sergeant reported that he had been to the Vida Works and that the manager confirmed the sending out of the crate. It contained a large duplicator, a speciality of the firm's. The machine had been ordered by letter from the Euston Hotel by a Mr James S. Stephenson. He enclosed the money, £62 10s., stating that they were to send it to the Morriston Road Goods Station in Swansea, labelled 'To be kept till called for.' It was to be there not later than on the 20th August, and he would call for it when the ship by which he intended to despatch it was ready to sail.

The news did not seem very hopeful to French, as over a belated lunch he discussed it with Howells.

'This opens a second line of inquiry at Ashburton,' he began, 'but I do not think somehow that we shall get much from it. I believe the real scent lies here.'

'Why so? I should have said it depended on what was in

the crate when it reached Swansea. And that's just what we don't know.'

'I agree. But to me that sergeant's report sounds as if things at Ashburton were O.K. If so, it follows that the body was put in some time during that lorry run from Swansea to Loughor. But that doesn't rule out inquiries at Ashburton. Even if I am right, something may be learned from the order for the machine.'

'Quite. Both ends will have to be worked. And how do you propose to do it?'

'Can't you guess?' French said blandly. 'Surely there can be but one answer. I couldn't hope to do it without the able and distinguished help of Superintendent Howells.'

The other laughed.

'I thought it was shaping to that. Well, what do you want me to do?'

'Trace the run, Superintendent. You can do it in a way I couldn't attempt. I would suggest that with a map we work out the area which could have been visited during that night, allowing time for unpacking the duplicating machine and putting the body in its place. Then I think this area should be combed. If murder has taken place you'll hear of it.'

'And you?'

'I shall go to Ashburton, learn what I can from the order, and if it seems worthwhile, follow it up in London. Then I'll come back here and join forces with you. Of course we shall have to get Superintendent Griffiths on the job also.'

After some further discussion this programme was agreed to. French, with the superintendent's help, was to estimate the area to be covered and to organise the search. Tomorrow was Sunday, and if by Monday evening nothing had come of it he was to leave Howells to carry on while he paid his visits to Ashburton and, if necessary, to London.

The longest unknown period of the lorry's operations being from 8.30 p.m. to 12.30 a.m. at night, this was taken as being the ruling factor in the case. During these four hours the machine had travelled from Neath to Gorseinon, a distance of about twenty-five miles. About two hours would be accounted for by the journey and the changing of the contents of the crate, leaving two more hours for additional running—an hour out and an hour back. This meant a radius of about twenty-five miles. The problem therefore was to make an intensive search of the country within, say, thirty miles of Swansea.

This was a large area, and the work involved the co-operation of a good many men. However, with Superintendent Howells's help it was arranged and by that evening operations were everywhere in progress.

During the whole of the next two days French remained on the job, working out possible routes for the lorry and making special inquiries along them. But no further information was obtained, and when Monday evening came, without result, he decided that unless he heard something next morning he would start for Ashburton.

But next morning news had come in which made a visit there essential. It appeared that about 9.30 on the evening in question the lorry had been seen standing in the same lane at Gorseinon in which three hours later the police patrol had found it. A labourer reported that he had passed it on his way home. As he approached the driver was sitting on the step, but on seeing him the man had jumped up and busied himself with the engine. The labourer had passed on out of sight, but his way taking him along a path at right angles to the lane, he had looked back across country and noticed the driver again seated on the step and lighting a cigarette. The position of the lorry was the same then as three hours later, and the conclusion that it had not moved during the whole period seemed irresistible.

But if so, it made it much less likely that the body had been put into the crate during the motor drive. The time available would have been so short that the area in which the change could have been made would have been very small indeed. The chances of a disappearance remaining unknown to the police would therefore have been correspondingly reduced. For the first time French began to consider seriously the possibility that the body had come from Devonshire.

While, therefore, Superintendent Howells in no way relaxed his efforts, French took an early train south. He was in a thoughtful mood as they pulled out of the station. This, it was evident, was going to be one of those troublesome cases in which an ingenious criminal had enveloped his evil deeds in a network of false clues and irrelevant circumstances to mislead the unfortunate detective officer to whom an investigation into them might afterwards be assigned. Confound it all! It was not long since he had got rid of that terribly involved affair at Starvel in Yorkshire, and here was another that bade fair to be as bad. However, such was life, and worrying wouldn't alter it. He was starting on an interesting journey, and he might as well forget his case and make the most of the scenery.

5

Messrs Berlyn and Pyke

Shortly before six o'clock that evening French stepped out of the train at the little terminus of Ashburton.

He had enjoyed his run, particularly the latter portion through the charming South Devonshire scenery, along the coast under the red cliffs of Dawlish and Teignmouth, and then inland through the well-wooded hills of Newton Abbot and Totnes. He was pleased, too, with the appearance of Ashburton, a town T-shaped in plan and squeezed down into the narrow Valleys between three hills. He admired its old-world air and its pleasant situation as he walked up the street to the Silver Tiger, the hotel to which he had been recommended.

After a leisurely dinner he went out for a stroll, ending up shortly after dark at the police station. Sergeant Daw had gone home, but a constable was despatched for him and presently he turned up.

'I went to the works at once, sir,' he explained in answer to French's question. 'They're out at the end of North Street. A big place for so small a town. They employ a hundred or more men, and a lot of women and girls. A great benefit to the town, sir.'

'And whom did you see?'

'I saw Mr Fogden, the manager. He turned up the information without delay. The duplicator was ordered from London and he showed me the letter. You can see it if you go up tomorrow. There was nothing out of the way about the transaction. They packed the machine and sent it off, and that was all they could tell me.'

Suspiciously like a wild-goose-chase, thought French, as he chatted pleasantly to the sergeant. Like his *confrère* at Burry Port, the man seemed more intelligent and better educated than most rural policemen. They discussed the weather and the country for some time, and then French said:

'By the way, Sergeant, the name of this Vida Works seemed vaguely familiar when you telephoned it. Has it been in the papers lately, or can you explain how I should know it?'

'No doubt, sir, you read of the sad accident we had here about six weeks ago—a tragedy, if I may put it so. Two of the gentlemen belonging to the works—Mr Berlyn, the junior partner, and Mr Pyke, the travelling representative—lost their lives on the moor. Perhaps you remember it, sir?'

Of course! The affair now came back to French. So far as he could recall the circumstances, the two men had been driving across Dartmoor at night, and while still several miles from home their car had broken down. They had attempted to reach the house of a friend by crossing a bit of the moor, but in the dark they had missed their way, and getting into one of the soft 'mires,' had been sucked down and lost.

'I read of it, yes. Very sad thing. Unusual too, was it not?'

'Yes, sir, for those who live about here know the danger and they don't go near these doubtful places at night. But animals sometimes get caught. I've seen a pony go down myself, and I can tell you, sir, I don't wish to see another. It was a slow business, and the worse the creature struggled the tighter it got held. But when it comes to human beings it's a thing you don't like to think about.'

'That's a fact, Sergeant. By the way, it's like a dream to me that I once met those two gentlemen. I wish you'd describe them.'

'They were not unlike, so far as figure and build were concerned; about five feet nine or five feet ten in height, I should say, though Mr Berlyn was slightly the bigger man. But their colouring was different. Mr Berlyn had a high colour and blue eyes and reddish hair, while Mr Pyke was sallow with brown eyes and hair.'

'Did Mr Berlyn wear glasses?' French asked, with difficulty keeping the eagerness out of his voice.

'No, sir. Neither of them did that.'

'I don't think they can be the men I met. Well, I'll go up and see this Mr Fogden in the morning. Goodnight, Sergeant.'

'Goodnight, sir. If there's anything I can do I take it you'll let me know.'

But French next morning did not go to the office equipment works. Instead he took an early bus to Torquay, and calling at the local office of the *Western Morning News,* asked to see their recent files. These he looked over, finally buying all the papers which contained any reference to the tragic deaths of Messrs Berlyn and Pyke.

He had no suspicions in the matter except that here was a disappearance of two persons about the time of the murder, one of whom answered to the description of the man who had called for the crate. No one appeared to doubt their death on the moor, but—their bodies had not been found.

59

French wished to know what was to be known about the affair before going to the works, simply to be on the safe side.

He retired to the smoking room of the nearest hotel and began to read up his papers. At once he discovered a fact which he thought deeply significant. The tragedy had taken place on the night of Monday, the 15th August. And it was on the following day, Tuesday, the 16th, that the crate had been despatched from Ashburton.

The case was exhaustively reported, and after half an hour's reading French knew all that the reporters had gleaned. Briefly the circumstances were as follow:

Charles Berlyn, as has been said, was junior partner of the firm. He was a man of about forty and he looked after the commercial side of the undertaking. Stanley Pyke was an engineer who acted as technical travelling representative, a younger man, not more than five-and-thirty. Each had a high reputation for character and business efficiency.

It happened that for some time previous to the date in question the Urban District Council of Tavistock had been in communication with the Vida Works relative to the purchase of filing cabinets and other office appliances for their clerk. There had been a hitch in the negotiations, and Mr Berlyn had arranged to attend the next meeting of the council in the hope of settling the matter. As some of the council members were farmers, busy during that season in the daytime, the meeting was held in the evening. Mr Berlyn arranged to motor over, Mr Pyke accompanying him.

The two men left the works at half-past five, their usual hour. Each dined early, and they set out in Mr Berlyn's car about seven. They expected to reach Tavistock at eight, at which hour the meeting was to begin. After their business

60

was finished they intended to call on a mill-owner just outside Tavistock in connection with a set of loose-leaf forms he had ordered. The mill-owner was a personal friend of Mr Berlyn, and they intended to spend the evening with him, leaving about eleven and reaching home about midnight.

This programme they carried out faithfully, at least in its earlier stages. They reached Tavistock just as the meeting of the Urban Council was beginning, and settled the business of the office appliances. Then they went on to the mill-owner's, arranged about the loose leaf forms, and sat chatting over, cigars and drinks until shortly before eleven. At precisely ten-fifty they set off on their return journey, everything connected with them being perfectly normal and in order.

They were never seen again.

Mrs Berlyn went to bed at her ordinary time, but waking up shortly before three and finding that Mr Berlyn had not returned, she immediately grew anxious. It was so unlike him to fail to carry out his plans that his absence suggested disaster. She hastily put on some clothes and went out to the garage, and on finding that the car was not there she woke the servant and said she was going to the police. Without waiting for the girl to dress she went out and knocked up Sergeant Daw at his little cottage.

Though the sergeant did his best to reassure her, he was by no means easy in his own mind. The road from Tavistock to Ashburton is far from safe, especially for night motoring. It is terribly hilly and winding, and at night extraordinarily deserted. An accident might easily happen, and in such lonely country hours might pass before its discovery.

The sergeant at once called a colleague, and the two men started off on motor bicycles to investigate. About eight miles out on the moor they came to Mr Berlyn's car standing close

61

up to the side of the road, as if drawn out of the way of passing traffic. It was heavily coated with dew, and looked as if it had been there for hours. The engine and radiator were cold, and there was no sign of either of its occupants.

At the side of the road was a patch of gravelly soil mixed with peat, and across it, leading from the road out over the moor, were two lines of footsteps. The prints were not sufficiently sharp to give detailed impressions, but the sergeant had no doubt as to whom they belonged. He tried to follow them over the moor, but the grass was too rough to allow of this being done.

But he soon realised what had happened. Three-quarters of a mile across the moor in the direction in which the footsteps pointed lived the senior partner of the Vida Company, Colonel Domlio. His was the only house in the neighbourhood, and it was therefore natural that if from a breakdown of the car or other reason the travellers had got into difficulties, they should go to him for help. But the house was not approached from the road on which they were travelling. The drive started from that which diverged at Two Bridges and led northwards to Moretonhampstead. To have gone round by the road, would therefore have meant a walk of nearly five miles, whereas fifteen minutes would have taken them across the moor. It was evident that they had adopted the latter course.

And therein lay their fate. Some quarter of a mile from the road were a number of those treacherous, vivid green areas of quagmire, to stumble into which is to run the risk of a horrible death. They were not quite in the direct line to the house, but in one of the mists which come up so frequently and unexpectedly it would not have been difficult for the men to lose their way. The sergeant at once knocked up

Colonel Domlio, only to learn that he had not seen or heard of either.

When the car was examined the cause of the stoppage was discovered. A short circuit had developed in the magneto which interfered with the sparking to such an extent that the cylinder charges could not be ignited.

French was a good deal disappointed by the account. He had hoped that he was on to the solution of his problem, but now he doubted it. That Berlyn had murdered Pyke and sent off his body in the crate had seemed at first sight a promising theory. But French could see no evidence of foul play in the story. It read merely as a straightforward narrative of an unfortunate mishap.

At the same time the coincidence of the dates was remarkable, and French felt that he could not dismiss the matter from his mind until he had satisfied himself that it really was the accident for which it had been taken.

He wondered if any tests were possible, and gradually four considerations occurred to him.

First, there was the breakdown of the car. If the breakdown had been an accident the whole affair was almost certainly an accident, for he did not think it possible that advantage could have been taken of an unexpected incident to commit the murder. The details of the disposal of the crate had been too well worked out to have been improvised. But if the breakdown had been faked it meant foul play.

Secondly, a valuable check in all such investigations was the making of a time-table. French felt sure that if murder had been committed the car must have gone from Tavistock to the works and back to where it was found. If not, he did not see how the body could have been taken to the works. Probably also it had waited at the works while the murderer

was substituting the body for the duplicator. Then the radiator must have been hot when the car was abandoned, and
it was cold when Sergeant Daw arrived on the scene. If French
could find out how long all these operations would have
taken he might find that they could not have been carried
out in the time available.

Thirdly, French wondered if in a place of the size of the
Vida Works there was no night watchman, and if there was,
how the contents of the crate could have been changed
without his knowledge.

Lastly, there was the question of the disposal of the duplicator. Assuming that murder had been done, it was extremely
probable that the murderer had found the duplicator packed
in the crate. How could he have got rid of so heavy and
cumbrous an object?

If these four points were investigated French thought he
would obtain sufficient information to settle the main question.
It was therefore with a second line of inquiries in his mind that
he returned to Ashburton and walked out to the Vida Works.

These stood a short distance beyond the town at the end
of North Street, and formed a rather imposing collection of
buildings, small but modern and well designed. The principal
block was of five storeys, showing narrow plasters of cream-
coloured concrete separating wide glazed panels. The remaining
buildings were single storey sheds. The place seemed spotlessly
clean and tidy.

French entered a door labelled 'Office,' and sending in his
private card, asked for Mr Fogden. He was shown into a
comfortably furnished room in which a youngish man with
a pleasant face sat at a table desk.

'Good afternoon, Mr French; won't you sit down? What
can I do for you, sir?'

'I should explain first who I am, Mr Fogden.' French handed over his official card. 'I have called on business which has already been brought to your notice by the local sergeant. It is about the crate which was sent by your firm to Mr James S. Stephenson at the Great Western Goods Station at Swansea.'

'I saw the sergeant when he called,' Mr Fogden answered a trifle shortly. 'That was yesterday, and I gave him all the information at my disposal.'

'So he told me, sir.' French's manner was very suave. 'My troubling you on the same business therefore requires a little explanation. I must ask you, however, to consider what I have to tell you confidential. That crate which you sent to Swansea was duly called for. It eventually reached Burry Port. There it was opened—by the police. And do you know what was found in it?'

Mr Fogden stared at the other with a rapidly growing interest.

'Good heavens!' he cried. 'You surely don't mean to say that it contained that body that we have been reading so much about in the papers recently?'

French nodded.

'That's it, Mr Fogden. So you will see now that it's not idle curiosity which brings me here. The matter is so serious that I must go into it personally. I shall have to investigate the entire history of that crate.'

'By Jove! I should think so. You don't imagine, I take it, that the body was in it when it left the works?'

'I don't, but of course I can't be sure. I must investigate all the possibilities.'

'That is reasonable.' Mr Fogden paused, then continued: 'Now tell me what you want me to do and I will carry out your wishes as well as I can. I have already explained to the sergeant that the crate contained a Vida No. 3 Duplicator, a special product of the firm, and that it was ordered by this Mr Stephenson in a letter written from the Euston Hotel. I can turn up the letter for you.'

'Thank you, I should like to see the letter, but as a matter of fact I should like a good deal more. I am afraid I must follow the whole transaction right through and interview everyone who dealt with it.'

'I get you. Right, I'll arrange it. Now, first as to the letter.'

He touched a bell and ordered a certain file to be brought him. From this he took out a letter and passed it to French.

6

The Despatch of the Crate

The letter was written on a single sheet of cream laid, court-sized paper, and bore the legend 'Euston Hotel, London, N.W.1' in blue type on its right top corner. It was typed in black and French could see that the machine used was not new and that some of the letters were defective and out of place. It was signed 'James S. Stephenson' in a hand which French instinctively felt was disguised, with blue black ink apparently of the fountain pen type. It read:

'*12 th August.*

'MESSRS. THE VIDA OFFICE EQUIPMENT
    MANUFACTURING CO. LTD.,
        ASHBURTON, SOUTH DEVON.

'Dear Sirs,—I should be obliged if you would kindly forward to Mr James S. Stephenson, Great Western Railway Goods Station, Morriston Road, Swansea, marked "To be kept till called for," one of your patent

Vida Electric Duplicators, No. 3, to take brief size. The motor to be wound for 220 volts D.C., and to have a flexible cord to plug into the main.

'Please have the machine delivered at Swansea not later than 19th inst., as I wish to ship it from there on the following day.

'I enclose herewith money order value £62 10s., the price, less discount, as given in your catalogue. Please advise receipt of money and despatch of duplicator to this hotel.

> 'Yours faithfully,
> 'JAMES S. STEPHENSON.'

There were here, French realised, several lines of inquiry. Something might be learned at the Euston Hotel. Unfortunately the fact that the letter was written on the hotel paper and the reply was to be sent there, did not mean that 'Stephenson' had stayed there: French remembered his own letter from the Charing Cross hotel to Dr Philpot in the Starvel case up in Yorkshire. But inquiries could not be omitted. Then there was the money order. It would be easy to learn the office at which it had been obtained, and there was at least the possibility that the purchaser had been observed. Lastly there was the typewriter. French felt sure that it could be identified from the irregularities of the type.

'I may have this letter, I suppose?' he asked.

'Of course.'

He put the paper slowly away in his pocket-book and then in his careful, competent way began to ask questions.

'You sent the receipt and notification of the despatch of the crate to the Euston Hotel?'

'Certainly.'

'What is the process of despatch? When that order came in, to whom did it go?'

'Well, I read it first and dropped it into a basket, from which it went automatically to the accounts department. Following the ordinary routine the money would be collected, and if all was O.K. an order would go to the sales department for the despatch of the goods. When the despatch had taken place a notification in duplicate would be returned to the office, and one copy, with the receipt, would be mailed to the purchaser. The whole thing is, of course, routine, and so far as I know that routine was carried out in this case. But we can see all concerned if you like.'

'That's just what I would like,' French declared.

'Come along, then.'

'There's another thing, Mr Fogden,' French interposed. 'I have told you my business because I wanted your help. But I am anxious that no one else suspects it. If I give out that the duplicator was stolen and that you have employed me to find the thief, will you back up the yarn?'

'Certainly. I am naturally anxious to have the affair cleared up. But do you think you can keep your real business secret?'

'I can for a time. But that may be long enough for me to get my man.'

In the sales department French was first shown a duplicator. It was an elaborate machine, with the usual large cylinder and ingenious devices for turning out copies at high speed.

'What does it weigh?' he asked, when he had duly admired it.

'About two hundredweight.'

'Do you always send them out in crates of the same kind?'

'Always. The crate is specially made for the purpose. Unfortunately it is an odd size, and cannot be used for any of the other products.'

This was interesting. Did it, French wondered, show an internal knowledge of the firm's methods on the part of 'Stephenson'?

'Now about the actual despatch. You say an order comes from the accounts department when anything is to be sent out. Could I see this particular order?'

Mr Fogden looked through a file, finally producing a tiny sheet of paper. But small as was the chit, it was comprehensive. On it were given not only all details of the duplicator and the address of the consignee, but also Mr Fogden's O.K., the initials of the storekeeper who had given out the machine and the crate, of the packer who had packed it, of the carter who had taken it to the station, and of the railway goods clerk who had received it, with the dates when all these things had been done.

'By Jove!' French remarked, when he had taken all this in, 'you don't leave much to chance in this establishment!'

'We believe in individual responsibility,' Mr Fogden explained. 'If anything goes wrong we can usually plant the blame on the right shoulders.'

'Well, it's a help to me at all events. Can I see these men who have initialed this order?'

'Certainly. Come down to the stores.' Mr Fogden led the way to a large room furnished with multitudinous bins containing thousands of articles neatly stacked, and each labelled with its code number and with a card showing the stock. Owing to its opposite walls being composed almost entirely of glass there was a brilliant light everywhere. French marvelled at the cleanliness and tidiness of everything, and expressed his admiration of the way the place was kept.

'This,' continued Mr Fogden, whose heart was evidently reached by French's comments, 'is what we call the part store. Here are the parts of all our machines arranged in sets. Here, for example, are small parts. Those bins carry lock rods for card indexes, those ball bearing rollers for file cases, those rings for loose leaf books, and so on. Over there you get the wooden parts, panels for vertical file cabinets, multiple bookcases, parts of desks and chairs. We carry a definite stock of each part, and every time it drops to a definite number an order automatically goes to the works department for a new lot to be made.'

'Good system.'

'We have to do it or we should get wrong. I'll show you now the erecting shop. This way.'

They passed into a large room where a score or more men were busily engaged in putting together machines of every type and kind. But they did not halt there long. After a general look round Mr Fogden led the way across the shop and through another door.

'This,' he said, 'is our completed articles store. Here we keep our products ready for immediate despatch. We stock a certain number of each class, and the same arrangement holds good with regard to the parts. Directly a number falls to the minimum an order automatically goes to the assembly department to build so many new pieces. That keeps our stock right. Of course, an order for a large number of pieces has to be dealt with specially. For example, we always keep a minimum of twelve No. 1 duplicators complete and ready to go out, and that enables us to supply incidental orders without delay. But when an order for fifty comes in, as we had yesterday from the Argentine, we have to manufacture specially.'

French murmured appreciatively.

'With regard to the No. 3. duplicators,' went on Mr Fogden, pointing to the machines in question, 'we always keep a minimum of three in stock. They are not in such demand as the No. 1's. Now let me see.' He compared the order with the bin or stock card. 'Only two of these have gone out since the one you are interested in. I dare say the men will remember yours.' He referred again to the order. 'Packed by John Puddicoombe. Here, Puddicoombe. A moment.'

An elderly man approached.

'Do you happen to remember packing a duplicator of this type on 15th of August last? It was a Monday and there's the docket.'

The man scratched his head. 'I don't know as I do, sir,' he answered slowly. 'You see, I pack that many and they're all the same. But I packed it all right if I signed for it.'

'Where did you pack it?' French asked.

'In packing shed next door,' the man replied, after an interrogatory glance at his chief.

'Come in and see the place,' Mr Fogden suggested, and they moved to a smaller room, the next in the series.

'You packed it in here,' French went on. 'Now, tell me, did you close up the crate here?'

'Yes, as soon as the duplicator was properly in I got the lid on. I always do.'

'Got the lid on and made it fast?'

'Yes, nailed it down.'

'And was the crate despatched that same day?'

'No,' Mr Fogden intervened. 'The dates show that it lay here that night. It was sent out the following day.'

'Ah, that's what I want to get at,' said French. 'Now, where did it lie all night?'

'Here,' the packer declared. 'It was packed here and lay here until the lorry came for it the next day.'

'But if you don't remember this particular case?' French persisted. 'Don't mind my asking. The matter is important.'

The packer regarded him with what seemed compassion, and replied with a tolerant forbearance.

'I know because that's what's always done, and there weren't no exception in the case of any machine,' he replied conclusively.

This seemed to end the matter as far as Puddicoombe was concerned, and French next asked to see the carter who had taken it to the station.

The man fortunately was available, and French questioned him minutely. He stated he remembered the occasion in question. On the Tuesday morning he had loaded up the crate, Puddicoombe assisting. It was lifted by a set of differential pulley blocks which, travelling on an overhead rail, carried it to the lorry. He had driven it to the station, unloading it in the goods shed, and had obtained the usual signature. He had not allowed it out of his sight all the time it was in his charge, and it was quite impossible that its contents could have been tampered with.

'I shall see the station people, of course,' French declared to Mr Fogden when they returned to the latter's office, 'though I don't suppose the crate could have been tampered with during the journey. What you have told me has satisfied me as to its stay here, except on one point. Could the duplicator have been taken out during the night?'

Mr Fogden believed it impossible.

'We have a night watchman,' he explained; 'quite a reliable

old fellow too. Nothing could have been done without his knowledge.'

'Could I see him?'

'Of course. But you'll have to wait while I send for him.'

After some time an office boy ushered in a wizened old man with a goatee beard who answered to the name of Gurney. He blinked at French out of a pair of bright little eyes like some wise old bird, and spoke with a pleasing economy of words.

He came on duty, he said, each evening at seven o'clock, relieving one of the late stokers, who kept an eye on things between the closing of the works at 5.15 p.m. and that hour. His first care was to examine the boilers of the electric power plant, of which he had charge during the night; then he invariably made an inspection of the whole premises. For part of the time he sat in the boiler house, but on at least three other occasions he walked round and made sure everything was in order. The boiler fires were banked and did not give much trouble, but he had to watch the pressure gauges and occasionally to adjust the dampers. At six in the morning he was relieved by the early stokers, and he then went home.

He declared that it would be impossible for anyone to tamper with the goods in the packing shed unknown to him. The packing shed and the boiler house were at opposite sides of a narrow yard, and should the light be turned on in the former no one in the latter could fail to see it.

He remembered the Monday night in question, because it was that on which Mr Berlyn and Mr Pyke had lost their lives. On that night he had come on duty as usual and had gone his customary rounds. He was very emphatic that no one had entered the works during his period of duty.

Though the man's character was vouched for by Mr Fogden, and though he made his statement without hesitation, French was conscious of a slight dissatisfaction. His perception of the reliability of witnesses had become so acute from long experience as to be practically intuitive. He did not think that Gurney was lying, but he felt that he was protesting more strongly than the occasion warranted. He therefore took him aside and questioned him severely in the hope of inducing some give-away emotion. But in this he failed. The watchman answered without embarrassment, and French was forced to the conclusion that his suspicions were unfounded. From the boiler house he saw for himself the effect of turning up the light in the packing shed, with the result that Gurney's statement on this point was confirmed. Then he examined the stokers who had been in charge before and after Gurney, but their statements as to visitors were the same as the watchman's. As far as oral testimony went, therefore, it was impossible that the crate could have been interfered with while it lay at the works.

French next betook himself to the station. But there he learned only what he expected. While no one actually remembered the transaction, its complete records were available. The crate had been received on Tuesday morning, the 16th of August, and had been unloaded in the goods shed and put immediately into a wagon for Plymouth. From the time it arrived until it left by the 11.35 a.m. goods train no one could have tampered with it, two porters being continuously about.

As after dinner that night French wrote up his report, he was conscious of a good deal of disappointment. The attractive theory that the remains were those of Pyke was not obtaining support. He had now gone into two of the four test-points he had considered, and the evidence on each of them was against it. Unless he could find some way round these difficulties, it followed that the body *must* have been put in after the crate had reached Swansea.

The other two test-points, however, remained to be investigated—the cause of the breakdown and the possible running time-tables of the car.

French decided therefore that unless there was news from Howells in the morning he would carry on with these.

7

Dartmoor

French saw that in order to get the information he required he must confide in someone who knew the locality. He therefore went down next morning to the police station to consult Sergeant Daw.

'Good morning, Sergeant,' he said with his pleasant smile. 'Do you think we could go into your office? I should like to have a chat with you.'

Daw was not accustomed to this mode of approach from superior officers, and he at once became mellow and ready to help.

'Quite at your service, sir,' he protested.

'I didn't tell you, Sergeant, just what I was after here. You've read about that body that was found in the sea off Burry Port?'

The sergeant looked up with evident interest.

'I just thought that was it, Mr French, when your 'phone message came through. Do you mean that the body came from the works here?'

'The crate came from here all right, but where the body

was put in I don't know. That's where I want your help. Can you give me any suggestions?'

The sergeant, flattered by French's attitude, wrinkled his brow in thought.

'Did anyone, for example, leave the place or disappear some five or six weeks ago?' went on French.

'No, sir,' Daw answered slowly. 'I can't say that they did.'

'What about Mr Berlyn and Mr Pyke?'

Daw's face showed first surprise and then incredulity.

'You don't suppose they were lost on the moor?' French continued.

'It never occurred to me to doubt it. Do you think otherwise yourself?'

'Well, look here, Sergeant.' French leaned forward and demonstrated with his forefinger. 'Those men disappeared on Monday night, the 15th of August. I say disappeared, because in point of fact they did disappear—their bodies were never found. On that same night the crate lay packed in the works, and next morning it was taken to the station and sent to Swansea. From that Tuesday morning until the body was found at Burry Port we cannot trace any opportunity of opening the crate. You must admit it looks suggestive.'

'But the accident, sir: the breakdown of the car?'

'That's it, Sergeant, you've got it in one. If the breakdown was genuine the affair was an accident, but if it was faked—why then we are on to a murder. At least that's how it strikes me.'

Daw was apologetic but evidently still sceptical.

'But do you suggest that both Mr Berlyn and Mr Pyke were murdered? If so, where's the second body?'

'What if one murdered the other?'

But this was too much for the sergeant.

'Oh, come now, sir,' he protested. 'You didn't know them. You couldn't suspect either of those gentlemen of such a crime. Not possibly, you couldn't.'

'You think not? But what if I tell you that the man who claimed the crate at Swansea answered the description you gave me of Berlyn?'

Sergeant Daw swore. 'I shouldn't have believed it,' he declared.

'Well, there are the facts. You will see, therefore, that I must have first-hand information about the whole thing. I've read all that the papers can tell me, but that's not enough. I want to go out on the moor with you and hear your story at the place where the thing happened. Particularly I want to test that matter of the breakdown. How can we get to know about that?'

'Easily enough, I think.' The man spoke with some relief, as if turning to a pleasanter subject. 'Makepeace has the car and he'll be able to tell us: that's the owner of one of the local garages.'

'Good. How did Makepeace get hold of it?'

'When we came in after finding it that night I sent young Makepeace out for it—that's the son. He couldn't start it, and he had to take out another car and tow it in. He took it to the garage for repairs, and it has lain there ever since. Then when Mrs Berlyn was leaving, Makepeace bought it from her. I understand he wants to sell it now.'

French rose.

'Good,' he said again. 'Then let us go to this Makepeace and see if it is still there. You might introduce me as a friend who wants a second-hand car and who might take Mr Berlyn's. If possible we'll get it out and do the same run that those men did that night. I want to get some times. Are you a driver?'

'Yes, I can handle it all right.'

The Makepeace garage was a surprisingly large establishment for so small a town. At least a dozen cars stood in the long low shed, and there were lorries and char-a-bancs in the yard behind. Daw hailed a youth who was polishing the brasswork of one of the 'sharries.'

'Your father about, John?'

Mr Makepeace, it appeared, was in the office, and thither the two men walked, to be greeted by a stout individual with smiling lips and shrewd eyes.

''Morning, Sergeant. Looking for me?'

The sergeant nodded. 'This is a friend of mine,' he explained, 'who is looking for a good secondhand car. I told him about Mr Berlyn's, but I didn't know whether you had it still. We came across to inquire.'

'It's here all right, and I can afford to sell it cheap.' Mr Makepeace turned to French. 'What kind of car were you wanting, sir?'

'A medium size four-seater, but I'm not particular as to make. If I saw one I liked I would take it.'

'This is a first-rate car,' Mr Makepeace declared firmly; 'one that I can stand over. But I'm afraid she's not very clean. I was going to have her revarnished and the bright parts plated. She'll be as good as new then. You can see her in the back house.'

He led the way to a workshop containing a variety of cars undergoing repairs. Just inside the door was a small dark blue four-seater touring car, looking a trifle the worse for wear. To this he pointed.

'A first-rate car,' he repeated, 'and in good order too, though wanting a bit of a clean up. As you can see, she's a 15-20 Mercury, two years old, but the engine's as good as the day it was made. Have a look over her.'

French knew something of cars though he was no expert. But by saying little and looking wise he impressed the other with his knowledge. Finally he admitted that everything seemed satisfactory, though he would require an expert's opinion before coming to a decision.

'Could I have a run in it?' he asked. 'I should, of course, pay for its hire. I want to go over to Tavistock, and if you could let me have the car it would suit. Mr Daw says he will take half a day's leave and drive me.'

Mr Makepeace agreed with alacrity, and when he understood that his prospective customer was ready to start then and there, he put his entire staff on to 'take the rough off her.' French stood watching the operation while he chatted pleasantly with the proprietor. Having duly admired the vehicle, he went on in a more serious voice:

'There's just one thing that puts me against taking her, and that's something that Mr Daw told me in the course of conversation. He said that on that night when Mr Berlyn met his death the car broke down, in fact that it was that breakdown which led indirectly to the accident. Well, I don't want a car that breaks down. If she's not realiable she's no good to me.'

Mr Makepeace looked pained and flashed a rather indignant glance at the sergeant.

'She did break down that night,' he admitted reluctantly, 'but there's no machinery on earth that won't *sometimes* go wrong. She failed from a most uncommon cause, and she might run for twenty years without the same thing happening to her again.'

'I'm not doubting your word, Mr Makepeace, but I shall want that clearly demonstrated before I think of her. What was it that went wrong?'

'Magneto trouble: armature burnt out.'

'What caused it?'

'It's hard to say; there was no defect showing outwardly. Careless handling, most likely. Some darned mechanic might have jabbed a screwdriver into the wire and covered up the mark. I've known that happen.'

'But it surely wouldn't run if that had been done?'

'Oh, yes, it might. If the insulation wasn't completely cut through it would run for a time. But eventually the short, would develop, causing the engine to misfire, and that would get worse till it stopped altogether.'

'That's interesting. Then you think the fault would only develop if there had been some original injury?'

'I don't say that. I have known cases of short circuits occurring and you couldn't tell what caused them.'

'I suppose you could do that sort of thing purposely if you wanted to?'

'Purposely?' Mr Makepeace shot a keen glance at his questioner.

'Yes. Suppose in this case someone wanted to play a practical joke on Mr Berlyn.'

Mr Makepeace shook his head with some scorn.

'Not blooming likely,' he declared. 'A fine sort of joke that would be.'

'I was asking purely from curiosity, but you surprise me all the same. I thought you could short circuit any electric machine?'

'Don't you believe it. You couldn't do nothing to short an armature without the damage showing.'

'Well, I'm not worrying whether you could or not. All I want is that it won't fail again.'

'You may go nap on that.'

82

'All right,' French smiled. 'Did you rewind the armature yourselves?'

'Neither unwound it or rewound it. That's a job for the makers. We sent it to London. It's an Ardlo magneto, and the Ardlo people have a factory in Bermondsey.'

'That so? I suppose the short circuit was the only trouble? The engine hadn't been hot or anything?'

'The engine was as right as rain,' Mr Makepeace asseverated with ill-repressed impatience.

'I'm glad to know that. I asked because I've known trouble through shortage of water in the radiator. I suppose there was plenty that night?'

'The radiator was full; my son noticed it particularly. You see, on account of the mascot sticking out behind, you have to take off the radiator cap before you can lift the bonnet. When he was taking off the cap he noticed the water.'

French turned as if to close the discussion.

'I don't think I need worry about the chance of more trouble with it,' he agreed. 'Surely, Mr Makepeace, you have her clean enough now? I think we'll get away.'

As they swung out along the Tavistock road French's heart had fallen to the depths. If what this garage owner said were true, the Berlyn-Pyke affair was an accident and he, French, was on the wrong track. However, he had made his plans, and he would carry them out. Banishing his disappointment from his mind, he prepared to enjoy his trip.

The road led from the west end of the town through scenery which was more than enough to hold his attention. The country was charmingly wooded, but extraordinarily hilly: never had French seen such hills. No sooner had they climbed interminably out of one valley than they were over the divide and dropping down an equally break-neck precipice into the next. French was interested in the notices to motor drivers, adjuring them to put their cars into lowest gear before attempting to descend. Three of these well-wooded valleys they crossed—the last the famous meeting of the waters, Dartmeet—and each had its dangerously narrow bridge approached by sharp right-angled bends. The climb beyond Dartmeet took them up on to the open moor, wild, lonely, rolling in great sweeps of heather-clad country like the vast swelling waves of some mighty petrified ocean. Here and there these huge sweeps ran up into jagged rocky crests, as if the dancing foam of the caps had been arrested in mid air and turned into grim shapes of black stone. Once before French had been on Dartmoor, when he had gone down to Princetown to see one of the unfortunates in the great prison. But he had not then been out on the open moor, and he felt impressed by the wide spaces and the desolation.

The sergeant's attention being fully occupied with his wheel, he proved himself a silent companion, and, beyond pointing out the various objects of interest, made no attempt at conversation. Mostly in silence they drove some eight or nine miles, and then suddenly the man pulled up.

'This is the place, sir.'

It was the loneliest spot French had yet seen. On both sides stretched the moor, rolling away into the distance. To the north the ground rose gently; to the south it fell to the valley of a river before swelling up to a line of more distant highlands. Some three miles to the west lay the grey buildings of Princetown, the only human habitations visible, save for a few isolated cottages dotted about at wide intervals. The road was unfenced and ran in a snaky line across the greens and browns of the heather and rough grass. Here and there spots of brighter green showed, and to these the sergeant pointed.

'Those are soft places,' he said. 'Over there towards the south is Fox Tor Mire, a biggish swamp, and there are others in the same direction. On the north side are small patches, but nothing like the others.'

'In which direction did the men go?'

'Northwards.' The sergeant walked a few yards down the road, expounding as he did so. 'The car was pulled in to the side of the road here. There is the patch of sandy soil that the footsteps crossed, and that is the direction they were going in.'

'Which way was the car heading?'

'Towards Ashburton.'

'Were the lamps lighted?'

'Yes, sir. Wing lamps, burning dimly, but good enough to show the car was there'

'It was a dark night?'

'Very dark for the time of year.'

French nodded.

'Now when you came out here tell me what you did.'

'I looked round, and when I couldn't see anyone, I felt the radiator and opened the bonnet and looked at and felt the engine. Both were cold, but I couldn't see anything wrong. Then I took the lamp off my bicycle and looked further around. I found the footsteps—if you've read the papers you'll know about them—and I wondered where they could be heading to. I thought of Colonel Domlio's and I went to the house and roused the colonel.'

'Across the moor?'

'Yes, sir.'

'But were you not afraid of the quagmires?'

'No. It was then a clear night, and I had a good acetylene lamp. I thought maybe the gentlemen had met with an accident on the way and that I'd better go over the ground. I walked carefully and kept on hard earth all the way.'

'Well, you aroused the colonel?'

'Yes, sir, and a job I had to do it. But he could give me no help.'

'Yes? And then?'

'Colonel Domlio wanted to come out with me, but I said there was nothing he could do. I left Constable Hughes with the car and ran back into Ashburton to give the news. I told Mrs Berlyn, and then I got all my men out with lamps and we went back and began a detailed search of the ground. We kept it up until the whole place had been gone over by daylight, but we found nothing.'

'Now this Colonel Domlio. What kind of man is he?'

'A rather peculiar man, if I may say so. He's practically the owner of the Vida Company, now Mr Berlyn's gone. He lives here alone, except for the servants. There's a man and his wife indoors and a gardener and a chauffeur outside. He must have plenty of money, the colonel.'

'There's nothing out of the way in all that. Why did you call him peculiar?'

'Well, just his living alone. He doesn't have much to say to the neighbours by all accounts. Then he catches insects about the moor and sits up half the night writing about them. They say he's writing a book.'

'What age is he?'

'About forty-five, I should say.'

'Well, that's all we can do here. Let's get on to Tavistock.'

French enjoyed the remainder of the drive as much as any he had ever taken. He was immensely impressed by the mournful beauty of the scenery. They passed Two Bridges, presently striking off from the Plymouth road. On the left the great grey buildings of the prison appeared, with rugged North Hessary Tor just beyond and the farm staffed by the prisoners in the foreground. The road led on almost due west until; after passing the splendid outlook of Moorshop and descending more break-neck hills, they reached cultivated ground and Tavistock.

They had driven fast, and less the time they had stopped on the road, the run had taken just sixty-three minutes. The car had behaved excellently, and if French had really been contemplating its purchase he would have been well satisfied with the test.

'I want to find out how long the radiator took to cool on that night,' French said. 'The point is to know whether the car could have done any further running after its trip from here to the place where it was abandoned. If it takes three hours or more to cool, it couldn't; if less, it might.'

'I follow, but I'm afraid that won't be easy to find out.'

'Why not?'

'Well, it depends on the weather and specially the wind. I used to drive, and I know something about it. If there's a wind blowing into the radiator it'll cool about twice as quickly as if the same wind was blowing from behind the car.'

'I can understand that,' French admitted. 'How was the wind that night?'

'A very faint westerly breeze—scarcely noticeable.'

'That would be behind the car. Then if we try it today in any pretty sheltered place we ought to get, roughly speaking,

87

the same result? The temperature's about the same today as it was that night, I should think?'

'That's so, sir, the weather conditions are as good for a test as you'll get. But even so it will be only a rough guide.'

'We'll try it anyway. Park somewhere and we'll go and have some lunch.'

They left the car in front of the fine old parish church while they lunched and explored the town. Then returning to the car, they sat down to wait. At intervals they felt the radiator until, just three and a half hours after their arrival, the last sensation of warmth vanished.

'That's three hours and thirty minutes,' Daw declared, 'but I don't think you would be wise to take that too literally. If you say something between three and four hours you won't be far wrong.'

'I agree, sergeant. That's all we want. Let's get home.'

That evening French sat down to write up his notes and to consider the facts he had learned.

The more he thought over these facts, the more dissatisfied he grew. It certainly did not look as if his effort to connect the Berlyn-Pyke tragedy with the crate affair was going to be successful. And if it failed it left him where he had started. He had no alternative theory on which to work.

He recalled the four points by which he had hoped to test the matter. On each of these he had now obtained information, but in each case the information tended against the theory he wished to establish.

First there was the breakdown of the car. Was that an accident or had it been pre-arranged?

Obviously if it had been an accident it could not have been part of the criminal's plan. Therefore neither could the resulting disappearance of Berlyn and Pyke. Therefore the murderer must have been out after some other victim, whose disappearance he had masked so cleverly that it had not yet been discovered.

Now Makepeace had stated definitely that the breakdown could not have been faked. Of course it would be necessary to have this opinion confirmed by the makers of the magneto. But Makepeace had seemed so sure that French did not doubt his statement.

The second point concerned the movements of the car on the fatal night. French began by asking himself the question: Assuming the murdered man were Pyke, how had his body been taken to the works?

He could only see one way—in the car. Suppose the murder was committed on the way from Tavistock. What then? The murderer would drive to the works with the dead man in the car. This, French believed, would be possible without discovery owing to the distance the works lay from the town. He would then in some way square the night watchman, unpack the duplicator, put the body in its place, load the duplicator into the back of the car, drive off, somehow get rid of the duplicator, return to the road near Colonel Domlio's house, make the two lines of footprints, and decamp.

At first sight this obvious explanation seemed encouraging to French. Then he wondered would there be time for all these operations?

Taking the results of the tests he had made and estimating times where he had no actual data, he set himself to produce a hypothetical time-table of the whole affair. It was a form of reconstruction which he had found valuable on many previous occasions. It read:

Tavistock depart	-	-	-	10.50 p.m.

A fast daylight run had taken 63 minutes—
for night, say 70. Add for actual murder;
5 minutes. Then—

Vida Works arrive	-	-	-	12.5 a.m.
Open gates and get car placed under differential, close gates	-	-	-	12.10 "
Square watchman and lift out body	-	-	12.25 "
Open crate carefully so as not to damage lid	-	12.30 "
Lift out duplicator and place it in car	-	-	12.40 "
Take outer clothes off body	-	-	-	12.50 "
Place body in crate	-	-	-	-	1 "
Make good the lid of crate	-	-	-	1.5 "
Take car out of works and lock gates	-	-	1.10 "

After leaving the works the murderer had to get rid of the duplicator. French could not estimate this item as he had no idea how the thing could have been done. But it had certainly taken half an hour. That would make it 1.40 a.m. At least another half hour would have been spent in returning to the site of the mock tragedy, bringing the time up to 2.10 a.m.

The engine and radiator had then gradually to cool, for there was no water on that part of the moor to cool them artificially. From his experiment French felt sure that this would have taken at least three hours. In other words there would have been traces of heat up till about five o'clock. And that at the very earliest possible.

But the sergeant found the car at 3.35 a.m, and it was then cold. It was therefore impossible that it could have been used to carry the victim to the works as French had assumed. And if it had not been so used how could the body have been transported? There was no way without introducing an accomplice and another car, which on the face of it seemed improbable.

It would, he saw, have been possible to have taken the body to the works in the car if the vehicle had immediately returned to the moor. But this not only postulated an accomplice, but overlooked the duplicator. If the car had been used to dispose of the duplicator it would have been warm when the sergeant found it.

The third point was the squaring of the night watchman. The more French thought over this, the more impossible it seemed. In an ordinary matter the man might easily have been corrupted, but unless he had some irresistible motive he would never have risked his neck by aiding and abetting a murder. And he could not have been deceived as to what was taking place. Even supposing that he had been at the time, next day's discovery would have made clear what he had assisted in.

But even supposing he had been squared, it did not clear the matter up. In this case French did not believe he could have sustained his interrogation without giving himself away. He would have guessed what lay behind the questions and would have shown fear. No, French was satisfied the man had no suspicion of anything so grave as murder, and it seemed impossible that the body could have been put into the crate without making the terrible fact clear.

The fourth test seemed equally convincing. If the body had been put into the crate in the works, where was the duplicator? It could not have been left in the works; the storekeeping methods would have revealed it long before this. Had it been taken out?

French could not imagine any way in which it could have been done. The duplicator was a big machine and heavy. It could not have been lifted by less than three or four people. Of course there was the differential pulley with its overhead rail, but even these would only have lifted it out of the crate on to a car or lorry. To have unloaded it secretly would involve the existence of a second differential in some place available only to the murderer, a far-fetched hypothesis, though no doubt possible.

But what finally convinced French was the consideration that if the murderer really had been able to dispose secretly of so bulky an object, he would surely have used this method to get rid of the body and thus have saved the whole complex business of the crate.

French felt deeply disappointed as he found himself forced to these conclusions. A promising theory had gone west, and he was left as far from a solution of his problem as when he took it up. Moreover, up to the present, at all events, the Yard had been unable to learn anything at the St Pancras or Euston Hotels of either 'John F. Stewart' or 'James S. Stephenson.' Evidently in this case as in most others there was no royal road to success. He must simply go on trying to amass information in the ordinary humdrum routine way, in the hope that sooner or later he might come on some fact which would throw the desired light on the affair.

Tired and not a little out of sorts, he turned in.

8

A Fresh Start

It is wonderful what an effect a good night's sleep and a bright morning will have on the mind of a healthy man. French had gone to bed tired and worried about his case. He woke cheery and optimistic, philosophic as to his reverses, and hopeful for the future.

On such a morning indeed it was impossible that anyone could be despondent. Though October had begun, the sun shone with a thin brilliancy reminiscent of early summer. The air, floating up gently from the garden in the rear of the hotel, was surprisingly warm and aromatic for the time of year. Birds were singing in the trees and there was a faint hum of insects from below. As he looked out of his window French felt that life was good and that to squander it in sleep was little better than a sin.

He breakfasted at his leisure, then lighting his pipe, he sauntered out into the little town to take what he called 'a turn' before settling down to the serious work of the day.

Though his conclusions of the previous evening still seemed incontrovertible, he was surprised to find that his sense of disappointment had vanished. At first he thought this was due simply to his night's rest, then gradually he realised the reason.

In his heart of hearts he distrusted these conclusions. In spite of the difficulties involved, he was not satisfied that the Berlyn-Pyke affair should be eliminated from the case.

The murderer had shown himself an extremely ingenious man. Could it not be that these seeming impossibilities were really intentionally designed to throw investigating detectives off the scent?

French reconsidered the strength of the coincidences otherwise involved.

A disappearance at a certain time and place was required to account for the body in the crate. At that very time and place, and there only, a disappearance was known to have occurred. French could not bring himself to dismiss the possibility of a connection between the two facts.

He decided that he had not exhausted the possibilities. He must learn more about Berlyn and Pyke.

For preliminary inquiries Sergeant Daw seemed the most hopeful source of information, and he lost no time in walking down to the police station and asking his help.

'I want to know who everybody is, Sergeant. You know the local people and you might tell me something which would give me the hint I am looking for.'

The sergeant did not think this likely, but he was willing to do anything to oblige.

'Very good. Then I'll ask questions. First of all, will you tell me what you can about Mr Berlyn?'

Daw put on his best police court manner and proceeded to deliver himself.

'Mr Berlyn was junior partner at the works. I understand

that some eight or nine years ago he and Colonel Domlio bought up nearly the whole of the stock between them. Mr Berlyn dealt with the commercial side and attended the office every day as if he was an official, but the Colonel looked on the business as a hobby. He acted as a sort of consulting engineer, and only went to the works when it pleased him. I believe there are other directors, but in practice they don't amount to anything.'

'Was Mr Berlyn liked?'

'As a matter of fact, sir, he wasn't altogether popular among the work-people. From what I've heard he wanted too much and he wouldn't make allowances for people making mistakes. It was get on or get out with him, and you know yourself, Mr French, that if that's pushed too far it doesn't always work. But he was straight enough, and what he said he stuck to.'

'A man like that would make enemies. Do you know of anyone he was on bad terms with?'

'No, sir. No one.'

'He hadn't his knife in Mr Pyke, for instance?'

'Not to my knowledge.'

'Was Mr Berlyn married?'

'Yes, four or five years ago. Very pleasant lady, Mrs Berlyn.'

'Any children?'

'No, sir.'

'Where did they live?'

'Out along the Buckland road about ten minutes walk from the works. Place called Soller. They say it's the name of some foreign town where he'd met the lady and popped the question, but of course I don't know anything about that.'

'Then he was a traveller, Mr Berlyn?'

95

'Yes; used to go away to France and such places when he had holidays.'

'Wise man,' French commented. 'And how did the match turn out?'

For the first time the sergeant hesitated.

'There, Mr French, you have me. I couldn't really tell you. From all accounts they got on as well as most people whose tastes differ. He was quiet and liked sitting at home in the evenings, and she wanted a bit of life. There's not much of what you might call gaiety in this town, as you may guess, but whatever there was Mrs Berlyn was in the centre of it. At first he used to go out with her to Torquay and so on, but he gradually gave that up and she had to find someone else to go with or stay at home.'

'And she found someone?'

'Any number. The gentlemen up at the works mostly. They were all glad to go with her. Colonel Domlio had been taking her about lately—I mean before Mr Berlyn's death, and before that it was Mr Pyke and sometimes Mr Cowls, the engineer. She was friends, too, with Dr and Mrs Lancaster; and I've seen her often out with people called Tucker that live close by.'

All this seemed suggestive to French; and his facile brain was already building up tentative theories.

'Was there ever any suggestion of anything between Mrs Berlyn and any of those men?'

'There was a bit of talk at one time, but I don't believe there was anything in it.'

'But there was talk. Just tell me what was said.'

'She was talked about with Mr Pyke. They certainly saw a deal of each other at one time. He was constantly at the house, and they went out motoring together. She was a top-hole driver.'

'You say they saw a deal of each other at one time. Did that not continue?'

'It was supposed to come to an end about four months before the tragedy. But that's only local gossip, and I can't vouch for it. All the same, I don't remember seeing them motoring since, except once when Mr Pyke's cousin came for three or four days.'

'And you have no idea what happened?'

'No, sir. Some said the lady heard of the talk and thought she had gone far enough, others that Mr Berlyn got wise to it, and others again that they just got tired of each other; I don't know. Whatever happened, it was all quite amicable, for I've seen them together different times since.'

'And was that the only time there was talk?'

'After that there was talk about her and Colonel Domlio. But you know, Mr French, in a place this size they're hard up for something to talk about. I don't believe there was anything in either story.'

'Tell me what was said anyway.'

'Well, that she used to go out to see him in the afternoons. The colonel was believed to be very fond of her, but she was only supposed to be amusing herself with him.'

'You say this took place recently?'

'That was the rumour.'

French shrugged.

'Safety in numbers, Sergeant. I agree it doesn't sound hopeful. Did Mr Berlyn seem upset about it?'

'Not that I ever heard of.'

'No good for us, Sergeant. Now about these others. Mr Pyke was not married, was he?'

No, Mr Pyke was not married, nor were Mr Cowls nor Mr Samuel nor Mr Leacock, other young men about the works with whom Mrs Berlyn had seemed on good terms. Mr Pyke had been with the firm for several years, and was said to be highly thought of. He was pleasant mannered and jolly and a general favourite. He lodged in the town; in fact his rooms were nearly opposite the hotel.

'Is Mrs Berlyn still here?'

'She left three or four days ago. There was an auction, and she waited till it was over. I heard she had gone to London.'

'Will she be well off?'

'I believe so. They say Mr Berlyn left her everything.'

'You spoke of Mr Pyke's cousin. Who is he?'

'A Mr Jefferson Pyke, a farmer in the Argentine. Rather like the late Mr Pyke, that's Mr Stanley, in appearance, but a bit taller and broader. He was on a visit to England, and was down here twice. First he came and stayed with Mr Stanley for three or four days about a couple of months before the tragedy: that was when Mrs Berlyn took them both out motoring. I wasn't speaking to him then, but I saw him with Mr and Mrs Berlyn and Mr Stanley in the car. Then the morning after the tragedy Mrs Berlyn gave me his London address and told me to wire for him. I did so, and he came down that evening. He stayed for three or four days in Torquay and came over to make inquiries and to look after Mr Stanley's affairs. A very nice gentleman I found him, and a good business man too.'

French noted the London address, and then asked what servants the Berlyns had.

'They had three, two house servants and the gardener.'

'Any of them available?'

'One of the girls, Lizzie Johnston, lives not far away. The others were strangers.'

French continued his inquisition in his slow, painstaking

way, making notes about everyone connected with the Berlyns and Pyke; but he learned nothing that confirmed his suspicions or suggested a line of research. It was true that in Mrs Berlyn he had glimpsed a possible source of trouble between her husband and Pyke. All the essentials of a triangle drama were there—except the drama itself. Mrs Berlyn might easily have hated her husband and loved one of these other men, but unfortunately for theorising detectives, if not for moralists, there was no evidence that she had done so. However, it was a suggestive idea and one which could not be lost sight of.

As these thoughts passed through French's mind a further consideration struck him, a consideration which he saw might not only prove a fifth test of the case he was trying to make, but which, if so, would undoubtedly be the most conclusive of them all. He turned once more to Daw.

'There's a point which is worrying me rather, Sergeant,' he declared. 'Suppose one of these two men murdered the other on that night. Now why would the murderer go to the trouble of getting the body into the works and sending it off in the crate? Could he not simply have thrown it into one of these mires?'

Daw nodded.

'I thought of that when you suggested your idea, but I don't believe there's anything in it. It wouldn't be so easy as it sounds. In fact, I couldn't see any way it could be done.'

'I'm glad to hear you say so, Sergeant. Explain, please.'

'Well, if you go into one of those places and begin to sink you throw yourself on your back. As long as your weight is on the small area of your feet you go down, but if you increase your area by lying on your back you reduce the weight per unit of area and you float—because it really is a kind of floating. You follow me, sir?'

'Quite. Go ahead.'

'Now, if you walk to a soft place carrying a body, you have doubled the weight on your feet. You will go down quickly. But the body won't go down. A man who tried to get rid of his victim that way would fail and lose his own life into the bargain.'

'That sounds conclusive. But I didn't know you could save yourself by throwing yourself down. If that is so, wouldn't Berlyn and Pyke have escaped that way? Why did you then accept the idea that they had been lost?'

'There were two reasons. First there was nothing to make me doubt it, such as knowing about the crate; and secondly, though the accident was not exactly likely, it was possible. This is the way I figured it out. Suppose one of these mists had come on: they do come on unexpectedly. One of the men gets into a soft place. Mists are confusing, and in trying to get out, he mistakes his position and flounders in farther. That's all perfectly possible. Then he calls to the other one, and in going to the first one's help, the other gets in also: both too far to get out again.'

'But you said it was a clear night?'

'So it was when I got there. But three or four hours earlier it might have been thick.'

'Now, Sergeant, there's another thing. Could the murderer not have used some sort of apparatus, a ladder or plank to lay on the soft ground, over which he could have carried the body and escaped himself? Same as you do on ice.'

'I thought of that too, but I don't believe it would be possible. A ladder wouldn't do at all: with its sharp edges it would go down under the weight. And I don't think a man could handle a big enough plank. It would have to be pretty wide to support the weight of two men, and it would have to be long to get beyond the edge of the mire. You see, Mr French, it's only well out into the big mires that a flat body will sink. Near the edges it would have to be kept upright with the weight on the feet. That couldn't be done off the end of a plank which would itself be sinking; in fact, I don't think it could be done at all.'

French nodded. This was certainly very satisfactory.

'Besides, sir,' Daw went on, 'think of a plank laid as you've suggested and with the end of it partly sunk. It'll not be easy to pull out, particularly when the ground you're pulling from is not very firm. You won't do it without leaving pretty deep footmarks, and the plank will leave a sort of trough where it was slid out. If that had been done that night the marks would have been there next morning, and if they had been there I should have seen them. No, sir, I think you may give up that idea. You couldn't get rid of a body by hiding it in a mire.'

'I'm uncommonly glad to hear you say so,' French repeated. 'If the thing had been possible it would have knocked my case into a cocked hat. Well, Sergeant, I've bothered you enough for one morning. I'll go along and have a word with Mrs Berlyn's maid.'

Lizzie Johnston lived with her mother in a little cottage on the hill behind the railway station. She proved to be a dark, good-looking girl of about five-and-twenty, and when French talked with her he soon discovered she was observant, and intelligent also.

She had lived, she said, with Mrs Berlyn for about two years, and French, in his skilful, pleasant way, drew her out on the subject of the household. It consisted of the two Berlyns, herself and cook, unless Peter Swann, the gardener, might be included.

Mr Berlyn she had not greatly liked. He was quiet in the house, but was rather exacting. He was not socially inclined, and preferred an evening's reading over the fire to any dinner party or dance. He had been civil enough to her, though she had really come very little in contact with him.

About Mrs Berlyn the girl was not enthusiastic either, though she said nothing directly against her. Mrs Berlyn, it appeared, was also hard to please, and no matter what was done for her, she always wanted something more. She was never content to be alone, and was continually running over to Torquay to amusements. After their marriage Mr Berlyn had gone with her, but he had gradually given up doing so and had allowed her to find some other escort. This she had had no difficulty in doing, and Mr Pyke, Mr Cowls, and others were constantly in attendance.

No, the girl did not think there had been anything between Mrs Berlyn and any of these men, though for a time Mr Pyke's attentions had been rather pronounced. But some four months before the tragedy they appeared to have had a disagreement, for his visits had suddenly fallen off. But it could not have been very serious, for he still had occasionally come to dinner and to play bridge. She remembered one time in particular when Mr Pyke had brought a relative; she heard it was a cousin. There were just the four, the two Pykes and the two Berlyns, and they all seemed very friendly. But there was a coolness all the same, and since it had developed Colonel Domlio had to some extent taken Mr Pyke's place.

About the Berlyns' history she could not tell much. Mr Berlyn had lived in the town for several years before his marriage. He seemed to have plenty of money. He had bought the house on the Buckland road just before the wedding, and had had it done up from top to bottom. It was not a large

102

house, but beautifully fitted up. At the same time he had bought the car. Peter Swann, the gardener, washed the car, but he did not drive it. Both Mr and Mrs Berlyn were expert drivers and good mechanics. Mrs Berlyn also used her push bicycle a good deal.

French then came to the evening of the tragedy. On that evening dinner had been early to allow Mr Berlyn to get away in the car at seven o'clock. It should have been the maid's evening out, but Mrs Berlyn had told her she would have to take the next evening instead, as some friends were coming in and she would be wanted to bring up supper. About eight o'clock Mr Fogden, Mr Cowls, a Dr and Mrs Lancaster, and three or four other people had arrived. She had brought them up coffee and sandwiches about half-past ten. They had left about eleven. She had gone to bed almost at once, and a few minutes later she had heard Mrs Berlyn go up to her room.

The next thing she remembered was being wakened in the middle of the night by Mrs Berlyn. The lady was partly dressed and seemed agitated. 'Lizzie,' she had said, 'it's nearly three o'clock and there's no sign of Mr Berlyn. I'm frightened. I've just been out to the garage to see if the car has come back, but it's not there. What do you think can be wrong?'

They hurriedly discussed the matter. Mr Berlyn was the last man to alter his plans, and both were afraid of an accident on that dangerous Tavistock road.

In the end they decided that Mrs Berlyn should knock up Sergeant Daw, who lived near. This she did, while Lizzie dressed. Presently Mrs Berlyn came back to say that the sergeant was going out to investigate. They had some tea and lay down without taking off their clothes. In the early morning a policeman brought the news of the tragedy.

Mrs Berlyn was terribly upset. But she grew calmer in time, and the arrangements for the auction and for her removal to London taking her out of herself, in a week she was almost normal.

She had been very nice to Lizzie at the last, giving her an excellent testimonial and an extra month's wages.

French thanked the girl for her information and rose as if to take his leave.

'I suppose Mrs Berlyn was something of a needlewoman?' he said carelessly. 'Someone told me she made her own dresses.'

Lizzie laughed contemptuously.

'Made her dresses, did she?' she repeated. 'I don't think. She didn't hardly know how to wear a thimble, she didn't. She wouldn't have sat down to a job of sewing, not for no person on earth she wouldn't.'

'Then who did the household mending?'

'Yours truly. Anything that was done I had to do.'

'But not the clothes surely? Who darned Mr Berlyn's socks, for instance?'

'Yours truly. I tell you Mrs Berlyn wouldn't have touched a sock or a bit of wool not to save her life.'

This was a piece of unexpected luck. French considered.

'I was just wanting a bit of mending done for myself,' he declared. 'Seeing that you're good at the job, would you be on to do it for me?'

Miss Johnston signified her willingness—on terms.

'Very well. You come down to the hotel after dinner tonight and ask for me. Or rather,' he paused, 'I have to come up in this direction after lunch today in any case, and I'll bring the clothes.'

No object in advertising the lines on which he was working,

he thought. The less that was known of his researches, the more hope there was of their proving fruitful.

A couple of hours later he returned with a small suitcase.

'Here are the clothes,' he said. 'I wish you'd see what they want, so that I'll know when I'm likely to get them.'

He laid four pairs of socks on the table, three brown pairs of his own and the grey pair found in the crate. The girl looked them over one by one. French watched her in silence. He was anxious, if possible, to give her no lead.

'There isn't much wrong with these,' she said presently. 'They don't want no darning.'

'Oh, but they have been badly mended. You see these grey ones have been done with a different coloured wool. I thought perhaps you could put that right.'

Miss Johnston laughed scornfully.

'You're mighty particular, mister, if that darning ain't good enough for you. I'd just like to know what's wrong with it.'

'You think it's all right?' French returned. 'If so, I'm satisfied. But what about these underclothes?'

The girl examined the clothes. They were almost new and neatly folded just as they had come back from the laundry, so that her contemptuous reply was not inexcusable. At all events it was evident that no suspicion that they were other than her visitor's had crossed her mind.

French, with his half-formed theory of Berlyn's guilt, would have been surprised if she had answered otherwise. The test, however, had been necessary and he felt he had not lost time. Mollifying her with a tip, he returned to the hotel.

9

A Step Forward

French believed that he had obtained all the available information about the Berlyns from his interview with the sergeant
and Lizzie Johnston. Pyke was the next name on his list, and
he now crossed East Street to the house in which the travelling representative had lodged. The door was opened by a
bright-eyed, bustling little woman, at sight of whom French's
emotional apparatus registered satisfaction. He knew the
type. The woman was a talker.

But when for the best part of an hour he had listened to
her, satisfaction was no longer the word with which to express
his state of mind. He had no difficulty in getting her to talk.
His trouble was to direct the flood of her conversation along
the channel in which he wished it to flow.

He began by explaining that he was staying at the hotel,
but that as he liked the district and might want to remain
for some time, he was looking about for rooms. He had
heard she had some to let. Was this so, and if it was, could
he see them?

It was so, and he could see them. She had had a lodger, a

very nice gentleman and a very good payer, but she had lost him recently. Mr—she had heard his name: was it not Mr French? Mr French must have heard about his dreadful death? His name was Mr Pyke. Had Mr French not heard?

Mr French had heard something about it. It seemed a very sad affair.

It was a very sad affair. Mr Pyke had gone out that evening as well as Mr French or herself, and he had never come back: had never been seen again. Terrible, wasn't it? And a terrible shock to her. Indeed she didn't feel the same even yet. She didn't believe she ever would. Between that and the loss of the letting . . .

What had he said before he started? Why, he hadn't said anything. At least he had said he wouldn't be home until about midnight, and for her not to forget to leave the hall door on the latch and to put some supper on the table in his room. And she had done. She had left everything right for him, and then she had gone to bed. And she had slept. She was a good sleeper, except that one time after she had had scarlet fever, when the doctor said . . .

Yes, the rooms were ready at any time. She believed in keeping her house clean and tidy at all times so that everything was always ready when it was wanted. She had once been in service with Mrs Lloyd-Hurley in Chagford, and she had learnt that lesson there. Mrs Lloyd-Hurley was very particular. She . . .

Mr Pyke's things? Oh, yes, they were gone. She thought that would be understood when she said the rooms were ready. She . . .

It was his cousin. His cousin had come down from London and taken everything there was. That was Mr Jefferson Pyke. Her Mr Pyke was Mr Stanley. Mr Jefferson was the only remaining relative, at least so she understood. He packed up everything and took it away. Except a few things that he said he didn't want. These she had kept. Not that she wanted them, but if they were going begging, as Mr French might say, why then . . .

No, she had only seen Mr Jefferson once before. He lived in the Argentine, or was it Australia? She wasn't rightly sure—she had no memory for places—but he lived away in some strange foreign country anyhow. He happened to be over on a visit and was going back again shortly. Her brother James lived in Australia, and she had asked Mr Jefferson . . .

So French sat and listened while the unending stream poured about his devoted head. At times, by summoning up all his resolution, he interposed a remark which diverted the current in a new direction. But his perseverance was rewarded, as from nearly all of these mutations he learned at least one fact. When at last, exhausted but triumphant, he rose to take his leave he had gained the following information:

Mr Stanley Pyke was a jolly, pleasant-mannered man of about five-and-thirty, who had lodged with the talkative landlady for the past four years. He had been connected with the works for much longer than that, but at first had had other rooms farther down the street. Hers, the landlady modestly explained, were the best in the town, and Mr Pyke's removal was an outward and visible sign of his prosperity. For the rest he was satisfactory as lodgers go, easy to please, not stingy about money, and always with a pleasant word for her when they met.

On the evening of the tragedy he had dined at 6.15 p.m. instead of seven, his usual hour. He had gone out immediately after, giving the instruction about the door and his supper. The landlady had gone to bed as usual, and the first intimation she had had that anything was wrong with the visit of the police on the following morning.

Someone, she did not know who, must have informed the cousin, Mr Jefferson Pyke, for that evening he turned up. He had stayed at Torquay for three or four days, coming over to Ashburton to see the police and make inquiries. On one of these visits he had called on her and stated that as he was the only surviving relative of his cousin, he would take charge of his personal effects. He had packed up and removed a good many of the dead man's things, saying he did not want the remainder and asking her to dispose of them.

It had not occurred to her to question Mr Jefferson Pyke's right to take her lodger's property. She had seen him once before, in Mr Stanley's lifetime. Some two months before the tragedy Mr Stanley had told her that his cousin was home on a visit from the Argentine—she believed it was the Argentine and not Australia—and that he was coming down to see him. He asked her could she put him up. Mr Jefferson had arrived a day or two later and she had given him her spare bedroom. He stayed for four days, and the cousins had explored the moors together. Mrs Berlyn, she had heard, had driven them about in her car. The landlady had found Mr Jefferson very pleasant; indeed, when the two men were together they had nearly made her die laughing with their jokes and nonsense. Mr Jefferson had told her that he owned a ranch in the Argentine and that he was thinking of starting flower gardens from which to supply the cities. He was then on his way back from the Scillies, where he had gone to investigate the industry. A week after Mr Jefferson left; Mr Stanley took his holidays, and he had told her he was going with his cousin to the south of France; to a place called

109

Grasse, where there were more gardens. He was only back some three weeks when he met his death.

All this was given to French with a wealth of detail which, had it been material to his investigation, he would have welcomed, but by which as it was he was frankly bored. However, he could do nothing to stop the stream, and he simulated interest as best he could.

'By the way, Mrs Billing,' he said, pausing on his way out, 'if I take these rooms could you look after the mending of my clothes? Who did it for Mr Pyke?'

Mrs Billing had, and she would be delighted to do the same for Mr French.

'Well, I have some that want looking after at the present time. Suppose I bring them over now, could you look at them?'

Five minutes later he returned with his suitcase and spread out the clothes as he had done for Lizzie Johnston an hour or two earlier. Like the maid, Mrs Billing glanced over them and remarked that there didn't seem to be much wrong.

French picked up the grey sock.

'But you see they have not been very neatly darned. This grey one has been done with a different coloured wool. I thought perhaps you could put that right.'

Mrs Billing took the grey sock and stared at it for some time, while a puzzled expression grew on her face. French, suddenly keenly excited, watched her almost breathlessly. But after turning it over she put it down, though the slightly mystified look remained.

'Here are some underclothes,' French went on 'Do these want any mending?'

Slowly the landlady turned over the bundle. As she did so incredulity and amazement showed on her bird-like features.

Then swiftly she turned to the neck of the vest and shirt cuffs and scrutinised the buttons and links.

'My Gawd!' she whispered hoarsely, and French saw that her face had paled and her hands were trembling.

'You recognise them?'

She nodded, her flood of speech for once paralysed.

'Where did you get them?' she asked, still in a whisper.

French was quite as excited as she, but he controlled himself and spoke easily.

'Tell me first whose they are and how you are so sure of them.'

'They're Mr Pyke's, what he was wearing the night he was lost. I couldn't but be sure of them. See here. There's the wool first. I darned that, and I remember I hadn't the right colour. Then these buttons.' She picked up the vest. 'I put that one on. See, it's not the same as the rest; it was the only one I could get. And then; if that wasn't enough; there are the cuff-links. I've seen them hundreds of times and I'd know them anywhere. Where did you get them?'

French dropped his suave, kindly manner and suddenly became official and for him, unusually harsh.

'Now, Mrs Billing,' he said sharply, 'I'd better tell you exactly who I am and warn you that you've got to keep it to yourself. I am Inspector French of New Scotland Yard; you understand, a police officer. I have discovered that Mr Pyke was murdered and I am on the track of the murderer.'

The landlady gave a little scream. She was evidently profoundly moved, not only by surprise and excitement but by horror at her late lodger's fate. She began to speak, but French cut her short.

'I want you to understand,' he said threateningly, 'that you must keep silence on this matter. If any hint of it gets about

111

it will be a very serious thing for you. I take it you don't want to be mixed up in a murder trial. Very well then; keep your mouth shut.'

Mrs Billing was terrified and eagerly promised discretion. French questioned her further, but without result. She did not believe her late lodger was on bad terms with anyone nor did she know if he had a birthmark on his upper arm.

French's delight at his discovery was unbounded. The identification of the dead man represented the greatest step towards the completion of his case that he had yet made. He chuckled to himself in pure joy.

But his brain reeled when he thought of his four test-points. If this news were true he had made some pretty bad mistakes! Each several one of his four conclusions must be false. As he remembered the facts on which they were based he had to admit himself completely baffled.

Presently his mood changed and a wave of pessimism swept over him. The identification of the underclothes was not after all the identification of the body. Such an astute criminal as he was dealing with might have changed the dead man's clothes. But when he reminded himself that the man who called for the crate resembled Berlyn, the thing became more convincing. However, it had not been proved, and he wanted certainty.

Fortunately there was the birthmark. French had examined it carefully and was satisfied, that it was genuine. Who, he wondered, could identify it?

The most likely person, he thought, was Jefferson Pyke. It would be worth a journey to London to have the point settled. That night therefore he took the sleeping-car express to Paddington.

Daw had given him the address—17b Kepple Street, off Russell Square, and before ten next morning he was there.

Jefferson Pyke was a clean-shaven man of about forty, of rather more than medium height and stoutly built. He was a study in browns: brown eyes, a dusky complexion, hair nearly black, brown clothes and shoes and a dark brown tie. He looked keenly at his visitor, then pointed to a chair.

'Mr French?' he, said, speaking deliberately. 'What can I do for you, sir?'

'I'll tell you, Mr Pyke,' French answered. 'First of all, here is my professional card. I want some help from you in an investigation I am making.'

Pyke glanced at the card and nodded.

'A case on which I was engaged took me recently to Ashburton, and while there I heard of the tragic death of Mr Pyke and Mr Berlyn of the Vida Works staff. I understand that Mr Pyke was a relative of yours?'

'That is so. My first cousin.'

'Well, Mr Pyke,' French said gravely. 'I have to inform you that a discovery has been made which may or may not have a bearing on your cousin's fate. A body has been found: the body of a murdered man. That body has not been identified, but there is a suggestion that it may be your cousin's. I want to know if you can identify it?'

Mr Pyke stared incredulously.

'Good heavens, Inspector! That's an astonishing suggestion. You must surely be mistaken. I went down to Ashburton directly I heard of the accident and there seemed no doubt then about what had happened. Tell me the particulars.'

'About a fortnight ago, as you may have noticed in the papers, a crate was picked up in the sea off Burry Port in

113

South Wales, which was found to contain the body of a murdered man. The face had been disfigured and there was no means of identification. However, I traced the crate and I learned that it was sent out from the Vida Works on the morning after your cousin and Mr Berlyn disappeared.'

'Good heavens!' Mr Pyke exclaimed again. 'Go on.'

'I made inquiries and the only persons known to have disappeared were those two men. You see the suggestion? I am sorry to have to ask you, but can you help me to identify the remains?'

Mr Pyke's face showed both amazement and horror.

'This is terrible news, Inspector. I need hardly say I hope you are mistaken. Of course you may count on me to do all I can.'

'You think you can identify the body, then?'

'Surely I ought to recognise my own cousin?'

'Otherwise than by the face? Remember the face has been disfigured. I might say, indeed, it is non-existent; it has been so savagely battered.'

'By heaven, I hope you will get the man who did it!' Pyke said hotly. 'But that does not answer your question.' He hesitated. 'If it is not possible to recognise the features, I'm not so sure. How do you suggest it might be done?'

French shrugged.

'Identification otherwise than by the features is usually possible. It is a matter of observation. Some small physical defect, a crooked finger, the scar of an old cut, or mole on the neck—there are scores of indications to the observant man.'

Mr Pyke sat in silence for a few minutes.

'Then I'm afraid I'm not very observant,' he said at last. 'I can't remember any such peculiarity in poor Stanley's case.'

'Nothing in the shape of the finger nails,' French prompted. 'No birthmark, no local roughness or discoloration of the skin?'

'By Jove!' Mr Pyke exclaimed with a sudden gesture. 'There is something. My cousin had a birthmark, a small red mark on his left arm, here. I remembered it directly you mentioned the word.'

'Then you have been fairly intimate with your cousin? Have you often see this mark?'

'Seen it? Scores of times. We were boys together, and I have noticed it again and again. Why, now I come to think of it, I saw it on these last holidays I spent with Stanley. We went to the south of France and shared a cabin in the steamer to Marseilles.'

'Could you describe it?'

'No, but I could sketch it.' He took a piece of paper and drew a rough triangle.

French laid his photograph beside the sketch. There could be no doubt that they represented the same object. Pyke took the photograph.

'That's it. I could swear to it anywhere. You've found Stanley's body right enough. Good heavens, Inspector, it's incredible! I could have sworn he hadn't an enemy in the world. Have you any clue to the murderer?'

Natural caution and official training made French hedge.

'Not as yet,' he answered, assuring himself that his ideas about Berlyn were hypothetical. 'I was hoping that you could give me a lead.'

'I?' Jefferson Pyke shook his head. 'Far from it. Even now I can scarcely credit the affair.'

'Well, I should like you to run over his associates and see if you can't think of any who might have hated him.

Now, to start with the senior partner: What about Colonel Domlio?'

Mr Pyke had never met him and knew nothing about him, though he had heard his cousin mention his name. French went on through the list he had made at Ashburton till, in the natural sequence, he came to Berlyn.

'Now, Mr Berlyn. Could he have had a down on your cousin?'

'But he was lost, too,' Pyke rejoined, then stopped and looked keenly at French. 'By Jove, Inspector, I get your idea! You think Berlyn may have murdered him and cleared out?' He shook his head. 'No, no, you are wrong. It is impossible. Berlyn wasn't that sort. I knew him slightly and I confess I didn't care for him, but he was not a murderer.'

'Why did you not like him, Mr Pyke?'

Pyke shrugged.

'Hard to say. Not my style, perhaps. A good man, you know, and efficient and all that, but—too efficient, shall I say? He expected too much from others: didn't make allowances for human errors and frailties. Poor Mrs Berlyn had rather a time with him.'

'How so?'

'Well, an example will explain what I mean. On this last holiday after Stanley and I got back to London we met Berlyn and his wife who were in town. The four of us dined together and went to a theatre. We were to meet at the restaurant at seven. Well, Mrs Berlyn had been off somewhere on her own, and she was five minutes late. What was that for a woman? But Berlyn was so ratty about it that I felt quite embarrassed. You see, he wouldn't have been late himself. If he had said seven, he would have been there—on the tick. He couldn't see that other people were not made the same way.'

116

'I follow you. You say that Mrs Berlyn had rather a time with him. Did they not get on?'

'Oh, they got on—as well as fifty per cent of the married people get on. Berlyn did his duty to her strictly, even lavishly, but he expected the same in return. I don't know that you could blame him. Strictly speaking, of course, he was right. It was his instinct for scrupulously fair play.'

'Your late cousin and Mrs Berlyn were very good friends, were they not?'

'We were both good friends with Mrs Berlyn. Stanley and I knew her as children. In fact it was through Stanley that Berlyn met her. I was in the Argentine at the time, but he told me about it. Berlyn was going for a holiday—one of those cruises round the Western Mediterranean. Stanley happened to have met Phyllis Considine, as she was then, in London, and she had mentioned she was going on the same trip. So he gave Berlyn an introduction. Berlyn, it appears, fell in love with her and was accepted before the cruise was over.'

'Do you think Berlyn could have been jealous of your cousin?'

'I'm sure he could not, Inspector. Don't get that bee into your bonnet. Stanley certainly went often to the house, but Berlyn was always friendly to him. I don't for a moment believe there was anything to be jealous about.'

'There was enough intimacy for them to be talked about.'

'In Ashburton!' Pyke retorted scornfully. 'In a little one-horse place like that they'd talk no matter what you did.'

'It was believed that there was something between them until about four months before the tragedy; then, for some unknown reason, the affair stopped.'

'That so?' Pyke retorted. 'Well, if it stopped four months before the tragedy, it couldn't have caused it.'

'Do you know where Mrs Berlyn is now?'

'Yes, in London, at 70b Park Walk, Chelsea, to be exact.'

French continued his questions, but without learning anything further of interest, and after cautioning Pyke to keep his own counsel, he took his leave.

So he had reached certainty at last! The body was Stanley Pyke's. He had admittedly made four ghastly blunders in his test-points and these he must now try to retrieve. There was also a reasonable suspicion that Charles Berlyn was the murderer. Splendid! He was getting on. As he went down to the Yard he felt he had some good work behind him to report.

10

London's Further Contribution

Now that he was in London, French decided that he should complete certain inquiries.

First, he should satisfy himself that everything possible had been done to trace the letter-writers of the Euston and St Pancras hotels and the purchaser of the money order for £62 10s. Next, he must visit the manufacturers of the Ardlo magneto and get their views on short circuited windings. Lastly, he must have an interview with Mrs Berlyn.

As it happened he took the last of these items first, and three o'clock that afternoon found him ascending the stairs of No. 70b Park Walk, Chelsea. The house was divided into a number of what seemed small but comfortable flats. Pretty expensive, French thought, as he rang.

A neatly dressed maid opened the door, and after taking in his card, announced that Mrs Berlyn would see him. He followed her to a tiny but pleasantly furnished drawing-room, and there in a few minutes he was joined by the lady of the house.

French looked at her with some curiosity. Of medium

height and with a slight, graceful figure, she still gave an impression of energy and competent efficiency. She was not beautiful, but her appearance was arresting and French felt instinctively that she was a woman to be reckoned with. Her manner was vivacious and French could imagine her dancing all night and turning up next morning to breakfast as cool and fresh and ready for anything as if she had had her accustomed eight hours' sleep.

'Inspector French, Scotland Yard,' she said briskly, glancing at the card in her hand. 'Won't you sit down, Mr French, and tell me what I can do for you?'

'Thank you, Mrs Berlyn. I am sorry to say I have called on distressing business. It may or may not concern your late husband. I am hoping for information from you which may decide the point.'

The lady's expression became grave.

'Suppose you give me the details,' she suggested.

'I am about to do so, but I warn you that you must prepare yourself for a shock. It is in connection with the tragedy by which Mr Berlyn and Mr Pyke were believed to have lost their lives.'

Mrs Berlyn started and her gaze became fixed intently on French.

'It has been discovered that Mr Pyke was not lost on the moor as was supposed. Of Mr Berlyn's fate nothing new has been learnt. But I deeply regret to inform you that Mr Pyke was murdered.'

'Stanley Pyke murdered! Oh, impossible!' Horror showed on the lady's face and her lips trembled. For a moment it looked as if she would give way to her emotion, but she controlled herself and asked for details.

French told her exactly what had occurred, from the discovery of the crate to Jefferson Pyke's identification of the birthmark.

'I'm afraid it must be true,' she said sadly, when he had finished. 'I remember that birthmark too. We were children together, the Pykes and I, and I have often seen it. Oh, I can't say how sorry I am. Who *could* have done such a terrible thing? Stanley was so jolly and pleasant and kind. He was good to everyone and everyone liked him. Oh, it is too awful for words!'

French made a non-committal reply.

'But what about my late husband?' Mrs Berlyn went on. 'You said nothing has been learned about him. But—if they were together—?'

She paused suddenly, as if seeing that a meaning which she had not intended might be read into her words. But French replied soothingly:

'That's one of the things I wanted to talk to you about, Mrs Berlyn. Did you know if either he or Mr Pyke had any enemies? You need not fear to tell me the merest suspicions. I will act only on knowledge that I obtain, but your suspicion might suggest where to look for that knowledge.'

'Are you suggesting that my husband might have been murdered also?' she said in a low voice.

'Not necessarily. I am asking if you can think of anything which could sustain that view?'

Mrs Berlyn could not think of anything. She did not know of anyone who had a grudge against either of the men. Indeed, only for the inspector's assurance, she could not have brought herself to believe that Mr Pyke had met so dreadful an end.

French then began pumping her in his quiet, skilful way.

But though she answered all his questions with the utmost readiness, he did not learn much that he had not already known.

Her father, she told him, was a doctor in Lincoln, and there she had known the Pykes. Stanley's mother—his father was dead—lived about a mile from the town, and he and his cousin Jefferson, who boarded with them, used to walk in daily to school. The three had met at parties and children's dances, and had once spent a holiday together at the seaside. The Pykes had left the town when the boys had finished their schooling and she had lost sight of them. Then one day she had met Stanley in London, and he told her that he was at the Vida Works. She had mentioned that she was going on a cruise to the Mediterranean, and he had said that his employer, Mr Berlyn, was going on the same trip and to be sure to look out for him. That was the way she had met Mr Berlyn. He had proposed to her on the trip, and she had accepted him.

French then delicately broached the question of her relations with Stanley Pyke. And here for the first time he was not satisfied by her replies. That there had been something more between them than friendship he strongly suspected. Indeed, Mrs Berlyn practically admitted it. As a result of French's diplomatic probing it came out that Mr Berlyn had shown marked disapproval of their intimacy and that about four months prior to the tragedy they had decided that for the sake of peace they should see less of each other. They had carried out this resolve, and Berlyn's resentment had apparently vanished.

French next turned to the subject of Colonel Domlio, but here Mrs Berlyn had as good as laughed. It appeared that the man had tried to flirt with her, but her opinion was evidently that there was no fool like an old fool. French had no doubt that any love-making that might have taken place was not serious, on the lady's side at all events.

Thinking that he had obtained all the information that he was likely to get, French at last rose to go. But Mrs Berlyn signed to him to sit down again, and said gravely:

'If that is all, Mr French, I want to ask you a question. I never think there is any use in pretending about things, and from your questions I cannot but guess what is in your mind. You think my late husband may have murdered Mr Pyke?'

'I take it from that, Mrs Berlyn, that you want a perfectly straight answer? Well, I shall give it to you. The idea, of course, occurred to me, as it would to anyone in my position. I am bound to investigate it, and I am going to do so. But I can say without reservation that so far it remains an idea.'

Mrs Berlyn bowed.

'Thank you for that. Of course, I recognise that you must investigate all possibilities, and I recognise too that you will not give any weight to what I am going to say. But I must tell you that if you suspect Mr Berlyn you are making a mistake. Though he was not perfect, he was utterly incapable of a crime like that—utterly. If you had ever met him you would have known that. I wish I could say or do something to convince you. Besides, if he were alive, why did he disappear? If he were guilty would he not have come forward with a story that Mr Pyke had gone alone across the moor and been lost in the mires?'

French had already noted the point as the chief difficulty in his theory and he admitted it fully. He added that Mrs Berlyn's statement had made an impression on him and that he would not fail to bear it in mind. Then promising to let her know the result of his inquiry, he took his leave.

He had not lied when he said her statement had impressed him. That it represented her firm conviction he had not the least doubt. And it certainly was a point in Berlyn's favour that such testimony should be forthcoming from his wife, when it was evident that their married life had been an indifferent success. Of course, it might be simply that the woman did not wish to be involved in the misery and disgrace which would come with proof of Berlyn's guilt. But French did not think it was this. Her thought had seemed to be for her husband rather than herself.

It was still fairly early in the afternoon and French thought he would have time to make another call. He therefore walked up the Fulham Road and took an east-bound district train at South Kensington. Half an hour later he was at the headquarters of the Ardlo Magneto Company in Queen Elizabeth Street.

When the managing director heard French's business he touched a bell.

'You had better see Mr Illingworth, our chief electrical engineer,' he said. 'I am afraid I could not help you in these technical matters.'

Mr Illingworth was a pleasant young man with a quiet, efficient manner. He took French to his office, supplied him with cigarettes, and asked what he could do for him.

French put his problem, recounting the inquiries he had already made.

'Those people told you quite correctly,' was Mr Illingworth's answer. 'Your question is this: Could a man drive a car up to a certain place and then short-circuit the magneto armature so that the car couldn't be started again? The answer is, Yes, but not without leaving marks.'

'But that's just my puzzle,' French returned. 'That's exactly what seems to have been done.'

'Well,' Mr Illingworth answered with a smile, 'you may take it from me that it wasn't.'

'Then in the case that I have described, the breakdown must have been a pure accident?'

'I should say, absolutely. Mind you, I don't say that a breakdown couldn't be faked without leaving traces: it could be. But not so as to stop the car then and there. The concealed injury would take time to develop.'

'That's a bit cryptic, isn't it? Can you make it clearer to a lay intelligence?'

'Well, it is possible to damage the insulation by jamming a needle into the armature winding between the wire and the iron core, and if you're careful it'll leave no mark. But if the damage is so slight as not to leave a mark it won't disable the magneto straightaway. In fact, the car will run as usual, and it may be a considerable time before any defect shows. But sparking takes place at the injury, perhaps at first only when the engine is working specially hard. This causes carbonisation of the insulation, leading eventually to complete breakdown. The car begins to misfire and it gradually grows worse until it won't run at all.'

'I follow you. I may take it then that it is possible to cause a breakdown without leaving a mark. The fault, however, is not produced immediately, but slowly grows, and no one can foretell when it will get bad enough to stop the car.'

'That's right.'

'Suppose the winding was short-circuited as you describe, could an electrician afterwards tell what had been done?'

'No. It might have happened through some carelessness in the original winding.'

'That seems pretty clear. Now, just one other point, Mr Illingworth. Those people, Makepeace, in Ashburton, sent the actual magneto up here to be overhauled. Can you trace it and let me know just what was wrong?'

'Certainly. We have records of every machine which passes through our hands.' He consulted an index, finally withdrawing a card. 'This is it. Sent in from John Makepeace, Ashburton, on Monday, 22nd August. Would that date work in?'

'Yes, that's all right.'

'We've not had another from Makepeace for five years previously, so it must be,' Mr Illingworth went on, rapidly turning over the cards. 'Well, it's just what we were speaking of. It failed from a short-circuit in the armature winding and it might have been caused purposely or it might not; there was nothing to indicate.'

French rose.

'That's good enough for me,' he declared.

He felt his brain reel as he considered the contradictory nature of the evidence he was getting. The breakdown of the car *had* happened, and at a time and place which made it impossible to doubt that it had been deliberately caused. To cause such a breakdown was mechanically impossible. That was the dilemma which confronted him. And the further he probed this contradiction, the more strongly he found its conflicting details confirmed.

In a dream he returned to the Yard and there with an effort switched his mind off the conundrum and on to the features of his case which had been dealt with from headquarters.

Inspector Tanner, it appeared, had handled these matters and by a lucky chance French found him just about to leave for home.

'I'll walk with you,' said French. 'I don't want to delay you, and what's more to the point, I want to get home myself.'

Tanner was a man who liked a joke, or at least, what he considered a joke. He now chaffed French on being unable to carry on his cases by himself, and they sparred amicably for some time before coming to business. But Tanner was also exceedingly able, and when he described what he had done at the hotels and post office, French was satisfied that no further information could be extracted from these sources.

All the next day, which was Sunday, the problem of the magneto remained subconsciously in French's mind, and when on Monday morning he took his place in the 10.30 a.m. Limited to return to Devonshire, he was still pondering it. In a dream he watched the bustle of departure on the platform, the arrival of more and ever more travellers, the appropriation of seats, the disposal of luggage. (That arma-ture *had* been tampered with. It must have been, because otherwise it would not have worked in with a pre-arranged crime.) Lord! What a pile of luggage for one woman to travel with! American, he betted. (But it could not have been done at the time. In no way could it have been made to fail just when it was wanted.) What price that for a natty suit? Why, the man was a moving chess-board! What was the connection between chess-board suits and horses? (It must have been tampered with: but it couldn't have been. That was the confounded problem.) There was the guard with his green flag, looking critically up and down and glancing first at his watch and then over his shoulder at the platform clock. It was just twenty-nine and a half minutes past. In another half minute . . .

Suddenly into French's mind flashed an idea, and he sat for a moment motionless, as with a sort of trembling eager-ness he considered it. Why, his problem was not a problem

127

at all! There was a solution of the simplest and most obvious kind! How had he been stupid enough not to have seen it?

As the guard waved his flag French sprang to his feet, and amid the execrations of the porters, he hurled himself and his baggage from the moving train. Then, smiling pleasantly at the exasperated officials, he hurried from the station, jumped into a taxi, and told the man to drive to the Ardlo Magneto Works in Queen Elizabeth Street.

'Sorry to trouble you so soon again, Mr Illingworth,' he apologised on being shown in, 'but I've thought of a way in which that car could have been disabled at the time and place required, and I want to know if it will hold water.'

'If your method covers all the factors in the case as you have described it, I should like to hear it, Mr French.'

'Well, it's simple enough, if it's nothing else. I take it that if the magneto of my car goes wrong I can buy another?'

'Why, of course, but I don't follow you.'

'They are all made to a standard—interchangeable?'

Mr Illingworth whistled.

'Gee, I'm beginning to get you! Yes, they're all made standard. There are several models, you understand, but all the magnetos of any given model are interchangeable.'

'Good! Now tell me, what's to prevent my man from buying a duplicate magneto, damaging the armature winding invisibly with a needle, and running it on his car till it gives up; then taking it off, carrying it as a spare, and putting it on again when he had got the car to the point of breakdown?'

'You've got it, Mr French! Great, that is! I didn't think it was possible, and there, as you say, it's as simple as A.B.C.'

'Well,' said French, 'then did he?'

Illingworth looked his question, and French went on:

'I'm looking to you for proof of the theory. First, do these

128

magnetos carry a number? If so, is there a record of the number fitted to each car? If so, what was the number supplied with Mr Berlyn's car? Next, is that the number that came in for repairs? Next, was there a magneto of that type ordered separately recently, and if so, by whom?'

'Steady on, Mr French,' Mr Illingworth laughed. 'What do you take me for? I'm not a detective. Now let's go over that again, one thing at a time. Magnetos carry a number, yes, and we have a note of the numbers supplied to the different car manufacturers. They can tell you the number of the magneto they put on any given car. What car are you interested in?'

'A 15-20 four-seater Mercury touring car, number 37,016, supplied through Makepeace to a Mr Berlyn of Ashburton.'

'Right. I'll ring up the Mercury people now.'

Mr Illingworth was indefatigable in his inquiries, but he was not prepared for the state of delighted enthusiasm into which his results threw French.

'That's got it,' the latter cried eagerly. 'A long shot, but a bull's eye! I have to thank you for it, Mr Illingworth, and you don't know how grateful I am.'

The first fact was not encouraging. The magneto which had been supplied originally with Mr Berlyn's car was the same that had been sent in by Makepeace with the short-circuited winding. So far, therefore, the breakdown might have been genuine enough. But it was the second item which had so transported French. A precisely similar magneto had been sold as a spare about a month earlier and under circumstances which left no doubt as to the motive. It had been ordered by a Mr Henry Armstrong, in a typewritten letter headed 'The Westcliff Hotel, Bristol,' and it was to be sent to the parcels office at St David's Station, Exeter, marked 'To be kept till called for.' The letter was being sent over by hand, and when French received it a few minutes later he saw that it had been typed by the same machine as that ordering the duplicator.

'That's fine, Mr Illingworth,' he repeated in high delight. 'That's one of my major difficulties overcome: I just want you to tell me one other thing. How long would it take to change the magneto—out in the country on a dark night?'

'It's a half hour's job for a skilled man. The actual lifting in and out of the machine is easy, but the setting is the trouble. The contact breaker, as I'm sure you know, has to be set so as to give the spark at the right point in the engine cycle. That takes a bit of time.'

'I follow that. But is there no way that the adjustable parts could be set beforehand to save that time?'

'That's right. They could be marked and everything set to the marks. That would speed things up.'

'By how much, should you say?'

'With everything marked, a man could do the whole thing in fifteen minutes.'

'Good,' said French. 'I guess that's everything at last.'

He returned to Paddington and caught the 1.30 p.m. express for Exeter. He was overjoyed at his progress. The issue was rapidly narrowing.

How rapidly it was narrowing struck him even more forcibly as he thought of a further point. The trick had been played with Berlyn's car. Could it have been done without Berlyn's knowledge? Could in fact, anyone but Berlyn have carried it out? French did not think so. It was beginning to look as if the solution of the whole problem were in sight.

At Exeter he went about the package. As far as book entries were concerned he was quickly satisfied. But no one remembered the transaction, nor could anyone recall inquiries having been made by a tallish, red-faced man with light hair and glasses.

Nothing daunted, French caught the last train from Exeter to Ashburton, full of an eager anxiety to get to grips with his remaining problems.

11

John Gurney, Night Watchman

French had now reconciled the apparent contradiction in regard to one of his four test-points. Obviously his next job was to clear up the other three.

As he considered on which he should first concentrate, his mind fastened on the one point which at the time had seemed not completely satisfactory: the slightly suspicious manner of Gurney, the night watchman. During the night, as he now knew, the body of Stanley Pyke had been taken to the works and put into the crate. It was impossible that this could have been done without Gurney's knowledge. Gurney must be made to speak.

Accordingly; after breakfast next morning, he set off to the man's house. He passed out of the town on the Newton Abbot road, then turning into a lane to the left, struck up the side of the valley. Soon he reached the cottage, a tiny place with deep overhanging eaves and creeper-covered walls. In front was a scrap of well-kept garden and in the garden was the man himself.

'Good morning, Gurney,' French greeted him. 'I thought you would have been in bed by now.'

'I be just going,' answered the old man. 'I came out an' begun a bit o' weeding, an' the time ran round without my noticing.'

'That's lucky for me,' said French heartily. 'I want a word with you. A nice place you've got here.'

'Not too bad, it ain't,' the other admitted, looking about him with obvious pride. 'The soil's a bit 'eavy, but it don't do so bad.'

'Good for your roses, surely? Those are fine ones beside the house.'

Gurney laid aside his hoe and led the way to the really magnificent bed of La Frances to which French had pointed. It was evident that these were the old man's passion. French was not a gardener, but he knew enough to talk intelligently on the subject and his appreciation evidently went straight to the watchman's heart. For some minutes they discussed horticulture, and then French wore gradually round to the object of his visit.

'Terrible business that about Mr Berlyn and Mr Pyke,' he essayed. 'It must have set this town talking.'

'It didn't 'alf, sir. Everyone was sorry for the poor gentlemen. They was well liked, they was.'

'And that was another terrible affair,' pursued French, after the local tragedy had been adequately discussed, 'that finding of the dead body in the crate. Extraordinary how the body could have been put in.'

'I didn't 'ear nought about that,' Gurney answered, with a sudden increase of interest. 'You don't mean the crate you was speaking about that day you was up at the works?'

'No other. Keep it to yourself and I'll tell you about it.' French became deeply impressive. 'That crate that I was inquiring about was sent from here to Swansea. There it was called for by a man who took it on a lorry to a place called Burry Port and threw it into the sea. A fisherman chanced to hook it, and it was brought ashore, more than a month later. And when it was opened the dead body of a man was found inside.'

'Lord save us! I read in the noospaper about that there body being found, but it fair beats me that the crate came from 'ere, it does.'

French continued to enlarge on the tale. That Gurney's surprise was genuine he felt certain. He could have sworn that the man had no inkling of the truth. But he marked, even more acutely than before, a hesitation or self-consciousness that indicated an uneasy mind. There was something; he felt sure of it. He glanced at the man with his shrewd, observant eyes and suddenly determined on directness.

'Look here, Gurney,' he said, 'come over and sit on this seat. I have something important to say to you.' He paused; as if considering his words. 'You thought a good deal of your employers, those two poor men who were lost on the moor?'

'An' I 'ad reason to. It weren't an accident 'appening in the execution of my dooty, as you might say, as made me lame and not fit to work. It was rheumatism, and they could 'ave let me go when I couldn't work no more. But they found this job for me, and they let me the 'ouse cheap. Of course it was Mr Berlyn as 'ad the final say, but I know as Mr Pyke spoke for me. It wasn't everyone as would 'ave done that, now was it, sir?'

Consideration on the part of an employer was not, French knew, to be taken as a matter of course, though it was vastly more common than the unions would have the public believe. But gratitude on the part of an employee was not so frequent, though it was by no means unique. Its exhibition, however,

134

in the present instance confirmed French in the course he was taking.

'Now, Gurney, do you know who I am?' he went on. 'I'm an Inspector from Scotland Yard, and I'm down here to try to solve these two mysteries. Because, Gurney, do you know what I think? I think that on that night the body of one of these two gentlemen was taken to the works and put into the crate.'

Gurney started and paled. 'Lord save us!' he muttered. 'But wot about the accident?'

'There was no accident,' French replied sternly. 'There was murder. Who committed it I don't know at present. Where the other body is, if there is another body, I don't yet know. But I have no doubt about one of the bodies. It was put into the crate on that night.'

Gurney moistened his dry lips.

'But—' he began, and his voice died away into silence.

'That's it,' French went on impressively. 'Now, Gurney, I'm not accusing you of anything. But you know something. You needn't attempt to deny it, because it has been plain to me from the first moment I spoke to you. Come now. Something out of the common took place that night. What was it?'

But Gurney did not deny the charge. Instead, he sat motionless with scared, unhappy eyes. French remained silent also, then he said quietly:

'What was it? Were you away from your post that night?'

'No, sir, not that. I was there all the time,' the other answered earnestly. Again he paused, then with a sudden gesture he went on: 'I didn't know nothing about what you 'ave been saying, but I see now I must tell you everything, even if I gets the sack over it.'

'You'll not get the sack if I can help it,' French said kindly, 'but go on and tell me all the same.'

'Well, sir, I did that night wot I never did before nor since. I slept the 'ole night through. I sat down to eat my supper in the boiler 'ouse, like I always does, an' I didn't remember nothing more till Peter Small, 'e was standing there shaking me. "Wake up," 'e says, "you're a nice sort of a night-watchman, you are." "Lord," I says, "I never did nothing like that before," an' I asks him not to say nothing about it. An' 'e didn't say nothing, nor I didn't neither. But now I suppose it'll come out, an' I'll get wot for about it.'

'Don't you worry about that,' French said heartily, 'I'll see you through. I'll undertake to get Mr Fogden to overlook this little irregularity on one condition. You must tell me everything that took place that night without exception. Go ahead now and let's have the whole of it.'

The old man gazed at him in distress.

'But there weren't naught else,' he protested. 'I went to sleep, an' that's all. If there were anything else took place, w'y, I didn't see it.'

'That's all right. Now just answer my questions. Go back to when you left your house. You took your supper with you?'

'Yes, sir.'

'Did you meet anyone on your way to the works?'

'Well, I couldn't rightly say. No one that I remember.'

'No one could have got hold of your supper anyway?'

The man started. 'You think it might 'ave been tampered with?' he queried. He thought for some moments, then shook his head. 'No, sir, I'm afraid not. I don't never let my basket out o' my 'and till I gets to the boiler 'ouse.'

'Very well. Now when you got to the boiler house?'

'I put it where I always does, beside one o' the boilers.'

'And you left it there?'

136

'While I made my rounds, I did. But there wasn't no one else in the works then.'

'How do you know?'

Gurney hesitated. In the last resort he didn't know. But he had not seen anyone and did not believe anyone had been there.

'But suppose someone had been hidden in the works,' French persisted, 'he could have doctored your supper while you were on your rounds?'

'If there 'ad been 'e might,' the man admitted. 'But I didn't see no one.'

'What time do you have your meal?'

Gurney, it appeared, had two meals during the night. Time hung heavily on his hands, and the meals made a break. He had his dinner about six, started work at seven, and had his first meal about eleven. His second meal he had about three, and he was relieved at six.

On the night in question he had his first meal at the usual time. Until then he had felt perfectly normal, but he had scarcely finished when he found himself growing overpoweringly sleepy, and the next thing he remembered was being wakened by the fireman at six the next morning.

'It's clear that your supper was doped,' French said. 'Now think, did nothing in anyway out of the common happen between six and eleven?'

Gurney began a denial, then stopped.

'There were one thing,' he said slowly, 'but I don't believe as 'ow it could have 'ad anything to do with it. A little before ten there was a ring at the office door. I went to open, but there weren't no one there. I didn't think naught of it, because children do ring sometimes just by way o' mischief. But there weren't no children there so far as I could see.'

'How far is this door that you opened from the boiler house?'

'At t'other end o' the building. Two 'undred yards maybe.'

'Is that the only door?'

'No, sir, there be a gate near the boilers for lorries, but people going to the office use the other.'

'Is the large gate locked at night?'

'Yes, sir.'

'Who keeps the key?'

'I do. There's a key in the office that any o' the gentlemen can get if they wants, but I carry one with me.'

For some moments French sat thinking, then a fresh point struck him.

'What did your supper consist of on that night?'

'Tea an' bread an' butter and a slice o' meat. I have a can o' tea. I leave it on the boiler and it keeps 'ot.'

'You mean that you don't make your tea separately for each meal. You drink some out of the can at the first meal and finish what is left at the second?'

'That's right, sir.'

'And the same with the food?'

'Yes, sir.'

'Now, on the night we're talking about you had only one meal. You slept through the time of the second. What happened to the tea and food that was left over?'

'We 'ad it for breakfast, my wife an' I.'

'That is what I wanted to get at. Now did either of you feel sleepy after breakfast?'

A mixture of admiration and wonder showed in the old man's eyes.

'Why no, we didn't, an' that's a fact,' he said in puzzled tones. 'An' we should 'ave, if so be as wot you think is true.'

This looked like a snag, but French reminded himself that

138

at the moment he was only getting information and his theorising could wait till later. He continued his questions, but without learning much more.

'Now, Gurney,' he said at last, 'under no circumstances are you to mention what we have been speaking of: not to your wife nor to Mr Fogden, nor to anyone. You understand?'

'I understand, sir, right enough.'

'Very good. Now I'm anxious to go into this matter further, and I'll call at the works tonight.'

'Right, sir. I'll be on the look-out.'

It was dark as French rang at the big gate of the works. Gurney soon appeared at the wicket and French followed him across the yard to the boiler house, a distance of perhaps forty yards. It was a fair-sized shed, housing five Babcock and Wilcox water-tube boilers, with mechanical stokers and the usual stoker engines and pumps. On a ledge of the warm brickwork near one of the ash openings stood the old man's can of tea, and his basket of food was placed on the repair bench close by. French took in these details, and then said:

'I want now to try an experiment. Will you lend me your key of the wicket. I will go out, lock the wicket behind me and go round to the office door and ring. When you hear the ring you go and open. Repeat everything exactly as you did that night so as to get back here at the same time. In the meantime I shall let myself in again by the wicket and see if I should have time to dope your tea and get away again before you appear. You understand?'

This programme was carried out. French went out and rang at the office door, then ran round to the large gate, let himself in through the wicket, found the can of tea, opened it and counted ten, closed it, and relocked the wicket. Then he began to time. Three minutes passed before Gurney appeared.

So that was all right. Anyone who had access to the key in the office could have doctored the watchman's food. Moreover, the fact that the Gurneys had breakfasted without ill effect on the remainder was not such a difficulty as French had at first supposed. The criminal might have doped the tea on his first visit and during his second poured away what was over and replaced it with fresh. In fact, if he were to preserve his secret, he must have done so. The discovery of the drugging would have started an inquiry which might have brought to light the whole plot.

Though French was enthusiastic about his discovery, he saw that it involved one disconcerting point. What about the theory of Berlyn's guilt? The ring at the office door had come shortly before ten. But shortly before ten Berlyn was at Tavistock. Therefore, some other person was involved. Was this person the murderer and had he made away with Berlyn as well as Pyke? Or was he Berlyn's accomplice? French inclined to the latter supposition. In considering the timing of the car he had seen that it could have been used to carry the body to the works, provided an accomplice was ready to drive it back to the moor without delay. On the whole, therefore, it looked as if the murder was the work of two persons, of whom Berlyn was one.

But whether principal or accomplice, it was at least certain that the man who had drugged Gurney's food knew the works intimately and had access to the key in the office. Only a comparatively small number of persons could fill these requirements, and he should therefore be quickly found.

Well pleased with his day's work, French returned to the hotel and spent the remainder of the evening in writing up his diary.

12

The Duplicator

The saying, 'it never rains but it pours,' is a popular expression of the unhappy fact that misfortunes never come singly. Fortunately for suffering humanity the phrase expresses only half the truth. Runs of good luck occur as well as runs of bad.

As French was smoking his after-breakfast pipe in the lounge next morning, it was borne in on him that he was at that time experiencing one of the most phenomenal runs of good luck that had ever fallen to his lot. Four days ago he had proved that the dead man was Pyke. Two days later he had learned how the breakdown of the car had been faked. Yesterday he had found the explanation of the watchman's inaction, and today, just at that very moment, an idea had occurred to him which bade fair to solve the problem of the disposal of the duplicator! Unfortunately nothing could be done towards putting it to the test until the evening. He spent the day, therefore, in a long tramp on the moor; then about five o'clock walked for the second time to Gurney's house.

'I want to have another chat with you,' he explained. 'I haven't time to wait now, but I shall come up to the works later in the evening. Listen out for my ring.'

He strolled back to the town, had a leisurely dinner, visited the local picture house, and killed time until after eleven. Then, when the little town was asleep, he went up to the works. Five minutes later he was seated with Gurney in the boiler house.

'I have been thinking over this affair, Gurney,' he began, 'and I am more than ever certain that some terrible deeds were done here on that night when you were drugged. I want to have another look round. But you must not under any circumstances let it be known that I was here.'

'That's all right, guv'nor. I ain't goin' to say nothing.'

French nodded.

'You told me that you had been a mechanic in the works before your rheumatism got bad. Have you worked at any of those duplicators like what was packed in the crate?'

'I worked at all kinds of erecting works: duplicators an' files an' indexes an' addressing machines, an' all the rest o' them. I knows them all.'

'Good. Now I want you to come round to the store and show me the different parts of a duplicator.'

Gurney led the way from the boiler house.

'Don't switch on the light,' French directed. 'I don't want the windows to show lit up. I have a torch.'

They passed through the packing shed and into the completed machine store adjoining. Here French called a halt.

'Just let's look at one of these duplicators again,' he said. 'Suppose you wanted to take one of them to pieces, let me see how you would set about it. Should I be correct in saying

142

that if five or six of the larger pieces were got rid of, all the rest could be carried in a handbag?'

'That's right, sir.'

'Now show me the bins where these larger parts are stocked.'

They passed on to the part store and across it to a line of bins labelled 'Duplicators.' In the first bin were rows of leg castings. French ran his eye along them.

'There must be fifty or sixty here,' he said slowly. 'Let's see if that is a good guess.'

On every, bin was a stock card in a metal holder. French lifted down that in question. It was divided into three sets of columns, one set showing in-comes, the second out-goes, and the third existing stock. The date of each transmission was given, and for each entry the stock was adjusted.

'Not such a bad guess,' French remarked slowly as he scrutinised the entries. 'There are just fifty-four.'

The card was large and was nearly full. French noticed that it went back for some weeks before the tragedy. He stood gazing at it in the light of his torch, while a feeling of bitter disappointment grew in his mind. Then suddenly he thought he saw what he was looking for, and whipping out a lens, he examined one of the entries more closely. 'Got it, by Jove! I've actually got it,' he thought delightedly. His luck had held.

One of the entries had been altered. A loop had been skilfully added to a six to make it an eight. The card showed that two castings had been taken out, which either had never been taken out at all or, more probably, which had been taken out and afterwards replaced.

Convinced that he had solved the last of his four test problems, French examined the cards of the other bins. In all of those referring to large parts he noticed the same

143

peculiarity: the entries had been tampered with to show that one more duplicator had been sent out than really was the case. The cards for the small parts were unaltered, and French could understand the reason. It was easier to get rid of the parts themselves than to falsify their records. The fraud was necessary only in the case of objects too big and heavy to carry away.

French was highly pleased. His discovery was not only valuable in itself, but he had reached it in the way which most appealed to his vanity—from his own imagination. He had imagined that the fraud might have been worked in this way. He had tested it and found that it had been. Pure brains! Such things were soothing to his self-respect.

He stood considering the matter. The evidence was valuable, but it was far from permanent. A hint that suspicion was aroused, and it would be gone. The criminal, if he were still about, would see to it that innocuous copies of the cards were substituted for these dangerous ones. French felt he dare not run such a risk. Nor could he let Gurney suspect his discovery, lest unwittingly the old man might put the criminal on his guard. He therefore went on:

'Now all I want is to make a sketch of each of these parts. The duplicator which went out in the crate may have been taken to pieces, and I want to be able to recognise them if they're found. I suppose I could get a sheet or two of paper in the storeman's desk?'

In one corner a small box with glass sides constituted an office for the storeman. French led the way thither. The door was closed but not locked. The desk, which he next tried, was fastened. But above it in a rack he saw what he was looking for, a pile of blank bin-cards. He turned back.

'It doesn't matter about the paper after all,' he explained.

'I see the desk is locked. I can make my sketches in my note-book, though it's not so convenient. But many a sketch I've made in it before.'

Chatting pleasantly, he returned to the bins and began slowly to sketch the leg casting. He was purposely extremely slow and detailed in the work, measuring every possible dimension and noting it on his sketch. Gurney, as he had hoped, began to get fidgety. French continued talking and sketching. Suddenly he looked up.

'By the way,' he said, as if a new idea had suddenly entered his mind, 'there is no earthly need for me to keep you here while I am working. It will take me an hour or two to finish these sketches. If you want to do your rounds and to get your supper, go ahead. I'll find you in the boiler house when I have done.'

Gurney seemed relieved. He explained that it really was time to make his rounds and that if French didn't mind he would go and do so. French reassured him heartily, and he slowly disappeared.

No sooner had his shuffling footsteps died away than French became an extremely active man. Quickly slipping the four faked cards from their metal holders, he carried them to the office. Then taking four fresh cards from the rack, he began slowly and carefully to copy the others. He was not a skilful forger, but at the end of half an hour's work he had produced four passable imitations. Two minutes later he breathed more freely. The copies were in the holders and the genuine cards in his pocket. Hurriedly he resumed his sketching.

French's work amounted to genius in the infinite pains he took with detail. In twenty minutes his sketches were complete and he effectually banished any suspicion which his actions might have aroused in Gurney's mind by showing them to him when he rejoined him in the boiler house. Like an artist, he proceeded to establish the deception.

'Copies of these sketches sent to the men who are searching for the duplicator will help them to recognise parts of it if it has been taken to pieces,' he explained. 'You see the idea?'

Gurney appreciated the point, and French, after again warning him to be circumspect, left the works.

The problem of what he should do next day was solved for French by the receipt of a letter by the early post. It was written on a half sheet of cheap notepaper in an uneducated hand and read:

> 'Ashburton.
> '12th October.
>
> 'DEAR SIR,—If you would come round some time that suits you I have something I could tell you that would maybe interest you. It's better not wrote about.
>
> 'LIZZIE JOHNSTON.'

French had received too many communications of the kind to be hopeful that this one would result in anything valuable. However, he thought he ought to see the ex-parlourmaid and once again he made his way to her cottage.

'It's my Alf,' she explained. 'Alf Beer, they call him. We're being married as soon as he gets another job.'

'He's out of a job, then?'

'Yes, he was in the sales department in the works; a packer, he was. He left there six months ago.'

'How was that?' French asked sympathetically.

'He wasn't well and he stayed home a few mornings and Mr Berlyn had him up in his office and spoke to him

146

something wicked. Well, Alf wouldn't take that, not from no man living, so he said what relieved his feelings and Mr Berlyn told him he could go.'

'And has he been doing nothing since?'

'Not steady, he hasn't. Just jobbing, as you might say.'

'Hard lines, that is. You say he had something to tell me?' The girl nodded. 'That's right,' was her reply.

'What is it, do you know?'

'He wouldn't say. I told him you was in asking questions and he seemed sort of interested. "Wants to know about Berlyn and Pyke and Mrs Berlyn's goings on with Pyke, does he," he sez. "I thought someone would be wanting to know about that before long. Well, I can tell him something," he sez.'

'But he didn't mention what it was?'

'No. I asked him and he sez "Value for cash," he sez. "He puts down the beans and I cough up the stuff. That's fair, ain't it," he sez. "Don't be a silly guff, Alf," I sez. "He's police and if he asks you questions, why you don't half have to answer them." "The devil I have," he sez. "I ain't done no crime and he hasn't nothing on me. You tell him," he sez, "tell him I know something that would be worth a quid or two to him." And so I wrote you that note.'

'Tell me why you thought I was police,' French invited.

Miss Johnston laughed scornfully.

'Well, ain't you?' she parried.

'That's hardly an answer to my question.'

'Well, everybody knows what you're after. They say you think Pyke was murdered on the moor and that Berlyn murdered him. Leastways, that's what I've heard said.'

This was something more than a blow to French and his self esteem reeled under it. For the *n*th time he marvelled at the amazing knowledge of other people's business to be found in country districts. The small country town, he thought, was the absolute limit! There he was, moving continually among the townspeople, none of whom gave the least sign of interest in his calling; yet evidently they had discussed him and his affairs to some purpose. The garrulous landlady, Mrs Billing, was no doubt responsible for the murder of Pyke becoming known, but the belief that he, French, suspected Berlyn of murdering him was really rather wonderful.

'It seems to me,' he said with a rather sickly smile, 'that your townspeople are better detectives than ever came out of Scotland Yard. So your young man thinks I'm police and wants to turn an honest penny, does he? Where am I to find him?'

'He'll be at home. He's living with his father at the head of East Street—a single red house on the left-hand side, just beyond the town.'

In the leisurely, holiday-like way he had adopted, French crossed the town and half an hour later had introduced himself to Mr Alfred Beer. Lizzie's Alf was a stalwart young man with a heavy face and a sullen, discontented expression. French, sizing him up rapidly, decided that the suave method would scarcely meet the case.

'You are Alfred Beer, engaged to Lizzie Johnston, the former servant at Mr Berlyn's?' he began.

'That's right, mister.'

'I am a police officer investigating the deaths of Mr Berlyn and Mr Pyke. You have some information for me?'

'I don't altogether know that,' Beer answered slowly. 'Just wot did you want to know?'

'What you have to tell me,' French said sharply. 'You told

Miss Johnston you had some information and I've come up to hear it.'

The man looked at him calculatingly.

'Wot do you think it might be worth to you?' he queried.

'Not a brass farthing. You should know that witnesses are not paid for their evidence. Don't you misunderstand the situation, Beer, or you'll find things mighty unpleasant. Come along, now. Out with it.'

'How can I tell you if you won't say wot you want?'

'I wouldn't talk to you any more, Beer, only I think you don't understand where you are,' French answered quietly. 'This is a murder case. Mr Pyke has been murdered. If you know anything that might help the police to discover the murderer and you don't tell it, you become an accessory after the fact. Do you realise that you'd get a good spell of years for that?'

Beer gave an uncouth shrug and turned back to his digging.

'I don't know nothing about no murder,' he declared contemptuously. 'I was just pulling Lizzie's leg.'

'You've done it now,' French said, producing his card. 'There's my authority as a police officer. You've wasted my time and kept me back from my work. That's obstruction and you'll get six months for it. Come along to the station. And unless you want a couple of years you'll come quietly.'

This was not what the man expected.

'Wot's that?' he stammered. 'You ain't going to arrest me? I ain't done nothin' against the law, I ain't.'

'You'll soon find out about that. Look sharp, now. I can't spend the day here waiting for you.'

'Aw!' The man shifted nervously. 'See, mister, I ain't done no harm, I ain't. I don't know nothing about no murder. I don't, honest.'

149

French was a trifle uneasy at the turn the interview had taken. Statements obtained by threats are not admitted as evidence and he felt he had been sailing rather near the wind. However, he had to get the information and he did not see what other way was open to him. At least, what he had done was better than to offer the man money.

'I don't want to be hard on you,' he went on, in more conciliatory tones. 'If you tell your story without any more humbugging I'll let the rest go. But, I warn you, you needn't start inventing any yarn. What you say will be gone into, and heaven help you if it's not true.'

'I'll take my davy it's true, mister, but it ain't about no murder.'

'Well, get along sharp and let's hear it.'

'It was one night about six months ago,' said Beer, now speaking almost eagerly. 'Me and Lizzie were walking out at that time. Well, that night we'd fixed up for to go for a walk, and then at the last minute she couldn't get away. Mrs Berlyn was goin' out or somethin' and she couldn't get off. We'd 'ad it fixed up that when that 'appened Lizzie would come down to the shrubbery after the rest 'ad gone to bed. Well, I wanted to see 'er that night for to fix up some little business between ourselves, so I went up to the 'ouse and gave the sign—three taps with a tree branch at 'er window. You understand?'

French nodded.

'Well, I went back into the shrubbery for to wait for her. It was dark, but a quiet night. An' then I 'eard voices an' steps comin' along the path. So I got behind a bush so as they'd not see me. There was a man and a woman, an' when they came close I knew them by their voices. It was Pyke and Mrs Berlyn. I stayed still an' they passed me close.'

150

'Go ahead. Did you hear what they said, or what are you getting at?'

'I 'eard wot they said when they were passing. "I tell you, 'e knows," she said. "I'm frightened," she said. "You don't know 'im. If 'e once thinks you've played 'im false 'e'll make a 'ell of a trouble." An' then Pyke says: "Nonsense," 'e said. "'E's not that sort. Besides," 'e said, "'e don't know anything. 'E knows we're friends, but that's all.' "No," she said, "I'm sure 'e knows, or 'e guesses anyway. We'll 'ave to separate," she said. 'E said they 'ad been careful enough, and then they went past an' I didn't 'ear no more.'

'That all?'

'That's all,' said Beer disgustedly. 'Ain't it enough?'

'Nothing to boast about,' French replied absently. He remembered that the man had been dismissed by Berlyn and he wondered if this statement was merely the result of spite. He therefore questioned him closely. But he was unable to shake him and he formed the opinion that the story was true.

If so, it certainly had a pretty direct bearing on the theory he was trying to evolve, for there could be little doubt as to who ''e' was. As he considered the matter he was surprised to find how complete that theory was and how much of it had been definitely established. There were gaps, of course, but there was no doubt as to its general correctness.

As French now saw it, the affair stood as follows:

Stanley Pyke and Phyllis Berlyn, friends during childhood, find that they love each other when they renew their acquaintance in later years. But it is then too late for the course of true love to run smooth, and a clandestine attachment follows. Berlyn learns of this some four months before the tragedy and as a result of his interference the two decide to discontinue their meetings—in public at all events. The flirtation with Colonel Domlio is possibly deliberately undertaken by Mrs Berlyn to prove to her husband that her interest in Pyke is over.

But the two find that they cannot give each other up and the intrigue is continued secretly. Berlyn, however, is not hoodwinked. He sees his friend betraying him and he determines on vengeance.

His first move is to get an accomplice to assist in the details. Here French admitted to himself that he was out of his depth. He could not imagine who the accomplice was or why he should have been required. But if Berlyn were guilty, the murder was clearly a two-man job. Simultaneous activities in different places proved it.

The arrangements about the crate are next made. French was aware that these had not yet been properly followed up; other matters had been more urgent. But they represented a second string to his bow which he would develop if necessary.

Then comes the night of the crime. While Berlyn and Pyke are at Tavistock the accomplice drugs the watchman's food. He then waits for the car. Pyke is sandbagged and his body carried into the works. One of the men then unpacks the crate, and taking the duplicator to pieces, returns the larger parts to stock. He has already doctored the cards as well as the corresponding books. He then strips the recognisable clothes off the body, puts the latter in the crate, smashes in the face, closes the crate and leaves all as before. Finally he escapes with Pyke's outer clothes and the smaller parts of the duplicator. He has only to get rid of these and his part in the ghastly business is complete.

In the meantime his confederate has driven the car out to a lonely part of the moor, changed the magneto and made the tracks leading from the road.

The facts which pointed to Berlyn's guilt were six-fold.

1. Berlyn in all probability was consumed by jealousy, one of the strongest of human motives for crime.

2. Berlyn had an unparalleled opportunity for the deed, which only he could have arranged.

3. It was not easy to see how anyone but Berlyn could have handled the magneto affair.

4. Berlyn had the necessary position in the Vida Works to carry out the watchman and stock-card episodes.

5. Berlyn answered the description of the man who had called for the crate.

6. Berlyn had disappeared, an incomprehensible action if he were innocent.

As French thought again over the accomplice he recognised that here was the snag in his theory. Motives of personal jealousy and private wrong leave no room for an accomplice. Moreover, it was incredible that a man who had shown such ingenuity could not have devised a scheme to carry out the crime single-handed.

But though French recognised that there were points in the case as yet unexplained, he saw that his own procedure was clear. He must start the search for Berlyn and he must learn the identity of the accomplice.

The first of these was easy. He had compiled a pretty accurate description of the junior partner and Daw had got hold of his photograph. An entry under the 'Wanted for Crime' heading of the *Morning Report* would start every police officer in the country on the search.

153

The second problem he found more difficult. Rack his brains as he would he could think of no one who might have helped Berlyn.

He thought his best plan would be an inquiry into the whereabouts at ten o'clock on the night of the crime of everyone whom it was possible to suspect. That, coupled with an investigation as to who was in London when the various letters were posted, should yield results.

The fact that a number of possible suspects had been at Mrs Berlyn's party from eight to eleven on the fatal evening seemed to rule them out. But French thought he should get some more definite information on the point. Accordingly, he went up to the works and asked for Mr Fogden, one of those whom Lizzie Johnston had mentioned as being present.

'I heard a peculiar story about Mrs Berlyn,' he said, *a propos* of nothing special when they had talked for some time. 'I was told she had a premonition of Mr Berlyn's death and was miserable and upset all that evening of the crime. A peculiar thing if true, isn't it?'

'Who told you that?' Mr Fogden asked sceptically.

'A chance remark in the bar of the Silver Tiger. I don't know the speaker's name; nor, of course, do I know if his story was true.'

'Well, you may take it from me that it wasn't. I was at Mrs Berlyn's that evening and there was nothing wrong with her that I saw.'

This gave French his lead. When he left the office he had obtained all the details of the party that he wanted. On the day before the crime Mrs Berlyn had 'phoned Mr Fogden to say that her husband was to be out on the following evening and that she would be alone, and asking if he and one or two of the others would come and keep

154

her company. Eight people had turned up, including himself, Cowls and Leacock from the works, a Dr Lancaster and his wife and two Miss Pyms and a Miss Nesbitt from the town. All these people were very intimate and the party was quite informal. Some of them had played billiards and the others bridge.

This information seemed to French to eliminate Fogden, Cowls and Leacock, as well, of course, as Mrs Berlyn herself. He spent the remainder of the day in racking his brains for other possible accomplices and in thinking out ways to learn their movements on the night in question.

Next morning he took up the matter of the whereabouts of all suspects when the incriminating letters were posted in London.

Fortunately the inquiry presented but little difficulty. A further application to Mr Fogden revealed the fact there was an attendance book at the works which all the officials signed, from Mr Fogden himself down. This book showed that everyone concerned was in Ashburton on the dates of posting. Even Stanley Pyke, who was absent five days out of six on his rounds, had been there. Further, Mr Fogden's diary showed that he had had interviews with Colonel Domlio on the critical days. From Lizzie Johnston, French learned that Mrs Berlyn had also been at home during the period.

French was more puzzled than ever. It looked as if someone must have been mixed up in the affair, of whose existence he was still in ignorance.

Just as he was about to step into bed that night an idea struck him which gave him sharply to think. As he considered it, he began to wonder if his whole view of the crime were not mistaken. He suddenly saw that the facts could bear a quite different interpretation from that which he had placed upon them, an interpretation, moreover, which would go far towards solving the problem of the accomplice.

Once again he swung from depression to optimism, as chuckling gently to himself he decided that next morning he would embark on a line of inquiry which up to the present he had been stupid enough entirely to overlook.

13

The Accomplice?

French's new idea had been subconsciously in his mind from the very first, but probably owing to his theory of the guilt of one of the two men supposed to be lost, he had never given it the consideration he now saw that it deserved.

Suppose that on the night of the tragedy the lines of footprints had not been faked. Suppose that after leaving the car the two men had walked across the moor *and reached Domlio's*. Suppose that Domlio was the moving spirit in the affair and Berlyn merely the accomplice.

This idea, French thought, would account not only for the facts which his previous theory had covered, but also for nearly all of those which the latter had failed to meet.

As before, the affair hinged on the fatal attractiveness of Phyllis Berlyn, but in this case Domlio was the victim. Suppose Domlio had fallen desperately in love with Phyllis and that she had encouraged him. So far from this being unlikely, the facts bore it out. Different witnesses had testified to the flirtation and Mrs Berlyn herself had not denied it.

Domlio then would see that there was a double barrier to

the realisation of his desires. There was, of course, Berlyn, but if Berlyn were out of the way there was still Pyke. How far Mrs Berlyn loved Pyke, Domlio might not know, but their 'affair' was common knowledge and he would want to be on the safe side. If murder were the way out in one case, why not in both? The risk was probably no greater, and once both his rivals were out of the way his own happiness was secured.

His plan decided on, he would approach his friend Berlyn with insidious suggestions as to the part Pyke was playing with his wife. Gradually he would let it be known that he also had occasion to hate Pyke, obviously for some quite different reason. He would feed the other's jealousy until, at last, Berlyn would be as ready for the crime as he was himself. Then he would put forward his proposals.

Pyke was a cause of misery in both their lives; they would combine to remove his evil influence.

Between them they would obtain and damage the spare magneto, then arrange the visit to Tavistock and the ordering of the crate and crane lorry. Berlyn would require Pyke to accompany him to Tavistock. All could be done without raising suspicion.

On the fatal night Domlio would go to the works and drug Gurney's supper. Later on, during the run back from Tavistock, Berlyn would stop the car and pretend to Pyke that it had broken down. He would suggest looking up Domlio, who would certainly run them into Ashburton in his own car. A light in the colonel's study would lead them direct to its French window, and Domlio would admit them without letting his servants know of their call.

Domlio would immediately get out his car and they would start for the town. A sandbag would be in the car and on the way Pyke would be done to death. The two men would then leave the car in some deserted place, and carrying the body to the works, would pack it in the crate. When the ghastly work was done they would return to the car, taking with them Pyke's suit and the small parts of the duplicator. These they would get rid of later. Lastly, they would change the magneto on Berlyn's car.

So far, French was well pleased with his new theory, but he realised that it contained a couple of nasty snags.

In the first place it did not account satisfactorily for the disappearance of Berlyn. Presumably Domlio had manœuvred his colleague into such a position that he could give him away to the police with safety to himself. Berlyn would therefore have to do the other's bidding, which would be to disappear and to get rid of the crate. This was possible, but there was not a shred of proof that it had happened.

Secondly, the theory did not explain how the letters were posted in London. However, though French was not entirely satisfied, he grew more and more convinced that he was on sure ground in suspecting Domlio. At all events his next job must be to test the point.

First he decided to find out what Sergeant Daw could tell him about the colonel, and early next morning saw him at the police station. The sergeant greeted him with a peculiar smile.

'I suppose, sir, you've heard the rumour that's going round?' he asked at once.

'What's that, Sergeant?'

'They say you've found out that Mr Berlyn murdered Mr Pyke out on the moor that night. Mrs Billing, Pyke's landlady, is supposed to have recognised the underclothes.'

French smiled.

'Well, it's quite true,' he admitted. 'I didn't mean to keep it from you, Sergeant, but I went off to London as soon as I discovered it. I warned Mrs Billing not to talk, but I hardly believed she could help herself.'

The sergeant was evidently upset.

'I'm sorry about the whole thing, Mr French. I should have thought Mr Berlyn was the last man who would do such a thing.'

'You may be right. Indeed, it's a matter arising out of that very point that I want to see you about. I have a notion there was a second person in it, someone who might even have taken the lead. Tell me,' French's voice became very confidential, 'what sort of a man is Colonel Domlio?'

The sergeant looked shocked.

'Colonel Domlio?' he repeated. 'Surely, sir, you don't mean to suggest that the colonel was mixed up in a murder?'

'You don't think it likely?'

'I don't, sir, and that's a fact. The colonel's a very quiet man and peculiar in some ways, but he's well respected in the district.'

'So was many a murderer.'

The sergeant was clearly sceptical, though anxious to be polite. He said he was sure Mr French would not speak without good reason, but his own view was evident.

'Well, tell me all you know about him anyway.'

Domlio, it appeared, was a man of about forty-five, short, thick-set and dark. (Not the man who called for the crate, thought French.) He was very well off, and, since his wife had died some six-years earlier, had lived alone with his servants in his house on the moor. He held sufficient Vida stock to give him a controlling interest in the firm, acted as consulting engineer and was usually referred to as the senior partner. Entomology was his pet hobby and it was believed that he was writing a book on the insect life of the moor.

He had four servants. Inside was John Burt, valet, butler and general factotum, and his wife, Sarah Burt, who combined the offices of cook and general servant. Outside was an ex-serviceman named Coombe, who acted as chauffeur and general handyman, and an old gardener called Mee. Mee lived with his wife and daughter in the gate lodge and Coombe boarded with them. All, so far as the sergeant knew, were reliable people of good character.

'I'll go out and see the colonel after lunch,' French announced. 'Could you lend me a push bicycle? I don't want all my movements reported on by the driver of a car.'

'I can borrow one for you, but it'll not be much use on these hilly roads.'

'It'll do all I want.'

A couple of hours later French set out. When near Colonel Domlio's gate he hid the bicycle in the brushwood and approached the house on foot. It was a smallish, creeper covered building, L-shaped, with thick walls and heavy, over-hanging eaves. At least a hundred years old, French thought. It stood some two hundred yards back from the road and was approached by a drive which wound between clumps of stunted trees and shrubs. In front was a small lawn of mown grass, while between the trees to the right French glimpsed the roofs of outbuildings. The place had a cared-for appearance. The woodwork of the house had been freshly painted, the flower-beds were tidy and the grass edges had recently been cut.

The door was opened by an elderly man in butler's dress, honest and kindly looking, but rather stupid. John Burt, evidently. He asked French to step inside while he took his card to his master.

The hall was of fair size, with a large, old-fashioned fireplace and lead lighted windows. French had not much time to observe it, for Burt called him almost immediately into a room on the left of the hall door.

It was long, low and delightfully furnished as a study. Bookcases lined the walls and a couple of deep, saddle-bag arm-chairs stood on the soft Chinese carpet in front of the fireplace. A collector's entomological cabinet was in one corner, with close by a table bearing books and a fine microscope. The room was evidently in the corner of the house, for there were French windows in adjacent walls. In one of these was a leather-topped desk and at the desk was seated a shortish man with a strong, clean-shaven face, iron-grey hair, and a not too amiable expression. He rose as French entered.

'Inspector French of Scotland Yard, is it not? I have heard that you were in the town.'

'That's correct, sir,' French answered, taking the chair to which the other pointed. 'You've probably heard enough, then, to guess my business?'

Colonel Domlio squared his shoulders.

'I heard you were investigating the deaths of Mr Berlyn and Mr Pyke. I don't know the object of this call.'

'I've come, Colonel Domlio, in connection with my investigation. I want to ask your help in it.'

'What do you wish me to do?'

'Two things, sir. In the first place I want any information you can give me about either of the two gentlemen you mentioned or anything which might throw light on the tragedy. Secondly, I would be obliged if you would answer the purely formal question that we inspectors have to ask all who were in any way connected with the victim of such a tragedy, Where were you yourself at the time of the occurrence?'

The colonel raised his eyebrows.

'Do you suspect me of murdering Mr Pyke?' he asked dryly.

'I think, sir, you needn't take up that line.' French's tone was also a trifle dry. 'I have explained that my question is a formal one, invariably put. You are not bound to answer it unless you wish.'

'If I don't you will suspect me in reality, so I don't see that I have much option. I was here, in this room.'

'Between what hours?'

'During the whole evening. I finished dinner about eight or a quarter past. Then I came in here and stayed here until I went to bed between one and two.'

'And no one came in during that time?'

'No one came in. I take nothing after dinner except a little whisky going to bed and I have everything I want in the cupboard there. I'm writing a book at present and I don't like to be disturbed in the evenings.'

'Then in the face of what you've said, I presume I needn't ask you if you heard any sound at the door or windows?'

'You need not.'

'Thank you,' said French, 'that disposes of one question. Now, the other. Can you tell me anything likely to be helpful to me about either of the two gentlemen?'

The colonel regretted that in this case also he could do nothing to oblige. He would answer Mr French's questions so far as he could, but he had nothing to volunteer. And French found that after half an hour's interrogation he had learnt just nothing whatever.

'There is one other matter to which I must refer,' he said.
'I regret the necessity, as it's somewhat delicate. Common
report says that Mrs Berlyn was on very intimate terms, first
with Mr Pyke and then with yourself. Would you tell me
how far that is true?'

The colonel squared his shoulders again and French
presently saw that it was an unconscious nervous trick.

'Is it really necessary that Mrs Berlyn's name should be
dragged in?' he asked stiffly.

'I'm afraid so. You will recognise that I am trying to find
motives.'

'I don't think you will find one there.'

'On the contrary, Colonel Domlio, I have evidence that Mr
Berlyn was acutely jealous.'

But the colonel was not to be drawn.

'That is news to me,' he declared.

'Well,' said French doggedly, 'I should like to have your
definite statement as to whether such jealousy would or would
not have been justified, in so far at all events as you yourself
were concerned.'

The colonel smiled sardonically.

'I state categorically that it would not have been
justified.'

'Very good, colonel. I have now only one other request to
make. I should like to interrogate your servants. Some of
them may have seen or heard something which might be
useful to me. Would you oblige me by calling them in and
instructing them to reply to me?'

For the first time an uneasy look appeared in the colonel's
eyes.

'Surely that is unnecessary?' he demurred. 'What could they
possibly tell you?'

'Nothing, I very greatly fear,' French admitted. 'But it is a routine inquiry, and as such I dare not omit it.'

With an evident ill grace Colonel Domlio rang the bell. French, sensing his opposition, had become keenly alert. It seemed to him that he might be on the brink of learning something important. But instantly he decided that he would postpone serious examination of the staff until he had them to himself.

The butler, Burt, answered the bell.

'This gentleman is Mr French, Burt,' said the colonel. 'He wants to ask you some questions. You might answer him so far as you can.'

'It was only to know whether you heard or saw anything unusual on the night of the deaths of Mr Berlyn and Mr Pyke,' French explained.

The man denied with what French thought was over-earnestness. Moreover, he looked acutely uneasy, even scared. French felt a sudden thrill, but he merely nodded and said:

'You didn't see any traces on the moor the next day?'

'Nothing whatever, sir,' said the man with evident relief.

'Thank you, that's all I want. Now, colonel, if I could see the others to put the same questions I should be finished.'

Mrs Burt and the two outside men were produced in turn and each denied having heard or seen anything unusual. Coombe and Mee, the chauffeur and gardener, were interested, but evidently nothing more. But Mrs Burt reproduced all the signs of uneasiness which her husband had exhibited, only in an intensified degree. She was obviously terrified when French questioned her, and her relief when her ordeal was over was unmistakable.

But French apparently saw nothing amiss, and when the quartet had gone he thanked Colonel Domlio for his

165

assistance and apologised for the trouble he had given. And in the colonel's manner he noticed the same repressed evidences of relief. That something had taken place that night of which the master of the house and the two domestics were aware, French was positive.

He left the house and regained the clump of brushwood in which he had hidden the bicycle. But he did not withdraw the machine. Instead, after a quick glance round he crept in beside it, pulling the bushes over him to make sure that he was invisible from the road. From his hiding place he could see the entrance to 'Torview,' as the colonel had named his house.

He was waiting on a pure chance, but after an hour he found that his luck was in. He heard the sounds of an engine being started up and presently saw a small green car turn out of the drive and disappear in the direction of Ashburton. In the car was Colonel Domlio.

French allowed another twenty minutes to pass, then crawling out of the brushwood, he returned to the house. Burt again opened the door.

'I'm sorry to trouble you again, Mr Burt,' he apologised with his pleasant smile, 'but I forgot to ask Colonel Domlio a question. Could I see him again, just for a moment?'

'Colonel Domlio went out about half an hour ago, sir.'

'Ah, that's very unfortunate.' French paused and looked disappointed, then brightened up. 'Perhaps you could give me the information, if you would be so kind? I don't want to have to come back another day.'

Burt was obviously disconcerted. But he tried to hide his feelings and reluctantly invited the caller into the study.

'Yes, sir?' he said.

French instantly became official and very stern. He swung

round, frowning at the other and staring him full in the face. Then he said harshly: 'It is you I want to see, Burt. You lied to me this afternoon. I have come back to hear the truth.'

The man started and fell back a pace, while dismay and something like terror showed on his features.

'I don't understand,' he stammered. 'What do you mean?'

'It's no use, Burt. You've given yourself away. You saw or heard something that night. What was it?'

'You're mistaken, sir,' he declared with a look of relief. 'I neither saw nor heard anything. I swear it.' And then, gaining confidence: 'I don't know what right you have to come here and tell me I was lying. I'm sure—'

'Cut it out,' French said sharply. 'Look here, Burt, if you have any information which might lead to the arrest of the murderer and you keep it back, it's conspiracy. You become an accessory after the fact. I'm not threatening you, but you can see for yourself where that would put you.'

Burt's jaw dropped, but French did not give him time to reply.

'Now, be advised by me and tell what you know. Mr Pyke was murdered that night, and perhaps Mr Berlyn as well. They were not lost on the moor, and it is believed they came here. Now, Burt, what about it?'

The man's face had grown pale, but he stuck to it that he had neither seen nor heard anything. French cut his protestations short.

'Fetch your wife,' he ordered.

The man's manner as he heard these words, coupled with Mrs Burt's evident fear when originally questioned, assured French that this time he was on the right track. With evident unwillingness the woman appeared.

'Now, Mrs Burt, I want to know what you heard or saw

on the night of the tragedy. There is no use in telling me there was nothing. Now, out with it!' And in terse language he explained what accessory after the fact meant and its penalty.

Mrs Burt was of less stern stuff than her husband. Under French's examination she was soon in tears, and presently, disjointed and in fragments, her story came out.

It appeared that on the night of the tragedy she slept badly, owing to some small indisposition. Shortly after one she woke in considerable pain. She endured it for a time, then thinking that perhaps a hot drink would help her, she decided to go down to the kitchen and heat some milk. She got up quietly so as not to awake her husband, and left the bedroom. A quarter moon dimly lit up the staircase and hall, so she carried no light. Just as she reached the head of the lower flight of stairs she heard the front door open. Startled, she drew back into the shadows, peering down at the same time into the hall. She was relieved to see that it was Colonel Domlio. He wore a hat and overcoat, and taking these off, he moved very quietly across the hall. Then she heard the click of the cloak-room door and slight sounds of movement as he approached the stairs. She slipped back into the passage which led to the servants' quarters and in a few seconds the colonel's bedroom door closed softly. This was a few minutes past two o'clock.

It was unusual for the colonel to be out at night and her woman's curiosity led her to examine the hat and coat. They were soaking wet. Rain was falling, but only very slightly, and she realised therefore that he must have been out for a considerable time.

She thought no more of the incident, and having had her hot milk, returned to bed. But she had not slept, and soon Sergeant Daw appeared with his story of the missing men.

This excited, but did not perturb her, but when a few minutes later she heard Colonel Domlio assuring the sergeant that he had spent the whole evening in his study until going up to bed, she felt that something was wrong. But it was not until the next day, when she had learnt the full details of what had happened and had talked the matter over with her husband, that any possible sinister significance of her employer's action occurred to her. Burt, however, had pointed out that it was not their business, and that their obvious policy was silence.

Mrs Burt did not state that she had coupled the colonel's nocturnal excursion with the tragedy, but French could sense that this was in both her and her husband's minds. He wondered what motive they could have suspected and further questions showed that it was connected with the colonel's intimacy with Mrs Berlyn. According to Mrs Burt this had been more serious than he had imagined. Mrs Berlyn had spent several afternoons and an occasional evening with the colonel in his study, and they were known to have had many excursions together on the moor. Since the tragedy, moreover, both the Burts noticed a change in their master. He had developed fits of abstraction and brooding and acted as if he had a weight on his mind.

Believing he had got all he could from the couple, French warned them to keep his visit to themselves, and immensely comforted Mrs Burt by assuring her that she had told him little that he had not known before. Then, saying he wished to have another word with the two outside men, he left the house and walked round to the outbuildings.

At the back of the main house was a large walled yard with an old-fashioned stone-built well in the centre and farm buildings along one side. Wheel-tracks leading into one of these indicated that it was the garage, and there, polishing up some spare parts, was Coombe.

French repeated his explanation about having forgotten to ask Colonel Domlio a question, then after chatting for some minutes he returned to the night of the tragedy. Putting up a bluff, he asked at what hours the colonel had taken out and brought back the car.

Coombe was considerably taken aback by the question and said at once that he knew nothing about it.

'But,' said French in apparent surprise, 'you must have known that the car was out?'

To his delight the man did not deny it. Oh, yes, he knew that, but he had not heard it pass and he didn't know when it had left or returned.

'Then how did you know it had been out? Did Colonel Domlio tell you?'

'No, he didn't say naught about it. I knew by the mud on the car and the petrol that had been used.'

'Pretty smart of you, that,' French said admiringly. 'So there was mud on her? Was she clean the night before?'

'No, he had her out in the afternoon and got her a bit dirty. But he said it was late and for me not to bother with her till the next day, and so I let her alone.'

'Naturally. And was much petrol gone?'

''Bout two gallons.'

'Two gallons,' French repeated musingly. 'That would run her about forty miles, I suppose?'

'Easy that, and more.'

'You live at the lodge gate, don't you, Coombe?'

'That's right.'

'Then the car must have passed you twice in the night. Surely you would have heard it?'

170

'I might not. Anyhow, I wouldn't if she went out the back way.'

All this was excessively satisfactory to French. The theory he had formed postulated that Domlio had secretly run his car to the works on the night of the tragedy. And now it looked as if he had done so. At least, he had taken the car out. And not only had he denied it, but he had arranged that the machine should be left dirty so that the fresh mud it might gather should not show. Furthermore, the hour at which he returned exactly worked in.

For a moment French was puzzled about the quantity of petrol which had been used. Forty miles or more was enough for two trips to the works. Then he saw that to carry out the plan Domlio must have driven there twice. First, he must have been at the works about ten to drug Gurney's tea. Then he must have gone in about midnight with Berlyn and Pyke. So this also fitted in.

French, always thorough, next interviewed Mee. But he was not disappointed when he found the man could tell him nothing. Keenly delighted with his progress, he renewed his directions to keep his visit secret and took his leave.

14

French Turns Fisherman

On reaching the road French returned to his clump of brush-wood and once more concealed himself. He was anxious to intercept Domlio before the latter reached home and received the account of the afternoon's happenings. A question as to the man's nocturnal activities would be more effective were it unexpected.

Though French enjoyed moorland scenery, he had more than enough of this particular view as he sat waiting for the colonel's appearance. Every time he heard a car he got up hopefully, only to turn back in disappointment. Again and again he congratulated himself that he had found a position which commanded the entrances of both front and back drives, or he would have supposed that his quarry had eluded him. For two hours he waited and then at last the green car hove in sight. He stepped forward with upraised arm.

'Sorry to stop you, colonel,' he said pleasantly, 'but I have had some further information since I saw you and I wish to put another question. Will you tell me, please, where exactly you took your car on the night of the tragedy?'

The colonel was evidently taken aback, though not so much as French had hoped.

'I thought I had explained that I wasn't out on that night,' he answered, with only a very slight pause.

'To be candid,' French rejoined, 'that's why I am so anxious to have an answer to my question. If there was nothing in the trip which would interest me, why should you try to hide it.'

'How do you know I was out?'

'You may take it from me, sir, that I am sure of my ground. But if you don't care to answer my question I shall not press it. In fact, I must warn you that any answers you give me may be used against you in evidence.'

In spite of evident efforts the colonel looked uneasy.

'What?' he exclaimed, squaring his shoulders. 'Does this mean that you really suppose I am guilty of the murder of Mr Pyke?'

'It means this, Colonel Domlio. You've been acting in a suspicious way and I want an explanation. I'm not making any charges; simply, I've got to know. Whether you tell me now or not is a matter for yourself.'

'If I don't tell you does it mean that you will arrest me?'

'I don't say so, but it may come to that.'

The colonel gave a mirthless laugh.

'Then I'm afraid I have no alternative. There is no mystery whatever about my taking out the car that night and I have no objection to telling you the whole thing.'

'But you denied that you had done so.'

'I did, and there I admit having made a foolish blunder. But my motive in doing so must be obvious.'

'I'm afraid not so obvious as you seem to think. However, having regard to my warning, if you care to answer my question I shall be pleased to hear your statement.'

'I'll certainly answer it. Possibly you know that I am interested in entomology? I think I told you I was writing a book about the insects of the moor?

'In order to get material for my book I make expeditions all over the moor. I made one on that day of the tragedy. I went to a little valley not far from Chagford where there are numbers of a certain kind of butterfly of which I wanted some specimens for microscopic purposes. While chasing one of these I had the misfortune to get a severe fall. My foot went into a rabbit hole and I crashed, as the airmen say. I was winded and it was some time before I could get up, but I was thankful not to have broken my leg, as I might easily have done. That put me off running for one day and I crawled back to the car and drove home.

'I was feeling a bit shaken and I went up to bed early that night, just before eleven. When I began to undress I found I had lost a miniature which I always carry and which I value extremely, not so much because of its intrinsic worth, but for sentimental reasons. Here it is.'

He took a small gold object from his pocket and passed it across. It was of a charming design, exquisitely chased and set with diamonds, and French saw at once that it was of considerable value. It contained the portrait of a woman; a beautiful, haunting face, clear-cut as a cameo. The whole thing was a wonderful example of artistic skill.

'My late wife,' Colonel Domlio explained as he replaced it in his pocket. 'As you can imagine, I was distressed by the loss. I could only account for it by supposing it had dropped out of my pocket when I fell. I thought over it for some time and then I decided to go out to the place then and there and have a look for it, lest some shepherd or labourer might find it in the early morning. I did so. I took out the car and a strong electric-torch and went back, and on searching the place where I fell I found it almost immediately. I came straight back, arriving shortly after two. Does that satisfy you?'

'No,' said French. 'Not until you explain why you denied having been out when Sergeant Daw asked you.'

'That, as I have said, was a mistake. But you can surely understand my motive. When I heard the sergeant's story I recognised at once that my having taken out the car was a very unfortunate thing for me. I felt sure that foul play would sooner or later be suggested and I thought I should be suspected. I couldn't prove where I had been and I was afraid I should not be believed when I explained.'

'I'm afraid that is not very clear. Why did you imagine that foul play would be suspected?'

Domlio hesitated.

'I suppose,' he said at last, 'things have gone so far there is no use in trying to keep anything back. I knew that there was bad blood between Berlyn and Pyke. The sergeant's news at once suggested to me that the trouble might have come to a head. I hoped not, of course, but the idea occurred to me.'

'Even yet I don't understand. What was the cause of the bad blood between those two and how did you come to know of it?'

'Surely,' Domlio protested, 'it is not necessary to go into that? I am only accounting for my own actions.'

'It is necessary in order to account for your own actions.'

Domlio squared his shoulders.

'I don't think I should tell you, only that, unfortunately, it is pretty well common property. I hate dragging in a lady's name, though you have already done it, but the truth is that they had had a misunderstanding about Mrs Berlyn.'

'About Mrs Berlyn?'

'Yes. She and Pyke saw rather too much of each other. I don't for a moment believe there was the slightest cause for jealousy, but Berlyn was a bit exacting and he probably made a mountain out of a molehill. I knew Mrs Berlyn pretty well myself and I am certain that Berlyn had no real cause for complaint.'

'You haven't explained how you came to know of the affair?'

'It was common property. I don't think I can tell you where I first heard of it.'

French considered for a moment.

'There is another thing, Colonel Domlio. You said that when you heard the sergeant's story you suspected the trouble between the two men had come to a head?'

'Might have come to a head. Yes.'

'Suppose it had. Why, then, did you fear that the sergeant might have suspected you?'

Again Domlio hesitated.

'That is a nasty question, Inspector,' he said at last, 'but from what you asked me in my study you might guess the answer. As a matter of fact, I had myself seen a good deal of Mrs Berlyn for some time previously. About this, there was nothing in the slightest degree compromising. All through we were merely friends. Not only that, but Berlyn knew of our meetings and excursions. When he could he shared them and he had not the slightest objection to our intimacy. But Daw wouldn't know that. For all I could tell, the excellent scandalmongers of the district had coupled Mrs Berlyn's name with mine. Berlyn was dead and gone and he could not state his views. My word would not be believed nor Mrs Berlyn's either, if she were dragged into it. I thought, at all events I had better keep secret a mysterious excursion which might easily be misunderstood.'

Not very convincing, French thought, as he rapidly considered what the colonel had told him. However, it *might* be true. At all events he had no evidence to justify an arrest. He therefore pretended that he fully accepted the statement, and wishing the colonel a cheery good-evening, stood aside to let the car pass.

As he cycled slowly into Ashburton he kept turning over in his mind the question of whether there was any way in which he could test the truth of Colonel Domlio's statement. Frankly, he did not believe the story. But unbelief was no use to him. He must prove it true or false.

All the evening he puzzled over the problem, then at last he saw that there was a line of research which, though it might not solve the point in question, yet bade fair to be of value to the inquiry as a whole.

Once again it concerned a time-table—this time for Domlio's presumed movements. Assume that Berlyn and Pyke reached the point at which the car was abandoned about 11.30 p.m. To convince Pyke of the *bona fides* of the break-down, Berlyn would have to spend some time over the engine, say fifteen minutes. In the dark they could scarcely have reached Torview in less than another fifteen; say that by the time Domlio had admitted them it was close on midnight. Some time would then be consumed in explaining the situation and in getting out the car; in fact, the party could scarcely have left Torview before 12.10 a.m. Running to the works would have occupied the most of another half hour, say, arrive 12.40 a.m. Domlio reached his house about 2.10 a.m., which, allowing half an hour for the return journey, left an hour unaccounted for. In this hour Pyke's murder must have been committed, the duplicator removed from the crate and the body substituted, the duplicator taken to pieces and the parts left in the store, fresh tea put into Gurney's flask, Pyke's clothes and the small parts of the duplicator got rid of and the magneto on Berlyn's car changed.

French wondered if all these things could have been done in the time. At last, after working out a detailed time-table, he came to the conclusion that they could, on one condition; that the clothes and duplicator parts were got rid of on the way to Torview, that is, if no time were lost in making a detour.

Where, then, could this have been done?

French took his map and considered the route. The Dart river was crossed three times and a part of the way lay through woods. But he believed that too many tourists strayed from the road for these to be safe hiding-places, though he realised that they might have to be searched later.

There remained two places, either of which he thought more promising; the works and Domlio's grounds.

The fact that elaborate arrangements had been made to get Pyke's body away from the works indicated that the disposal of it there was considered impossible. Nevertheless, French spent the next day, which was Sunday, prowling about the buildings, though without result.

This left Domlio's little estate, and early the following morning French borrowed the sergeant's bicycle and rode out to his former hiding-place outside the gates. History repeated itself, for after waiting for nearly two hours he saw Domlio pass out towards Ashburton.

As the car had not been heard by either Coombe or Mee on the night of the tragedy, it followed that it had almost certainly entered by the back drive. French now walked up this lane to the yard, looking out for hiding-places. But there were none.

He did not see any of the servants about and he stood in the yard, pondering over his problem. Then his glance fell on the old well and it instantly occurred to him that here was the very kind of place he was seeking. There was an old wheel-pump beside it, rusty and dilapidated, working a rod to the plunger below. He imagined the well was not used, for on his last visit he had noticed a well-oiled force pump a hundred yards away at the kitchen door.

The well was surrounded by a masonry wall about three feet high, coped with roughly-dressed stones. On the coping was a flat wooden grating, old and decaying. Ivy covered about half of the wall and grating.

French crossed the yard, and leaning over the wall, glanced down. The sides were black with age and he could distinguish no details of the walls, but there was a tiny reflection from the water far below. Then suddenly he noticed a thing which once again set him off into a ferment of delight.

The cross-bars of the grating were secured by mortar into niches cut in the stone. All of these bore signs of recent movements.

Satisfied that he had at last solved his problem, French quietly left the yard, and recovering his bicycle, rode back to the police station at Ashburton.

'I want your help, Sergeant,' he said as Daw came forward. 'Can you get some things together and come out with me to Colonel Domlio's tonight?'

'Of course, Mr French.'

'Good. Then I want a strong fishing-line and some hooks and some twenty-five or thirty yards of strong cord. I want to try an experiment.'

'I'll have all those ready.'

'I want to be there when there's no one about; so as the colonel sits up very late, I think we'll say three o'clock. That means we ought to leave here about one-fifteen. Can you borrow a second bicycle?'

The sergeant looked completely mystified by these instructions, but he answered, 'Certainly,' without asking any questions. It was agreed that they should meet in the evening at his house, sitting up there until it was time to start.

Having explained at the hotel that he had to go to Plymouth and would be away all night, French started out for a tramp on the moor. About eleven he turned up at Daw's cottage and there the two men spent the next couple of hours, smoking and chatting.

Shortly before three they reached Torview. They hid their bicycles in the brushwood and walked softly up the back drive to the yard. The night was fine and calm, but the sky was overcast and it was very dark. Not a sound broke the stillness. Silently they reached the well and French with his electric torch examined the wooden cover.

'I think if we lift together we can get it up,' he whispered. 'Try at this side and use the ivy as a hinge.'

They raised it easily and French propped it with a billet of wood.

'Now, Sergeant, the fishing line.'

At the sergeant's cottage they had tied on a bunch of hooks and a weight. French now let these down, having passed the line through one of the holes in the grating to ensure its swinging free from the walls. Gradually he paid out the cord until a faint plop announced that the water had been reached. He continued lowering as long as the cord would run out, then he began jerking it slowly up and down.

'Swing it from side to side, Sergeant, while I keep jerking it. If there's anything there we should get it.'

For twenty minutes they worked and then, just as French was coming to the conclusion that a daylight descent into the well would be necessary, the hooks caught. Something of fair weight was on the line.

'Let it stay till it stops swinging, or else we shall lose the hooks in the wall, Mr French,' the sergeant advised, now as keenly interested as was French himself.

'Right, Sergeant. The water will soon steady it.'

After a few seconds French began to pull slowly up, the drops from the attached object echoing loudly up the long funnel. And then came into the circle of the sergeant's torch a man's coat.

It was black and sodden and shapeless from the water, and slimy to the touch. They lifted it round the well so that the wall should be between them and the house and examined it with their electric torches.

In the breast pocket was a letter-case containing papers, but it was impossible to read anything they bore. A pipe, a tobacco-pouch, a box of matches and a handkerchief were in the other pockets.

Fortunately for French there was a tailor's tab sewn into the lining of the breast pocket and he was able to make out part of the legend: 'R. Shrubsole & Co., Newton Abbot.' Beneath was a smudge which had evidently been the owner's name, but this was undecipherable.

'We'll get it from the tailor,' French said. 'Let's try the hooks again.'

Once again they lowered their line, but this time without luck.

'No good,' French declared at last. 'We'll have to pump it

out. You might get the depth and then close up and leave it as we found it. We'd better bring a portable pump, for I don't suppose that old thing will work.'

They replaced the grating and the billet of wood, and stealing silently out of the yard, rode back to Ashburton.

With the coat wrapped in paper and packed in his suitcase, French took an early 'bus to Newton Abbot. There he soon found Messrs Shrubsole's establishment and asked for the proprietor.

'It's not easy to say whose it was,' Mr Shrubsole declared when he had examined the coat. 'You see, these labels of ours are printed; that is, our name and address. But the customer's name is written and it would not last in the same way. I'm afraid I cannot read it.'

'If it had been possible to read it I should not have come to you, Mr Shrubsole. I want you to get at it from the cloth and size and probable age and things of that kind. You can surely find out all those things by examination.'

This appeared to be a new idea to Mr Shrubsole. He admitted that something of the kind might be done, and, calling an assistant, fell to scrutinising the garment.

'It's that brown tweed with the purple line that we sold so much of last year,' the assistant declared. He produced a roll of cloth. 'See, if we lift the lining here it shows clear enough.'

'That's right,' his employer admitted. 'Now can we get the measurements?'

'Not so easy,' said the assistant. 'The thing will be all warped and shrunk from the water.'

'Try,' French urged with his pleasant smile.

An orgy of measuring followed, with a subsequent recourse to the books and much low-voiced conversation. Finally, Mr Shrubsole announced the result.

182

'It's not possible to say for sure, Mr French. You see, the coat is shrunk out of all knowing. But we think it might belong to one of four men.'

'I see your difficulty, Mr Shrubsole, but if you tell me the four it may help me.'

'I hope so. We sold suits of about this size to Mr Albert Cunningham, of 27 Acacia Street, Newton Abbot; Mr John Booth, of Lyndhurst, Teignmouth; Mr Stanley Pyke, of East Street, Ashburton; and Mr George Hepworth, of Linda Lodge, Newton Abbot. Any of those any good to you?' Mr Shrubsole's expression suddenly changed. 'By Jove! You're not the gentleman that's been making these discoveries about Mr Berlyn and Mr Pyke? We've heard some report that some Scotland Yard man was down and had found out that that tragedy was not all it was supposed to be. That it, sir?'

'That's it,' French replied, feeling that it was impossible to keep his business private. 'But I don't want it talked about. Now, you see why I should like to be sure whether that was or was not Mr Pyke's coat.'

But in spite of the tailor's manifest interest, he declared that the point could not be established. He was fairly sure that it belonged to one of the four, but more than that he could not say.

But French had no doubt whatever, and well pleased with his progress, he left the shop and took the first 'bus back to Ashburton.

15

Blackmail

'Have you been able to get the pump, Sergeant?' asked French as he reached the police station that afternoon.

'I've got the loan of one, Mr French, or at least I'll get it first thing tomorrow. From a quarry close by. It's a rotary hand-pump, and Mr Glenn, the manager, tells me that it will throw far faster than anything we'll want.'

'We shall have to fix it down in the well?'

'Yes, the well's forty-two feet deep. It's thirty to the water and there's twelve feet of water. But there'll be no trouble about that. The beams that carry the old pump will take it too.'

'You think they're strong enough?'

'We'll just have to try them.'

'What about ladders?'

'I've got a fifty-foot length of rope ladder from the same quarry.'

'Good. What time can we start tomorrow?'

'I shall have the pump by half past eight.'

'Then we should be at the colonel's shortly after nine.'

This time French thought it would be wise to have Domlio present at their experiment. He therefore rang him up and made an appointment for nine-thirty.

Early next morning a heavily-loaded car left Ashburton. In addition to the driver it contained French, Daw, and two constables in plain clothes, as well as a low, squat pump with detachable handle, an immense coil of armoured hose, another huge coil of rope ladder, a candle lantern and several tools and small parts.

'Another rush to Klondyke,' said French, at which priceless pearl of humour Daw smiled and the plain-clothes men guffawed heavily.

'I should have thought that tailor could have fixed up the ownership of the coat,' Daw remarked presently. 'Shouldn't you, sir?'

'Of course, Sergeant. But we shall get it all right, even if we have to do all the work ourselves. I thought it wasn't worth troubling about. It's pretty certain the coat is not the only thing that was thrown into the well and we shall get our identification from something else.'

The car was run into the yard, unloaded and dismissed, while French went to the hall door and asked for Colonel Domlio.

'Sorry to trouble you at this hour, colonel, but I want you to be present at a small experiment I am carrying out.' He watched the other keenly as he spoke. 'Will you, please, come out into the yard, where I have left Sergeant Daw and some men?'

Surprise showed on the colonel's face, but not, so far as French could see, apprehension.

'This is very interesting, Inspector. I'm glad I'm at least being informed of what is taking place on my own ground. I shall certainly see what you are doing.'

As they turned the corner and the purpose of the visit became apparent to Domlio his surprise seemed to deepen, but still there was no appearance of uneasiness. The police had lifted the cover of the well and were getting the pump rigged. Coombe and Mee had joined the others and stood speechlessly regarding the preparations.

'Ah, an invasion? I presume, Inspector, you have adequate authority for these somewhat unusual proceedings?'

'I think you'll find that's all right, sir. With your permission, we're going to pump out the well.'

'The removal of the well-cover and the pump rather suggested something of the kind, but for the moment I can't quite recall the permission.'

'I feel sure that, under the circumstances, you won't withhold it. Better lower that lantern with the candle, Sergeant, before you send a man down. We want to be sure the air is good.'

'If it's not an impertinence,' Domlio remarked, with ironic politeness, 'I should be interested to know why you are not using the existing pump.'

'I didn't think it was in working order. Is the well used?'

'An explanation, complete, no doubt, but scarcely satisfying. It did not occur to you to try it?'

'No, sir. Too noisy. But what about the well?'

'Ah, yes, the well. The well is used—in summer. We have a gravity supply from the hill behind the house, but it fails in summer; hence pumping from the well.'

This statement was very satisfactory to French. It cleared up a point which had been worrying him. If it were possible to get rid of the clothes by throwing them down the well, why had Pyke's body not been disposed of in the same way? But now this was explained. The condition of the water in the following summer would have led to investigation.

'Try the fixed pump, Sergeant. It may save us rigging the other.'

But a test showed that the valve leathers were dry and not holding, and they went on with their original programme.

French had been puzzled by the colonel's attitude. If beneath his cynical manner he were consumed by the anxiety which, were he guilty, he could scarcely help feeling, he was concealing it in a way that was little short of marvellous. However, the preparations would take time and it was impossible that, if the man knew what would be found, he could hide all signs of tension.

The candle, lowered to the surface of the water, burned clearly, showing that the air was fresh. The rope ladder was then made fast to the stonework and Sergeant Daw climbed down. Presently he returned to say that the beams on which the old pump rested were sound. The new pump was therefore lowered and one of the constables sent down to begin work.

Getting rid of the water turned out a bigger job than French had anticipated. Slowly the level dropped. At intervals the men relieved each other, French and Daw taking their turns. By lunch time the water had gone down seven feet, though during the meal it rose six inches. After that they worked with renewed energy to get the remaining five feet six inches out before dusk.

'You have a second well, have you not, colonel?' French inquired. 'I noticed a pump near the kitchen door.'

'Yes, we use it for drinking purposes. This is only good enough for washing the car, and so on.'

On more than one occasion Domlio had protested against what he called the waste of his time in watching the work. But French insisted on his remaining till the search was complete.

About four o'clock the water was so far lowered as to allow an investigation of the bottom and the sergeant, squeezing past the man at the pump, went down with his electric torch. French, leaning over the wall, anxiously watched the flickering light. Then came the sergeant's voice: 'There's a waistcoat and trousers and shoes here, Mr French.'

'That all?' called French.

'That's all that I see. It's everything of any size, anyhow.'

'Well, tie them to the rope and we'll pull them up.'

How Domlio would comport himself when he saw the clothes was now the important matter. French watched him keenly as the dripping bundle appeared and was carried to a bench in the garage.

Though the day's work prepared the man for some such *dénouement,* he certainly appeared to French to be genuinely amazed when the nature of the find was revealed.

'Good heavens, Inspector! What does this mean?' he cried, squaring his shoulders. 'Whose are these and how did you know they were there?'

French turned to the plain-clothes men. 'Just wait outside the door, will you?' he said, then went on gravely to the other: 'That is what I have to ask you, Colonel Domlio.'

'Me?' The man's sardonic calm was at last broken. 'I know nothing about them. The thing is an absolute surprise to me. I swear it.' His face paled and he looked anxious and worried.

'There is something I should tell you,' French continued. 'On considering this Berlyn-Pyke case I formed a theory. I don't say it is correct, but I formed it from the facts I had learnt. According to that theory you took out your car on the night of the tragedy, drove into Ashburton, picked up Mr Pyke's coat, waistcoat, trousers, shoes, and certain other things, brought them here and threw them into the well. A

188

moment, please.' He raised his hand as Domlio would have spoken. 'Rightly or wrongly, that was my theory. But there was a difficulty. You had stated to the sergeant that you had not gone out that night. I came here and found that that statement was not true; you had been out. Then I made further inquiries and learned that you had taken out your car. You explained that, but I regret to say that I was unable to accept your explanation. I thought, however, that the presence or absence of these objects in the well would settle the matter. I looked at the well and saw that the cover had recently been moved. Two nights ago Sergeant Daw and I came out, and after trying with a line and fish-hooks, we drew up a coat—Pyke's coat. Now, colonel, if you wish to make a statement I will give it every consideration, but it is my duty again to warn you that anything you say may be used in evidence against you.'

'What? Are you charging me with a crime?'

'Unless you can satisfy me of your innocence you will be charged with complicity in the murder of Stanley Pyke.'

The colonel drew a deep breath.

'But, good heavens! How can I satisfy you? I don't even know what you have against me, except this extraordinary business which I can make neither head nor tail of. You must know more about it than you have said. Tell me the rest.'

'You tell me this: Was your statement about the loss of the locket on that night true?'

Colonel Domlio did not reply. He seemed to be weighing some problem of overwhelming difficulty. French waited patiently, wondering how far his bluff would carry. At last the colonel spoke.

'I have lied to the sergeant and to you, Inspector, with what I now believe was a mistaken motive. I have been turning over the matter in my mind and I see that I have no alternative but to tell you the truth now or to suffer arrest. Possibly things have gone so far that this cannot be avoided. At all events, I will tell you everything.'

'You are not forgetting my warning, Colonel Domlio?'

'I am not forgetting it. If I am acting foolishly it is my own look out. I tried to put you off, Inspector, to save bringing Mrs Berlyn's name further into the matter, because, though there was nothing against her character, I was sure you would have bothered her with annoying questions. But though I thought it right to lie with this object, I don't feel like risking prison for it.'

'I follow you,' said French.

'You will remember then what I told you about Mrs Berlyn, that she had been seeing a good deal, first of Pyke and then of myself. I'm sorry to have to drag this in again, but otherwise you wouldn't understand the situation.

'About, let me see, four months before the tragedy Mrs Berlyn came out here one afternoon. She said that she had been in London to a lecture on entomology and that she had been so much interested that she had read one or two books on the subject. She said that she knew I was doing some research in it and she wondered whether I would let her come and help me and so learn more. I, naturally, told her I should be delighted, and she began to come out here quite often. On different occasions she has accompanied me on the moor while I was searching for specimens, and she has spent several afternoons with me in my library mounting butterflies and learning to use the microscope. This went on until the day of the tragedy.'

Colonel Domlio paused, squared his shoulders and continued:

'On that morning I had received by post a letter addressed in a strange hand and marked "Personal." It was signed "X.Y.Z." and said that the writer happened to be walking about 4 p.m. on the previous Tuesday in the Upper Merton glen at a certain point which he described; that he had seen me with Mrs Berlyn in my arms; that having a camera he had at once taken two photographs, one of which had come out well; and that if I cared to have the negative he would sell it for fifty pounds. If I wished to negotiate I was to meet him on the Chagford-Gidleigh road at the gate of Dobson's Spinney at one o'clock that night. Should I not turn up, the writer would understand that I was not interested and would take his picture to Mrs Berlyn, who, he thought, would prefer to deal rather than have it handed to Mr Berlyn.

'For a time I could not think what was meant, then I remembered what had taken place. We had been, Mrs Berlyn and I, searching for a certain butterfly at the place and time mentioned. Suddenly she had cried out that she had seen a specimen and she had rushed after it past where I was standing. Just as she reached me she gave a cry and lurched against me. "Oh, my ankle," she shouted, and clung to me. She had twisted her foot in a rabbit hole and she could not put her weight on it. I supported her in my arms for a few seconds, and it must have been at this moment that my blackmailer came on the scene. I laid Mrs Berlyn down on the grass. She sat quiet for some minutes, then with my arm was able to limp to the car. She said her ankle was not sprained, but only twisted, and that she would be all right in a few hours. Next day when I rang up to inquire she said it was still painful but a good deal better.

'At first I was doubtful whether I should act on the letter, then I thought that if there was a genuine photograph it would be better for me to deal with the Owner. I therefore went out to the rendezvous at the time mentioned. But I might have saved myself the trouble, for no one was there. And from that day to this I never heard another word about the affair, nor did I mention it to a soul. Indeed, the Berlyn-Pyke tragedy put it out of my head, and the same thing, I suppose, robbed the photograph of its value.'

'You told me,' said French, 'something about Mrs Berlyn's relations with Mr Pyke and yourself, saying that I would not understand your story otherwise. Just what was in your mind in that?'

'Because these relations complicated the whole situation. Do you not see that? Had everything been normal I could have treated the thing as a joke and shown the photograph to Berlyn. As things were, he would have taken it seriously.'

French felt a little puzzled by this statement. If the man were lying it was just the sort of story he would expect to hear, except for one thing. It was capable of immediate confirmation. If it were not true, he would soon get it out of Mrs Berlyn.

'I don't want to be offensive, colonel,' he said, 'but by your own admission you have twice lied about what took place that night. Can you give me any proof that your present statement is true?'

Domlio squared his shoulders.

'I can't,' he admitted. 'I can show you the letter and you can ask Mrs Berlyn, but I don't know that either of those would constitute proof.'

'They wouldn't in themselves, but from either I might get some point which would. Now, I'll tell you what we'll do. We'll see first whether Sergeant Daw has made any further discoveries, then you can show me the letter and we'll drive out to the place where Mrs Berlyn fell.'

'That's easily done.'

They returned to the well and there to French's satisfaction found the missing duplicator parts laid out on the coping of the wall.

'Excellent, sergeant. That's all we want. I take it you will get the pump away? You needn't wait for me. I'm going out with Colonel Domlio.'

While Coome was bringing round the car the two men went to the study for the letter. It was just as the colonel had described and French could see no clue to the sender.

They ran out then to the Upper Merton glen and Domlio pointed out the spot at which the alleged incident had taken place. French insisted on his describing the occurrence in the most minute manner. He wished to form an opinion as to whether the man was relating what he had seen or inventing the details as he went along.

After half an hour of close questioning on the lines of the American third degree, French had to admit that the affair had either happened as Domlio had said or that it had been rehearsed with great care. On no point was he able to trip the colonel up, and knowing the difficulty of inventing a story in which every detail is foreseen and accounted for, he began to think the tale true. At all events, with the mass of detail he now possessed, a similar examination of Mrs Berlyn should set the matter at rest.

French was in a thoughtful mood as they drove back to Torview. He was up against the same old question which had troubled him so many times in the past. Was his suspect guilty or was he the victim of a plot?

The evidence against the man was certainly strong. Seven

separate facts pointed to his guilt. French ran over them in his mind:

1. Domlio had the necessary qualifications for partnership in the crime. He knew the *dramatis personæ* and he was acquainted with the works. He could have ordered the duplicator, and arranged for Berlyn and Pyke to visit Tavistock on the night in question.

2. He was out in his car on that night at the time and for the distance required.

3. He had denied this.

4. When cornered, he had told a false story of a search for a lost locket.

5. The clothes of the dead man had been found in the very place where French imagined Domlio would have hidden them.

6. There was a quite adequate motive if, as might well be, Domlio was really attached to Mrs Berlyn.

7. There was no other person whom French knew of who could have been Berlyn's confederate.

Many and many a man had been hanged on far less evidence than there was here. With this mass of incriminating facts an arrest was amply justifiable. Indeed, a conviction was almost assured.

On the other hand, every bit of this evidence was circumstantial and could be explained, on the assumption of Domlio's innocence, by supposing him to be the victim of a conspiracy on the part of the real murderer.

French wondered if he could make the man reveal his own outlook on the affair.

'Tell me, colonel,' he said, 'did it not strike you as a strange thing that Mrs Berlyn should stumble at just the point which ensured her falling into your arms?'

Domlio slackened speed and looked round aggressively.

'Just what do you mean by that?'

'As a matter of fact,' French answered sweetly, 'what I mean is: Was the accident genuine or faked?'

The colonel squared his shoulders indignantly.

'I consider that a most unwarrantable remark,' he said hotly; 'and I shall not answer it. I can only suppose your abominable calling has warped your mind and made suspicion a disease with you.'

French glanced at him keenly. The man was genuinely angry. And if so, it tended in his favour. Real indignation is difficult to simulate and would not be called forth by an imaginary insult.

'If you think my remark unwarrantable, I shall withdraw it,' French said with his pleasant smile. 'I simply wanted to know whether you yourself believed in it. I think you do. Well, colonel, I think that's all we can do tonight. I'm sorry to have given you all this annoyance, but you can see I had no option.'

They had reached the gate of Torview. Domlio stopped the car.

'Then you are not going to arrest me?' he asked with barely concealed anxiety.

'No. Why should I? You have accounted in a reasonable way for the suspicious circumstances. So far as I can see, your explanation is satisfactory. I can't expect any more.'

The colonel gave a sigh of relief.

'To be quite candid,' he admitted, 'I scarcely hoped that you would accept it. After what has occurred, I can't expect you to believe me, but for what it's worth I give you my word of honour that what I have told you this time is the truth. I may tell you that I have been afraid of this very development, ever since the tragedy. How are you getting to Ashburton? Shall I run you in?'

'It would be very good of you.'

It was with considerable uneasiness that French saw Colonel Domlio drive off from the hotel in Ashburton. He had backed his judgment that the man was innocent, but he recognised that he might easily have made a mistake. At the same time Domlio could scarcely escape, otherwise than by suicide, and he felt sure that his mind had been so much eased that he would not attempt anything so drastic. As soon, however, as the car was out of sight he walked to the police station and asked Daw to have a watch kept on the man's movements.

16

Certainty at Last

That night as French was writing up his diary the question he had asked Domlio recurred to him. 'Tell me, colonel,' he had said, 'did it not strike you as strange that Mrs Berlyn should stumble at just the point which ensured her falling into your arms?' He had asked it to test the colonel's belief in the incident. Now, it occurred to him that on its merits it required an answer.

Had the incident stood alone it might well have passed unquestioned. But it was not alone. Two other matters must be considered in conjunction with it.

First, there was the coincidence that at the precise moment a watcher armed with a camera should be present. What accident should take a photographer to this secluded glen, just when so compromising a tableau should be staged? Was there here an element of design?

Secondly, there was the consideration that if suspicion were to be thrown on Domlio he must be made to take out his car secretly on the fatal night. And how better could this be done than by the story of the photograph? Once again, did this not suggest design?

If so, something both interesting and startling followed. Mrs Berlyn was privy to it. And if she were privy to it, was she not necessarily implicated in the murder? Could she even be the accomplice for whom he, French, had been searching?

There was, of course, her alibi. If she had been at the party at her house at ten o'clock she could not have drugged Gurney's tea. But was she at her house?

Experience had made French sceptical about alibis. This one certainly seemed water-tight, and yet was it not just possible that Mrs Berlyn had managed to slip away from her guests for the fifteen or twenty minutes required?

It was evident that the matter must be tested forthwith, and French decided that, having already questioned Mr Fogden, he would interview the Dr and Mrs Lancaster whom Lizzie Johnston had mentioned as also being members of the party. They had lived on the Buckland road, half a mile beyond the Berlyns', and next morning French called on them.

Dr Lancaster, he had learned from Daw, was a newcomer to the town, a young medical man who had been forced by a break-down in health to give up his career. He received French at once.

'I want to find out whether any member of the party could have left the house about ten o'clock for fifteen or twenty minutes,' French explained. 'Do you think that you or Mrs Lancaster could help me out?'

'I can only speak for myself,' Dr Lancaster smiled. 'I was there all the time, and I'm sure so was Mrs Lancaster. But I'll call her and you can ask her.'

'A moment, please. Surely you can speak for more than yourself? Were you not with the others?'

'With some of them. You see, what happened was this. When we went in Mrs Berlyn said that she had been disappointed in that three London friends, who were staying at Torquay and whom she expected, had just telegraphed to say they couldn't come. That made our numbers wrong. She had intended to have three tables of bridge, but now as some of us played billiards she suggested one bridge table and snooker for the other five. She and I, and, let me see, Fogden and a Miss Pym, I think, and one other—I'm blessed if I can remember who the other was—played snooker. So I wasn't with the other four between the time that we settled down to play and supper.'

'What hour was supper?'

'About half-past ten, I think. We broke up when it was over—rather early, as a matter of fact. We reached home shortly after eleven.'

'And you played snooker all the evening until supper?'

'No. After an hour or more we dropped it and played four-handed billiards.'

'Then some player must have stood out?'

'Yes. Mrs Berlyn said she must go and see how the others were getting along. She watched us play for some time, then went to the drawing-room. She came back after a few minutes to say that supper was ready.'

'Now, Dr Lancaster, just one other question. Can you tell me at what time Mrs Berlyn went into the drawing-room?'

'I really don't think I can. I wasn't paying special attention to her movements. I should say perhaps half an hour before supper, but I couldn't be sure.'

'That's all right,' said French. 'Now, if I could see Mrs Lancaster for a moment I should be done.'

Mrs Lancaster was a dark, vivacious little woman who seemed to remember the evening in question much more clearly than did her husband.

'Yes,' she said, 'I was playing bridge with Miss Lucy Pym, Mr Cowls and Mr Leacock. I remember Mrs Berlyn coming in about ten. She laughed and said, "Oh, my children, don't be frightened. I couldn't think of disturbing such a serious game. I'll go back to our snooker." She went away and presently came back and called us to the library to supper.'

'How long was she away, Mrs Lancaster?'

'About twenty minutes, I should think.'

This seemed to French to be all that he wanted. However, he thought it wise to get the key of the Berlyns' house and have a look at the lay-out. The drawing-room was in front with the library behind it, but between the two there was a passage with a side door leading into the garden. He felt satisfied as to the use to which that passage had been put on the night in question. He could picture Mrs Berlyn fixing up the uneven number of guests, among whom would be some who played billiards and some who did not. The proposals for snooker and bridge would almost automatically follow, involving the division of the party in two rooms. Mrs Berlyn, as hostess, would reasonably be the odd man out when the change was made from snooker to billiards. The result of these arrangements would be that when she slipped out to the works through the side door each party would naturally assume she was with the other, while if any question as to this arose, her re-entry at supper time would suggest to both that she had gone out to overlook its preparation.

These discoveries justified French's theory, but they did not prove it, and he racked his brains for some test which would definitely establish the point.

At last an idea occurred to him which he thought might at least help.

In considering Mrs Berlyn as her husband's accomplice he had been doubtful whether there would have been sufficient time for the various actions. If, after Berlyn's arrival at the works with the body, Mrs Berlyn had driven the car back to where it was found, changed the magneto and made the footprints, he did not believe she could have walked home in time to wake the servant at the hour stated. Nor did he believe that Berlyn, after disposing of the body in the works, would have been able on foot to make Domlio's in time to hide the clothes in the well before the sergeant's call.

He now wondered whether Mrs Berlyn's bicycle could have been pressed into the service. Could the lady have brought the machine to the works, lifted it into the tonneau of the car, carried it out on the moor and ridden back on it to the works? And could her husband have used it to reach, first Domlio's, and then Plymouth or some other large town from which he had escaped?

To test the matter, French returned to Lizzie Johnston and asked her if she knew what had become of the bicycle.

But the girl could not tell him. Nor could she recall when or where she had seen it last. She supposed it had been sold at the auction, but in the excitement of that time she had not noticed it.

'Where did Mrs Berlyn get it, do you know?'

'From Makepeace's. He has bicycles, same as motors. He'll tell you about it.'

Half an hour later French was talking to Mr Makepeace. He remembered having, some five years earlier, sold the machine to Mrs Berlyn. He looked up his records and after considerable trouble found a note of the transaction. The bicycle was a Swift, number 35,721. It had certain dimensions and peculiarities, of which he gave French details.

French's next call was with the auctioneer who had conducted the sale of the Berlyn effects. Mr Nankivell appeared *au fait* with the whole case and was obviously thrilled to meet French. He made no difficulty about giving the required information. A bicycle had not been among the articles auctioned, nor had he seen one during his visits to the house.

This was all very well as far as it went, but it was negative. French wanted to find someone who could say definitely what had happened to the machine. He consulted with Sergeant Daw and at last came to the conclusion that if Peter Swann, the gardener-chauffeur, could be found, he might be able to give the information. Daw believed he had gone to Chagford and he telephoned to the sergeant there, asking him to make inquiries.

In the afternoon there was a reply to the effect that the man was employed by a market gardener near Chagford and French at once took a car over to see him. Swann remembered the bicycle well, as he had had to keep it clean. He had seen it in the wood-shed on the day before the tragedy, but next morning it was gone. He had looked for it particularly, as he wished to use it to take a message to the town, and he had wondered where it could have got to. He had never seen it again. He had not asked about it as he had not considered that his business.

Once again French experienced the keen delight of finding his deductions justified by the event. In this whole case he had really excelled himself. On several different points he had imagined what might have occurred, and on a test being made, his idea had been proved correct. Some work, that!

As he did not fail to remind himself, it showed the highest type of ability.

The next thing was to find the bicycle. He returned for the night to Ashburton and next morning went down to see the superintendent of police at Plymouth. That officer listened with interest to his story and promised to have a search made without delay. When he had rung up and asked for similar inquiries to be made in the other large towns within a cycle ride of the moor, French found himself at a loose end.

'You should have a look round the place,' the superintendent advised. 'There's a lot to see in Plymouth.'

French took the advice and went for a stroll round the city. He was not impressed by the streets, though he admired St Andrew's Church, the Guildhall and some of the other buildings in the same locality. But when, after wandering through some more or less uninteresting residential streets, he unexpectedly came out on the Hoe, he held his breath. The promenade along the top of the cliff was imposing enough, though no better than he had seen many times before. But the view of the Sound was unique. The sea, light blue in the morning sun, stretched from the base of the cliff beneath his feet, out past Drake's Island and the long line of the Breakwater to a clear horizon. On the right was Mount Edgcumbe, tree-clad to the water's edge, while far away out to the south-west was the faint white pillar of the Eddystone lighthouse. French gazed and admired, then going down to the Sutton Pool, he explored the older part of the town for the best part of an hour.

When he presently reached the police station he was delighted to find that news had just then come in. The bicycle had been found. It had been pawned by a man, apparently a labourer, shortly after the shop opened on the morning of

Tuesday, the 16th August; the morning, French reminded himself delightedly, after the crime. The man had stated that the machine was his daughter's and had been given two pounds on it. He had not returned since, nor had the machine been redeemed.

'We're trying to trace the man, but after this lapse of time I don't suppose we shall be able,' the superintendent declared. 'I expect this Berlyn abandoned the machine when he reached Plymouth, and our friend found it and thought he had better make hay while the sun shone.'

'So likely that I don't think it matters whether you find him or not,' French returned.

'I agree, but we shall have a shot at it, all the same. By the way, Mr French, it's a curious thing that you should call today. Only yesterday I was talking to a friend of yours; an ass, if you don't mind my saying so, but married to one of the most delightful young women I've ever come across. Lives at Dartmouth.'

'Dartmouth?' French laughed. 'That gives me a clue. You mean that cheery young optimist, Maxwell Cheyne? He is an ass, right enough, but he's not a bad soul at bottom. And the girl's a stunner. How are they getting along?'

'Tip-top. He's taken to writing tales. Doing quite well with them, too, I believe. They're very popular down there, both of them.'

'Glad to hear it. Well, Superintendent, I must be getting along. Thanks, for your help.'

Next day he showed the bicycle to Lizzie Johnston, and was delighted when she unhesitatingly identified it as Mrs Berlyn's.

French was full of an eager optimism as the result of these discoveries. The episode of the bicycle, added to the break-down of the alibi, seemed definitely to prove his theory of Mrs Berlyn's complicity.

But when he considered the identity of the person whom Mrs Berlyn had thus assisted, he had to admit himself staggered. That Berlyn had murdered Pyke had seemed an obvious theory. Now, French was not so certain of it. The lady had undoubtedly been in love with Pyke. Surely, it was too much to suppose she would help her husband to murder her lover?

Had it been the other way round, had Phyllis and Pyke conspired to kill Berlyn, the thing would have been easier to understand. Wife and lover against husband was a common enough combination. But the evidence against this idea was strong. Not only was there the identification of the clothes and birth-mark, but there was the strong presumption that the man who disposed of the crate in Wales was Berlyn. At the same time, this evidence of identification was not quite conclusive, and French determined to keep the possibility in view and test it rigorously as occasion offered.

And then another factor occurred to him, an extremely disturbing factor, which bade fair to change his whole view of the case. He saw that even if Pyke had murdered Berlyn it would not clear up the situation. In fact, this new idea suggested that it was impossible either that Pyke could have murdered Berlyn or that Berlyn could have murdered Pyke.

What, he asked himself, must have been the motive for such a crime? Certainly not merely to gratify a feeling of hate. The motive undoubtedly was to enable the survivor to claim Phyllis as his wife and to live with her in good social standing and without fear of his rival. But the crime, French reminded himself, had a peculiar feature. The staged accident on the moor involved the disappearance of *both* actors, the murderer as well as the victim. If, then, the murderer disappeared, he could not live with Phyllis. If either Berlyn or Pyke were guilty, therefore, he had carried out the crime in a way which robbed him of the very results for which he had committed it.

French saw that he was up against a puzzling dilemma. If Berlyn had murdered Pyke it was unlikely that Mrs Berlyn would have assisted. If, on the other hand, Pyke had murdered Berlyn, Mrs Berlyn's action was clear, but not Pyke's, for Pyke could get nothing out of it.

French swore bitterly, as he realised that in all probability his former view of the case was incorrect, and that he was once again without any really satisfactory theory on which to work. Nor did some hours' thought point the way to a solution of his problem.

At least, however, he saw his next step. Mrs Berlyn was the accomplice of *someone*. That someone was doubtless alive and biding his time until he thought it safe to join the lady. If so, she was pretty sure to know his whereabouts. Could she be made to reveal it?

French thought that, if in some way he could give her a thorough fright, she might try to get a warning through. It would then be up to him to intercept her message, which would give him the information he required.

This meant London. Next day, which was Saturday, he travelled up to Paddington.

17

'Danger!'

Before leaving Plymouth, French had wired to Mrs Berlyn, asking for an interview for the following Monday morning. On reaching the Yard he found a reply. If he called round about half-past ten the lady would see him. He rang his bell for Sergeant Carter.

'I shall want you with me today, Carter,' he explained. 'Have a taxi ready at 10.15 a.m.'

As they were driving towards Chelsea he explained the business.

'It's to help me to shadow a woman, a Mrs Phyllis Berlyn. Lives at 70b Park Walk. There's her photograph. When I go in you keep this taxi and be ready to pick me up when I want you.'

If he were to tap a possible S.O.S., he must begin by finding out if his victim had a telephone. He therefore got out at the end of Park Walk, and, passing the house, turned into an entry leading to the lane which ran along behind the row. The absence of wires, front and rear, showed that the house was not connected up. Then he went to the door and knocked. Mrs Berlyn received him at once.

'I am very sorry, madam,' he began gravely, 'to have to come on serious and unpleasant business. In my inquiries into the death of Mr Pyke, certain facts have come out. These facts require an explanation, and they point to you as being perhaps the only person who can give it. I have, therefore, called to ask you some questions, but I have to warn you that you are not bound to answer them, as in certain eventualities anything you say might be used against you.'

Mrs Berlyn looked startled.

'Whatever do you mean, Inspector?' she demanded. 'You don't mean against me personally, I suppose, but against my husband? I do not forget the terrible suggestion you made.'

'I mean against you personally, madam. As I say, I want an explanation of certain facts. If you care to give it I shall hear it with attention, but if you would prefer to consult a solicitor first, you can do so.'

'Good gracious, Inspector, you are terrifying me! You are surely not suggesting that you suspect me of complicity in this awful crime?'

'I make no accusations. All I want is answers to my questions.'

Mrs Berlyn grew slowly dead white. She moistened her dry lips.

'This is terrible,' she said in low tones. French had some twinges of conscience; for, after all, he was only bluffing. He recognised, however, that the greater the effect he produced, the more likely he was to get what he wanted. He therefore continued his third degree methods.

'If you are innocent, madam, I can assure you that you have nothing to fear,' he encouraged her, thereby naturally increasing her perturbation. 'Now, would you like to answer my questions or not?'

She did not hesitate. 'I have no option,' she exclaimed in somewhat shaky tones. 'If I do not do so your suspicions will be confirmed. Ask what you like. I have nothing to hide, and therefore cannot give myself away.'

'I am glad to hear you say so,' French declared grimly. 'First, I want you to give me a more detailed account of your relations with Colonel Domlio.'

'Why,' the lady explained, 'I told you all about that on your last visit. Colonel Domlio was very friendly, exceedingly friendly, I might say. But we had no relations,' she stressed the word, 'in the sense which your question seems to indicate.'

'How did your friendship begin?'

'Through my husband. He and Colonel Domlio were old friends and it was natural that we should see something of the Colonel. He visited at our house and we at his.'

'That was when you first went to Ashburton, was it not?'

'Not only then. It was so all the time I lived there.'

'But I don't mean that. I understand that about four months before the tragedy your friendship became much more intense, if I may use the word?'

'Intense is certainly not the word, but it is true that we met more frequently after the time you mention. I thought I had explained that. It was then that my husband became dissatisfied about my perfectly harmless friendship with Mr Pyke. As I told you, Mr Pyke and I decided to see less of each other. I was therefore thrown more on my own resources and, frankly, I was bored. I filled a little more of the time with Colonel Domlio than formerly. That is all.'

'Who began this increased intimacy?'

'Our intimacy was not increased. We saw more of each other—a very different thing. I began it; in this way. In

209

London I heard some lectures on insect life. I was interested in the subject and I asked Colonel Domlio to let me see his collection. We began to talk about it, and it ended in my going out with him occasionally to look for specimens on the moor and also in my helping him to arrange them afterwards. That was the beginning and end of what you are pleased to call our "intimacy."'

The look of fright had left Mrs Berlyn's eyes and she was speaking now with more of her usual assurance.

'You sprained your ankle one day?'

'I twisted it slightly. It was painful for a few hours, but not really much the worse.'

'You fell?'

'I did not fall. I should have done so, but Colonel Domlio sprang forward and caught me and helped me down on to the grass. In a few minutes I was better.'

'Now, Mrs Berlyn,' and French's voice was very grave, 'what you have to do is to convince me that that fall into Colonel Domlio's arms really was an accident.'

For a moment the lady looked at him uncomprehendingly, then she flushed angrily.

'Oh,' she cried with a gesture of disgust, 'how dare you? This is insufferable! I shall not answer you. If you are coming here to insult me I shall apply for protection to your superiors at Scotland Yard.'

'If I were you I should keep away from Scotland Yard as long as you can,' French advised dryly. 'In a case like this heroics will not help you any. Tell me, did you know there was a photographer watching the incident?'

'No,' she answered sullenly, while again her face showed fear.

'You knew there wasn't?'

'I didn't know anything about it.'

'But you are not surprised to hear of the photographer?'

'I am. At least, I should be if you assured me one was there.'

'Did you know that the handwriting of Colonel Domlio's letter has been identified?'

Once again the colour ebbed away from her face.

'What letter?' she cried faintly. 'I don't know what letter you mean or what you are talking about. You have made me quite confused with your questions. I scarcely know what I am saying.'

French felt that he had got the effect he wanted. He therefore reassured her by a few innocuous questions, then with a change of manner he apologised for having given unnecessary annoyance and took his leave.

The taxi was standing far down the street with the bonnet open and the driver bending over the engine. French got in and with Carter sat watching the house.

For half an hour they waited, then Mrs Berlyn appeared, and walking to King's Road, turned in the direction of Sloan Square. Presently she hailed a taxi, causing French to congratulate himself on his prevision.

Mrs Berlyn drove to Victoria, and hurriedly paying off their own man, the detectives followed her into the station. With a rapid look round she made her way to the telephone boxes and disappeared into one of them.

'I'll drop out here, Carter,' French said. 'You stick to the woman and as far as possible keep in touch with the Yard.'

Approaching the boxes, French slipped into a convenient doorway and watched until Mrs Berlyn reappeared. As soon as she was out of sight he entered the box she had left.

'Inspector from Scotland Yard speaking,' he told the operator. 'Keep the number of that last call. It's wanted in connection with a murder case. I'll get you the authority to divulge. Now, give me Scotland Yard, please.'

He put through the request for the number, then returned to the Yard to wait for the reply. After a short delay he received both number and name: Thomas Ganope, Newsagent and Tobacconist, 27 Oakley Street, off Russell Street.

In half an hour he reached the place. Ganope's was a small untidy shop and Ganope a ruffianly looking man with purple cheeks and a cast in his left eye. He was the only occupant of the shop.

'Can I use your telephone?' French asked, laying a shilling on the counter.

'Sure.'

French rang up his wife to say that he had mislaid Mr Walker's address and could she let him have it again, a code message designed for such occasions and to which no attention was paid, but which enabled him to use a telephone without arousing suspicion, as well as a writing pad, should such be available. For in this case his quick eye had seen such a pad on the instrument and from many a pad he had read the last message to be written from the impression left on the paper. On chance therefore he made a pretence of noting the mythical Mr Walker's address, and removing the top sheet, put it in his pocket book. Then he turned to Mr Ganope.

'Say,' he said confidentially, 'what would you charge for taking in telephone messages and sending them to an address? Private, you know.'

Mr Ganope looked him over keenly with one of his shrewd little eyes.

'A bob a message, if it's near by.'

'That's a lot. Do you never do it for less?'

Mr Ganope seemed disgusted.

'If you can get anyone to do it for less you'd better go to them,' he advised sourly.

'I might manage the money if I was sure the thing would be done right,' French went on. 'How do you send out the messages? I mean, is your arrangement reliable? Do you do it yourself or have you a messenger?'

'Wot do you tyke me for, mister? Do you think the shop would run itself while I was away? You don't need to worry. You pay your bob and you'll get your message all right.'

'Not good enough for me. I want to know what kind of messenger you'd send before I trust my business to you.'

'See 'ere,' the man declared. 'I've been doing this business for long enough to know all about 'ow it's done. I've a good boy, if you must know. You give 'im a penny or two a time if you're nervous, and you needn't be afryde but you'll get all there's for you.'

French laid five shillings on the counter.

'Right,' he said. 'There's for the first five messages. Send to Mr James Hurley, care of Mr William Wright, Tobacconist, corner of Bedford Place and Ivy Street.'

'I know it,' declared Ganope, pocketing the money.

Mr William Wright was a distant connection of Mrs French's and French knew that he would help him in the matter. He nodded to Ganope and walked across to Ivy Street.

'Hallo, Joe! Some time since we've seen you here,' was Mr Wright's greeting. 'Come in behind and let's hear the news.'

'I want you to do me a good turn, William,' French answered. 'There's a boy I want to get hold of, and I've fixed it that he'll come here asking for Mr Hurley. Will you put him on to me when he turns up? That's all.'

'Surely, Joe,' and Mr Wright turned the conversation to more intimate matters.

'Just let me use your 'phone,' French asked presently. 'Something I forgot.'

'Surely, Joe.'

Going into the little office at the back of the shop, French rang up Ganope.

'Message for Hurley,' he explained in falsetto tones. 'Mr James Hurley.'

'Right,' came from the other end.

'"Cargo will be in at ten-fifteen tomorrow." That's all. Repeat, please.'

Mr Ganope repeated slowly, evidently as he wrote, and French settled down with his pipe to await the advent of the messenger.

In less than half an hour a sharp, foxy-looking boy turned up and Mr Wright sent him into the sitting-room to French.

'Hallo, sonny. You from Ganope's?'

'Huh-huh,' said the boy. 'Name of Hurley?'

'That's right. You have a message for me?'

'Huh-huh.' He slowly drew an envelope from his pocket, watching French expectantly.

French produced sixpence.

'There you are, sonny. Wait half a sec till I read this. There may be an answer.'

He tore open the envelope and glanced at its contents.

'No, there's nothing,' he went on. 'You're kept busy, I'm sure?'

214

'Huh-huh.'

'And maybe you don't get too much money for it, either?'

The boy indicated that this was a true summary of his case.

'Well, how would half a crown for a little job for me suit you?'

The gleam in the boy's eyes was sufficient answer.

'It's just a bit of information between you and me. No one else would know anything about it. It wouldn't take you two minutes to give it to me. Are you on?'

'Ain't I, guv'nor. You just try me.'

French took some money out of his pocket and slowly counted out two single shillings and a sixpence. These he laid on the table in a little pile.

'Tell me, sonny,' he said. 'You had to take a message out this morning shortly after eleven?'

'Huh-huh.'

'Where did you take it to?'

'You won't tell the old man?'

'I'll not, sonny. I give you my word.'

'Name o' Pyke, 17 Kepple Street.'

In spite of his training as an officer of the Yard, French started. Pyke! He remained for a moment lost in thought. Pyke! Could this be the solution at last? Could Mrs Berlyn have transferred her somewhat facile affections to Jefferson Pyke? Could these two be guilty of the murder of both Stanley and Berlyn?

Here was a promising idea! In the first place it was the solution to the dilemma which had so greatly puzzled him. The crime had been committed to enable the murderer to live with Phyllis in good social standing. Therefore, the murderer could not have disappeared. Therefore, it could

215

not have been either Berlyn or Pyke. That had been French's problem.

But if Jefferson Pyke and Phyllis had been accomplices all these difficulties vanished. Berlyn and Pyke had disappeared because they were dead. The murderer had survived to enjoy the fruits of his crime. All the facts seemed to be met.

In itself, also, this new theory was likely enough. Jefferson and Phyllis had been playmates and an old attachment might easily have flamed up anew on their meeting at Ashburton. If so, there was the motive for Berlyn's murder. Stanley Pyke might also have been in the way. Possibly Phyllis was so far entangled with him that to break loose would have turned him into a dangerous enemy. Possibly the accomplices feared that he might guess their crime. Under the circumstances it was easy to see that their only safe scheme might well have been to remove both men.

The details also worked in. Phyllis could have obtained the information about the works necessary for the disposal of the body. Jefferson was of the size and build of the man who had called for the lorry and crate at Swansea, and though his colouring was different, this could have been altered artificially. He could be biding his time until he was sure the affair had blown over to take Phyllis out to his estancia in the Argentine.

Another point occurred to French. Alfred Beer had stated, no doubt in all good faith, that the conversation he had overheard in the Berlyn's shrubbery was between Mrs Berlyn and Stanley Pyke, and French had naturally assumed that the ''e' referred to was Berlyn. But were he and Beer correct? Might the scene not equally well have been between the lady and Jefferson and might ''e' not have been Stanley? French decided to look up his notes of the matter at the earliest opportunity.

He had little doubt that at long last he was on to the truth. Jubilantly he handed over the half-crown to Ganope's boy and dismissed him with the assurance that he would never hear of the matter again.

As to his next step there could be no question. He walked quickly to Kepple Street and asked if Mr Jefferson Pyke was at home.

Pyke was out, but was expected shortly. Hugging himself for his luck, French said that if he might, he would like to wait for Mr Pyke. The landlady remembered his previous visit and made no difficulty about showing him up to her lodger's sitting-room.

Before the door closed behind her French saw that his lucky star was still in the ascendant. There, on the chimney-piece, stood a note addressed 'Mr Jefferson Pyke' in the same handwriting as that for 'Mr James Hurley.'

French carried an old razor-blade in his pocket and in less than a minute the envelope was open. The note read:

'Danger. Meet me tonight at old time and place.'

French swore softly in high delight. He had them now! Here was convincing proof of their guilt.

But it was insufficient to bring into court. He must get something more definite. With skilful fingers he re-closed the envelope and put it back where he had found it. Then he settled down to wait for Pyke.

In less than ten minutes the man appeared. French, smiling his pleasant smile, greeted him apologetically.

'Sorry to trouble you again, Mr Pyke, but I want to ask

you for a little further help in this Ashburton affair. I have made a discovery, but first I must ask you to keep what I have to say to yourself.'

Pyke nodded.

'Of course, Mr French. Sit down, won't you, and tell me what I can do for you.'

'All I want is a little information,' French declared, taking the proffered chair. 'I may tell you between ourselves that certain facts suggest that Colonel Domlio may have been involved. Can you tell me anything that might help me to a decision, anything that your cousin told you or that Mr Berlyn may have said in your presence?'

Pyke shook his head.

'Colonel Domlio?' he repeated, 'Why, no. I never thought of such a thing and neither Stanley nor Berlyn ever said anything which might give colour to it.'

French continued to question him long enough to convince him that this was really the business on which he had called. Then he tried to discount the effect which Mrs Berlyn's note would have when at last the man had an opportunity to read it.

'I've been to see Mrs Berlyn on this matter,' he explained. 'I'm afraid I was rather rude to her, but I just had to frighten her in order to satisfy myself as to whether or not she suspected the colonel. But, at least, I apologised afterwards. I think she forgave me.'

'And did she suspect Domlio?'

'No, I'm sure she did not. And that counts in the colonel's favour, for she knew him pretty well. Aren't you thankful you're not a detective, Mr Pyke?'

They chatted easily for some moments and then French, thinking that some information about the other's former movements might be useful, turned the conversation to travel.

'You had a pleasant trip to the south of France with your late cousin, I understand?' he remarked. 'I wonder if you'd tell me something about it? I've just done enough travelling myself to whet my appetite for more and the idea of the south of France absolutely fascinates me. What part did you go to?'

'The Riviera and Provence,' Pyke answered with a subtle change of manner. Up to the present he had been polite, now he was interested. 'I can tell you, Inspector, that if you're fond of travelling you should try those districts. You'd enjoy every moment of it.'

'It's not doubt of that which keeps me away. Money and time are my trouble. Did you get as far as Italy?'

'Yes. I'll tell you our itinerary if you care to hear it. We went round to Marseilles by long sea. A jolly sail, that. Then—'

'Good weather?' French interposed. He wanted plenty of detail so that he could check the statements up.

'It was dirty when we left Birkenhead and choppy in the Irish Sea. But it quieted down as we got across the Bay, and from St Vincent to Gata the sea was like a mirror—an absolute flat calm without a ripple showing. Glorious! Then after Gata we ran into fog, which wasn't so nice. But we got to Marseilles on time.'

'Birkenhead? That's the Bibby Line, isn't it?'

'Yes, we went on the *Flintshire*. Fine boat of 16,000 tons.'

'I've heard those boats well spoken of. I envy you, Mr Pyke. Then, from Marseilles?'

'From Marseilles we went straight through to San Remo. We spent three or four days there, then worked back to Grasse, that's a small town where they make perfume, between Nice and Cannes, but a bit inland. I'm considering going into the flower trade and I wanted to see the gardens. A wonderful sight all that country must be with flowers in the season!'

'I've read about it,' French assured him. 'It's one of the places I've got on my list. Flowers and pretty girls, eh?'

'That's right. We had a dandy specimen to show us round the perfume factory.'

'I guess I'll see that factory,' French declared. 'Are there good hotels in a small place like that?'

'We stayed at the Metropole and it was quite all right. Then we worked slowly up through Provence, staying a night in different towns; Marseilles, Nîmes, Arles, Avignon, and so on to Paris. I've got all mixed about the places, we saw so many. An interesting country that, Inspector! There are buildings standing there for sixteen hundred years and more. Wonderful! First chance you get you should go down and see for yourself. But don't do it as we did.'

'How do you mean?'

'Don't go from place to place, staying in each for a night. Stay at a centre; Avignon is a first-rate one, there are day char-a-banc trips that let you see all these places, and you don't have the nuisance of packing and going to a fresh hotel every day.'

'That's a point, certainly. Thanks for the tip. Where do you recommend staying in Paris?'

If Pyke recognised that French was merely pumping him he gave no sign, but replied readily:

'We stayed at the Regina and found it quite good. But we just broke the journey for a night. Next day we came on here.'

'To these rooms?'

'No, I hadn't taken them then. We stayed a night at the Houston. That's the night I had such a joke on Stanley.'

'That sounds interesting.'

'I don't know how he did it, but while he was dressing he knocked the basin off the stand and it broke, and soaked his shoes and deluged the room. You know, they have old-fashioned separate basins there, not running water as you get abroad. I imagine he must have set the basin down on a corner of the towel, and when he picked up the towel it twitched the basin off. The wretched thing must have been cracked for it went into two pieces. But they charged him for it, all right.'

'Rough luck, Mr Pyke. And after that you both thought one night enough to stay?'

Pyke laughed.

'I wanted rooms,' he explained. 'Next day I found these and moved in.'

'I suppose your late cousin went back to Ashburton at the same time?'

'Not quite directly, I think. He went to see some people near Bath; I believe he said for two days only, but I'm not sure.'

'Do you soon return to the Argentine, Mr Pyke?'

'I've not made up my mind. I like this country and I'm half thinking of settling down here and growing flowers for the London market. I'm sick of ranching anyway and I've instructed my solicitors to begin negotiations for the sale of my property. Of course, I'll have to go out to see to that, but I think I'll come back very soon.'

They continued chatting about the Roman remains in Provence, until at last French looked at his watch and said he must go.

He was jubilant as to his progress. He believed that he had accounted for his presence and that Pyke suspected nothing. He had also obtained enough information to check practically the whole of the man's movements from his departure with Stanley for his holiday down to the present time. The end of the affair was in sight. And that evening, he promised himself, should see him a step further on his road.

18

On Hampstead Heath

French telephoned for a relief to take over the shadowing of Pyke during the afternoon, but by six o'clock he was back in Kepple Street, with the intention of being, if possible, present at the rendezvous of his new suspects.

'He's not shown up since,' Sergeant Harvey explained. 'No one called, but one person left the house, a girl of about twenty. She returned in about two hours.'

'Tall, good-looking girl, fair hair and blue eyes?' French suggested. 'I know her; the landlady's daughter. I saw her when I called. That'll do, Harvey, you can get away. I shall manage alone.'

It was a fine evening, but cold. The last glimmerings of daylight were disappearing from the sky and outside the radius of the street lamps stars began to show. It looked as if there would be frost later.

To keep a secret watch on a house in a city street is a feat requiring no little skill. Though French had reached the stage in which he left most of such work to his underlings, he was a past master in the art. Yet, as first seven, then eight, then nine struck from the surrounding clocks it required all his ingenuity to give the appearance of being detained on some ordinary and unimportant business. He strolled up and down, hiding in alley-ways and behind projecting, corners and moving on at intervals from one such place of vantage to another. He had engaged a taxi in case his quarry should do the same, and for a good part of the time he employed the old device of sitting back in its deepest recesses, while the driver gave a lengthy first-aid to his refractory engine.

At last, when he had become stiff with cold and was cursing mentally but steadily at the delay, Pyke appeared and started off quickly towards Russell Square. French drew back into the entry in which he was taking cover and allowed him to pass, then having signed to his driver to keep him in sight, he followed the quarry as closely as he dared. Pyke turned down Montague Street, walking by New Oxford Street and Charing Cross Road to Charing Cross Station. He seemed about to enter the station, but suddenly glancing round, he turned to the right and dived down the steps to the Hampstead and Highgate tube. French had already settled up with his driver and he followed without delay.

Keeping close behind, French shadowed his man to the platform and entered the next coach of the Hampstead train which the other boarded. At each station he watched the alighting passengers, but it was not until Hampstead was reached that Pyke appeared. Twenty feet apart, the two men passed out into the street and up the hill towards the Heath.

At the wide space at the entrance to the Heath, French fell further behind. Pyke was now strolling easily along, as if out for a breath of air before bed. He passed in towards the left near Jack Straw's Castle, taking one of the side paths which led to the wilder areas. Here were fewer people and French dropped back till he could just see the man's light fawn coat like a faint smudge against the dark background of the trees.

Some four or five hundred yards from the entrance, down in the hollow, there are a number of thick clumps of bushes. Round one of these Pyke passed and instantly became invisible. French stopped in his turn, and tiptoeing to the nearer side of the clump, began stealthily to creep nearer. Though a certain amount of starlight showed in the open, among the bushes it was pitchy black. There was no wind and, in spite of the vast city surrounding the place, scarcely a sound broke the stillness. French crept on, stopping every few seconds to listen intently. Presently he heard movements close by. There were faint footsteps, as if of a man pacing up and down, and occasional soft scraping of leaves and snapping of small twigs. Crawling under a bush, French crouched down and waited.

For close on fifteen minutes the man paced backwards and forwards, while French grew stiff in his cramped position. Then light footsteps were heard on the path alongside the clump and a woman cleared her throat. The man moved out and said something in a low voice, to which the other replied. Then French heard Pyke say: 'Come behind the shrubs. There is no one about and we shan't be heard.'

They moved close, to French, though not so near as he would have liked. Listening intently, he could hear a good deal, though not all, of their conversation. The woman was Mrs Berlyn and she was saying: 'He suspects something; I'm sure of it. I've been just sick with terror all day. I thought I must see you and this seemed the only way. I was afraid he might follow me if I met you publicly.'

There was a murmur of Pyke's voice, but French could not distinguish the words nor could he hear Mrs Berlyn's reply. Then he heard Pyke say: 'I don't think so. The note was there on the chimney-piece, but I'm quite certain it hadn't been opened. I examined it carefully.'

Mrs Berlyn's intonation sounded like a question.

'Yes, I rang up Ganope and he said that no inquiries had been made,' Pyke rejoined. 'It's all right, Phyllis, I'm sure. Why, French explained that he had frightened you deliberately in order to find out your real opinion of Domlio.'

They seemed to turn away, for during some moments French could only hear the murmur of their voices. Then apparently they approached again.

'. . . I thought it was Charles he suspected,' Mrs Berlyn was saying, 'then today I thought it was myself. He knows a lot, Jeff. He knows about Colonel Domlio's letter and the photograph.'

'Yes, but that's all immaterial. He doesn't know what really happened that night, and he won't know.'

'But if he arrests us?'

'Let him! As far as I am concerned he can do nothing. He can't break down the evidence of all those people in Manchester with whom I spent the night of the murder. You, I admit, haven't such a water-tight alibi, but it is impossible that he can prove you committed a crime of which you are absolutely innocent. And he can't connect you with Charles. Remember that we've no reason to suppose he has the least idea that Charles is alive.'

'If he finds that out he'll suspect Charles and then he'll suspect me as his accomplice.'

'I dare say,' Pyke admitted, 'but he won't find out. Poor old Charles! I said to him on that last day—'

The two moved off again, for Pyke's voice died down into an unintelligible murmur. Again, for some moments, French could not distinguish what was said, then the words came more clearly.

'No,' Pyke was saying, 'I have a better plan than that. Tomorrow I'll call at the Yard to see French and I'll confess to the murder. I'll say that my misery through remorse and suspense is worse than anything I could afterwards suffer and that I just can't bear it any longer. Lots of murderers have done that and he'll suspect nothing. He'll, of course, arrest me. Admittedly, he may arrest you also. This, of course, I should infinitely regret, but you will agree there is no other way. He'll then think he has solved his problem and he'll look no further afield. Before going to the Yard I'll communicate with Charles, and Charles can make his get-away. Then, when Charles has had time to get out of the country, I shall produce my Manchester witnesses and prove my innocence. The case against you will then break down.'

'That's all right, except for two things,' Mrs Berlyn returned. 'If Charles believed he could get out of the country he would have done it long ago. Secondly, why, if you prove your innocence, will the case against me break down?'

'Those are easily answered. By the time Charles was well enough to travel suspicion had been aroused and every policeman in the country was on the look-out for the Ashburton murderer. If I confess, the watch at the ports will be relaxed. Besides—'

Again the words became unintelligible. There was a faint sound of slowly pacing feet and the voice dwindled. But after a short time the footsteps again grew louder.

'. . . under the circumstances,' Mrs Berlyn was saying, 'but, of course, if Charles is taken we shall be accused of being his confederates.'

'Very possibly. But, Phyllis, what can we do? We know old Charles is innocent, though things look so badly against him. We can't let him down. We must do what we can to help him and take the risk.'

'I know. I know. But isn't the whole thing just *awful*! What have we done that we should get into such a position? It's too much.'

Her voice, though carefully repressed, was full of suffering and French could picture her wringing her hands and on the verge of tears. Pyke comforted her, though not at all in the tone of a lover, then went on:

'It's time that we went back, old girl. Until I get the warning to Charles we mustn't risk being seen together; therefore, you'd better go on by yourself. I'll follow in ten minutes.'

They bade each other an agitated farewell, and then Mrs Berlyn's light footsteps sounded on the path. For another quarter of an hour Pyke remained among the trees, his presence revealed by occasional movements and by the whistling under his breath of a melancholy little tune. Then, at last, he also moved away and French was able to stretch his aching limbs. Carefully he followed his man back to the tube-station and, eventually, to his rooms in Kepple Street.

He did not know what to make of the conversation to which he had just listened. The statements made were so surprising and unexpected that at first sight he was inclined to dismiss the whole thing as a blind, deliberately arranged to throw him off the scent. Then he saw that for several reasons this could not be. In the first place, neither Phyllis nor Berlyn knew he was listening. In the second, such a plant would require careful pre-arrangement, and since his visit to Pyke the latter had had no opportunity of communicating with Phyllis Berlyn. Then there would be no object in such a scheme. They surely did not imagine that because of it French would relax his watch on them. Moreover, if it were false, its falseness would be demonstrated on the very next day. No, French felt the interview must be genuine.

And if so, what a completely new view it gave of the crime! Berlyn, Phyllis and Jefferson Pyke all apparently mixed up in the affair, and all innocent! Who, then, could be guilty? French had to own himself completely puzzled. If this view were correct the murderer must be someone whom he had not yet seriously considered.

Unless it could be Domlio, after all. Nothing that the two had said directly precluded the possibility. Of course, in this case it was difficult to see why they should not denounce Domlio, if it would free themselves and Berlyn from suspicion. But then again they might suspect Domlio, even, perhaps, be reasonably certain of his guilt, and yet unable to prove it.

French continued to turn the matter over in his mind, and the more he did so the more he leaned to the opinion that Domlio must be after all the murderer. All the arguments which had before led him to this conclusion recurred to him with redoubled force and the difficulties in the theory seemed more and more easily surmountable. Domlio's motor drive on the night of the crime, his denial of the trip, the hiding of the clothes and duplicator parts in the well, his depressed and absorbed manner—these really were not accounted for by any theory other than that of the man's guilt. And Domlio might easily have invented the story of the photograph and produced the letter to account for his nocturnal excursion.

Puzzled and worried, French began to believe that he was on the wrong track in London and that he must return to Devon and try once more to get the truth from Domlio. But he would not relax his watch on Mrs Berlyn and Pyke. Pyke he would himself shadow next day, so that if he communicated with Berlyn he, French, would learn the latter's whereabouts.

He turned into the nearest telephone booth, and ringing up the Yard, arranged for reliefs for himself and Sergeant Carter. Then, Sergeant Deane having taken over the watch in Kepple Street, he went home.

Next morning he called at the Yard for Carter and about nine o'clock the two men reached Kepple Street.

'That'll do, Deane. You may get away,' French greeted the night man. 'Nothing stirred, I suppose?'

'Nothing, sir. No one in or out the whole night.'

'Now, Carter,' French went on, 'it's your show mostly today. Pyke knows me and I'll have to keep in the background. You stay about here and I'll get a taxi and wait round the corner. If I see your signal I'll come along.'

Time soon began to drag for the watchers. Evidently their man was in no hurry. Ten o'clock came, then eleven, then eleven-thirty, and still he made no sign. French began to grow seriously uneasy.

At last he could stand it no longer. He got out of his taxi and strolled up to Carter.

'Go up to the door and ask for him, Carter. If he sees you, say I sent you to ask if he would call round at the Yard any time this afternoon.'

Taking his subordinate's place, he watched him walk up to the door and knock. In a moment the door was opened and Carter disappeared.

For several minutes he remained inside, while French, growing more and more anxious every second, remained pacing impatiently up and down. Then Carter reappeared, and without any attempt at secrecy, beckoned to French.

'What is it?' the latter whispered sharply as he joined the sergeant on the door-step. 'Anything wrong?'

'I'm afraid so, sir. We can't make him hear.'

French swore. A wave of misgiving swept over him. Why, in heaven's name, hadn't he arrested the man last night when he had the chance? He pushed into the house, to meet an anxious landlady in the hall.

'I am Inspector French of Scotland Yard,' he explained quickly. 'Where is Mr Pyke?'

'Lawks!' said the landlady, recognising her former visitor. 'Are you police? And I thinking you were a friend of Mr Pyke's all the time.'

'Yes, madam, I am a police officer and I want to see Mr Pyke at once. Where is he?'

The anxious look returned to the woman's face.

'He's in his room,' she explained. 'But he's not had his breakfast and he won't answer my knocking. He said last night that he had a chill and that he wouldn't get up this morning and for me not to disturb him. But that's no reason why he shouldn't answer a knock.'

'Which is his room?' said French grimly. This would be a lesson to him to avoid his confounded trick of waiting till he was sure. If this man had slipped through his hands any chance of that chief inspectorship was gone—if his job itself remained.

They went to a first-floor room at the back of the house and French knocked peremptorily. There was no reply.

'Down with the door, Carter. Put your shoulder to it with me.'

Despite the protests of the landlady, both men threw themselves on the door. With a tearing sound the screws of the keeper drew out and the door swung open.

The room was empty.

It was a large room, comfortably furnished as a bed-sitting-room. It was not disarranged in any way, but the lower sash of the window was fully up. French hurriedly crossed to it and looked out. It gave on the yard and about four feet below the sill was the roof of a small shed. This shed ran along the side of the yard at right angles to the main house, its further gable being against the wall between the yard and the lane which passed at the back of the houses. The roof of the shed formed a direct passage from the room to the lane.

Though French had no doubt that Pyke had escaped by this route, he dropped out of the window and crawled over the roof tiles, searching for traces. These he speedily discovered. Someone had passed a short time previously.

His chagrin was too deep for words. Even the lurid phrase, with which in times of stress he was wont to relieve his feelings, now proved utterly inadequate. He was aghast at the extent to which he had been hoodwinked.

For it was now evident that Pyke had known he had been shadowed to Hampstead Heath and that the whole conversation there had been designed to put him, French, off the track. Pyke was a cleverer man than he had thought. It seemed scarcely possible that the interview had been pre-arranged, and yet French could not imagine its being an improvisation. The whole thing was very puzzling.

However, at least one thing was clear. Jefferson Pyke and Mrs Berlyn were the criminals for whom he was seeking. And he was on a hot scent. He would get Mrs Berlyn at once and Pyke with very little delay. The man had less than twelve hours' start. He turned to Carter.

'Wait here for me, Carter,' he directed. 'Have a look round and learn anything you can, but without disturbing things. I shall be back presently.'

He ran out of the house, and calling up his taxi, was driven to Park Walk. There he soon spotted the man who was shadowing Mrs Berlyn.

'Anything to report, Jeffries?' he demanded quickly. 'She's still there, all right?'

'Still there, Mr French. No one left the house since I came on duty.'

'Good. Then come with me.'

He rang at the door, and when the servant opened, asked for Mrs Berlyn.

'She's not up, sir,' the girl returned. 'Last night she said she had a chill and did not want to be called or disturbed this morning. She said she probably wouldn't want anything until lunch and not to bring up breakfast as she was going to take a sleeping draught and might not be awake.'

Though still inadequate to relieve his feelings, French swore his lurid oath.

'Go and wake her now,' he ordered the scandalised girl. 'Here, I'll go to the door with you.'

The girl seemed about to object, but French's tone overawed her. Hesitatingly, she led the way.

'Knock,' said French. 'Or wait; I will.' He gave a rousing knock at the door.

There was no answer.

'She too, by thunder!' he growled, rattling the handle. The door was locked.

'Your shoulder, Jefferies!' and for the second time in half

an hour French burst open the door of a bedroom. As in the former case, the room was empty.

But here there was no open window. Not only was the sash latched, but when French opened it and looked out he found that it was thirty feet above the pavement and that there was nothing to assist a descent.

A glance at the door explained the mystery. The key was missing. Evidently the occupant had left the room by the door, locking it behind her and removing the key. And the maid was able to supply the further information required. The girl, on coming down that morning, had found the yard door unlocked. Though she thought she had fastened it on the previous evening, she had supposed she must have overlooked it.

French hurried down the narrow yard to the door which led out on the passage behind the houses, only to find that here again the door was locked and the key missing. Again and again he cursed himself for having underestimated the ability of these two people. Had he had the slightest idea that they had followed his progress so minutely, he would have employed very different methods. Even if he had not arrested them he would have seen to it that they did not escape. The shadowing he had adopted would have been effective under normal conditions, but not where the victims were alive to their danger and ready to make a desperate bid for safety.

But French was too sensible to cry over spilt milk. He had blundered. Very well, it could not be helped. What he had to do now was to retrieve his error at the earliest moment possible. How could he most quickly get on the track of these criminals?

He returned to the house and made a rapid search for any clue that the lady might have left, but without result. Then leaving Jefferies in charge, he drove back to Kepple Street.

19

The Bitterness of Death

'Any luck, Carter?' French asked quietly as he re-entered Pyke's room.

'No, sir. He has taken a suit-case with him, a brown leather one of medium size. I got the description from Mrs Welsh. She says she noticed it here yesterday afternoon and it's gone now. And he has taken all his outer clothes, his suits and overcoats and shoes, but most of his socks and underclothing are here in these drawers. I've been through everything, but I've not found anything useful.'

'Let's have a look.'

French hastily ran through the missing man's effects. 'Most of this stuff is foreign,' he observed as he glanced over the clothes. 'You see the Argentine marking on the collars and shirts. No, I don't think there's much to help us there. No books or papers?'

'None, sir. But there's a big heap of burnt paper in the grate.'

'So I saw. We'll go through it, later on. Now, ask the landlady to come here. Just sit down, Mrs Welsh, will you? I want to know if you can tell me anything to help me to find your lodger. I'm sorry to say he is wanted on a very serious charge; murder, in fact. Therefore, you will understand how necessary it is that you should tell me all you know.'

Mrs Welsh was thunderstruck, declaring again and again that she would not have believed it of so nice a gentleman. She was also terrified lest her rooms should suffer through the inevitable publicity. But she realised her duty and did her best to answer French's questions.

For a long time he gained no useful information, then at last an important point came out, though not in connection with his immediate objective.

Having given up for the moment the question of Pyke's destination, French was casting around to see if he could learn anything connecting him with the crime when he chanced to ask, had Mr Pyke a typewriter?

'Not lately, he hadn't,' Mrs Welsh answered; 'but he did have one for a time. I don't know why he got it, for I never knew him to use it. But he had it there on the table for about three weeks.'

'Oh,' said French, interested. 'When was that?'

'I couldn't say exactly. Three months ago or more, I should think. But my daughter might remember. Vera is a typist and she was interested in the machine more than what I was. I'll call her, if you like. She is at home on holidays.'

Vera Welsh was the pretty girl with fair hair and blue eyes whom French had already seen. She smiled at him as she appeared in answer to her mother's call.

'We were talking of Mr Pyke's typewriter,' he explained. 'Can you tell me what make it was?'

'Yes, I noticed it when I was dusting the room. It was a Corona Four.'

'And when did he get it?'

The girl hesitated. 'Between three and four months ago,' she said at last, with a reserve which aroused French's interest.

'Between three and four months?' he repeated. 'How are you so sure of that? Was there anything to fix it in your mind?'

There was, but for some time the girl would not give details. Then at last the cause came out.

It seemed that on the day after Vera had first noticed the machine she had had some extra typing to do in the office which would have necessitated her working late. But on that day her mother had not been well and she had particularly wanted to get home at her usual time. The thought of Mr Pyke's typewriter occurred to her, together with the fact that he had left that morning on one of his many visits to the country. She had thereupon decided to borrow the machine for the evening. She had brought her work home and had done it in his sitting-room. She did not remember the actual day, but could find it from her records in the office.

'Very wise, if you ask me,' French said sympathetically. 'And what was the nature of the work you did?' He found it hard to keep the eagerness out of his voice.

'Just a copy of some tenders we had from America. I am in a hardware shop in Tottenham Court Road and it was about American lawn mowers and other gardening machines.'

'I understand. I suppose you don't know what the copies were required for?'

'Just for filing. The originals had to be sent away and these were wanted for reference.'

French rose to his feet. Certainly, the luck was not entirely against him.

'Put your hat on, if you please, Miss Welsh, and come along with me to your office. I must see that copy. I can't tell you how much you have helped me by telling me of it.'

The girl at first demurred, as she feared her employer might have views of his own as to the taking of important papers home from the office. But French assured her that he would see she did not suffer for her action. In fact, before she knew what was happening she was in a taxi on the way to the place.

On reaching the senior partner's office French was as good as his word. He explained the importance of his seeing the type-script, and saying that Miss Welsh had risked her job in the interests of justice, begged that the matter might not be held against her.

Mr Cooke shook his head over the incident, but admitting to French that the girl was satisfactory, he agreed to overlook it. Then he rang for the papers in question.

Ten seconds with his lens was enough for French. Here at last was the proof he had been looking for! The typing was that of the notes to the Vida works and to the magneto company.

'I'm pretty glad to get this paper, Mr Cooke,' he declared. 'Now, do you think you could let me keep it? Miss Welsh could perhaps type another copy for you?'

Mr Cooke was obliging and in ten minutes the precious document was handed over. Stopping only to get the girl to certify on it that she had made it with Pyke's machine, French hurried her away.

'I'll drive you home, Miss Welsh,' he said with his pleasant smile. 'You have been of the greatest help. Now, I wonder if you could do something else for me,' and he began repeating the questions he had already put to her mother.

Almost at once he got valuable information, though once again not on the matter immediately at issue.

It appeared that on the previous afternoon Pyke had called

the girl into his room and asked her if she would do a small commission for him. It was to take a letter to a lady in Chelsea. It concerned, so he said, an appointment to dine that evening, so that she would see that it was urgent. The matter was private and she was not to give the note to anyone but the lady herself, nor was she to mention it. To compensate her for her trouble and to cover the cost of taxis and so on, he hoped she would accept a ten-shilling note. She had not thought this strange, as she knew him to be liberal in money matters. But she had wondered that a note about a dinner appointment should be so bulky. The envelope was of foolscap size and must have contained at least a dozen sheets. She had taken it to the address it bore and handed it to the lady—Mrs Berlyn, 70b Park Walk, Chelsea. She had not mentioned the matter to anyone.

Here was the explanation of the conversation French had overheard on Hampstead Heath. With a little thought he was able to follow the man's mental processes.

In the first place it was evident that Pyke had realised that he was suspected, as well as that French had opened Ganope's note. He would guess therefore that French would shadow him continually until his meeting with Mrs Berlyn, and would try to overhear what passed thereat. He would also see that for that very reason he was safe from arrest till the meeting had taken place, when this immunity would cease.

But he wanted the night in which to escape. How could he stave off arrest until the following day?

Clearly, he had solved his problem by writing out the conversation, possibly with stage directions, as a playwright writes out the dialogue in his play. In it he had pledged himself to a visit to Berlyn on the morrow. If he could make French swallow the yarn he knew that arrest would be

postponed in order that French might learn the junior partner's whereabouts. He had then sent Mrs Berlyn her 'lines,'
and she had learnt them like any other actress. French ruefully
admitted to himself that, in spite of the absence of a rehearsal,
the two had presented their little piece with astonishing
conviction.

On reaching the Yard, French's first care was to set the
great machine of the C.I.D. in operation against the fugitives.
Among his notes he already had detailed descriptions of each,
and he thought he would be safe in assuming that Pyke
would wear his collar up and his hat pulled low over his
eyes. Mrs Welsh had described the suit-case, and, burdened
by this, French thought there was a reasonable chance of the
man having been noticed.

A number of helpers were soon busy telephoning the
descriptions to all the London police stations as well as to
the ports. Copies were also sent for insertion in the next
number of the *Morning Report*. In a day or so all the police
and detectives in the country would be on the look-out for
the couple.

With Mrs Welsh's help French made a list of the clothes
likely to be in the suit-case. As these would have had a
considerable weight, he thought it unlikely that Pyke would
have walked very far. He therefore despatched three sets of
men, one to make inquiries at the adjoining railway and tube
stations, another to comb the neighbouring hotels and
boarding houses, and the third to search for a taxi driver
who might have picked up such a fare in one of the near-by
streets.

It was not until these urgent matters had been dealt with
that he turned to consider his second line of inquiry. Of
Jefferson Pyke himself he knew practically nothing. What

was the man's history? Why was he remaining in England? Particularly, where had he been at the time of the crime and while the crate was at Swansea.

He began operations by writing to the Lincoln police for all available information about Phyllis Considine, as well as Stanley and Jefferson Pyke. Then he sent a cable to the Argentine, asking the authorities there for details about Jefferson. He wired to the police at San Remo, Grasse, and in Paris, asking whether the cousins had stayed during the month of July at the various hotels Jefferson had mentioned. Lastly, he rang up the Bibby Line offices to know if they could help him to trace two passengers named Pyke who had sailed from Liverpool to Marseilles on their *Flintshire* about four months previously.

The Bibby people replied first. They said that the *Flintshire* had been home, but had left again for Rangoon. However, if Mr French would call at their office they would show him the passenger list and perhaps give him other required information.

In an hour French was seated with the manager. There he inspected the list, which bore the names of Stanley and Jefferson Pyke, and he was assured that two gentlemen answering to these names had actually sailed.

'If that is not sufficient for you, it happens that you can get further evidence,' the manager went on. 'Mr Hawkins, the purser of the *Flintshire*, broke his arm on the homeward trip. He went off on sick leave and, if you care to go down to Ramsgate, you can see him.'

'I shall be only too glad,' French said.

Armed with an introduction from the manager, French travelled down next morning to the Isle of Thanet. Mr Hawkins was exceedingly polite and gave him all the information in his power. He remembered the Pykes having sailed on the last trip from Birkenhead to Marseilles. Stanley Pyke he had not come in contact with more than in the normal way of business, though they had once chatted for a few moments about the day's run. But he had seen a good deal of Jefferson. He, Mr Hawkins, had spent a year in the Argentine in Jefferson's district and they had found they had many acquaintances in common. He had formed a high opinion of Jefferson, both as a man of the world and a rancher. Both the cousins had seemed in every way normal, and several of the passengers had expressed regret when the two left the ship at Marseilles.

On reaching London, French drove to the Houston. Showing his credentials he asked whether two gentlemen, a Mr Stanley and a Mr Jefferson Pyke, had stayed there for one night towards the end of the previous July.

It was not to be expected that the reception clerk would remember either visitor. But she soon turned up the register. The names appeared on July 21st, both having been written by Stanley.

'That's scarcely good enough for me,' said French. 'It doesn't prove that they were both here.'

'Practically, it does,' the clerk returned. 'You see, each was allotted a room. If the rooms had not been occupied the allocation would have been cancelled, for at that time we were turning people away every night. But we can soon settle it.' She looked up her account-books. 'Here,' she went on, after a moment, 'are the accounts in question. Mr Stanley occupied No. 346 and Mr Jefferson, No. 351. The accounts were paid separately. I receipted Mr Stanley's and Miss Hurst, another of our staff, receipted Mr Jefferson's. Curiously,' she went on, 'I remember Mr Stanley paying. He broke the basin in his room and we had some discussion as to whether he would be charged for it. He was, in the end.'

This would have seemed ample confirmation of Jefferson's statement to most people, but French, with his passion for thoroughness, decided to see the chambermaid. She remembered the incident and remembered also that the gentleman's friend had occupied No. 351, as on her bringing his hot water in answer to his ring, he had said he was late and would she go and wake his friend in No. 351. She had done as requested, but the friend was already up.

From the Houston, French walked to Kettle Street. Yes, Mr Jefferson had taken the rooms on the 22nd July last, and though he had been frequently away for a day or two at a time, he had lived there ever since. Moreover, Mrs Welsh's records enabled her to say that he had been absent not only on the night of the crime, but also on the date when the crate was disposed of at Swansea.

On his return to the Yard, French found that replies had come in from Paris and the Riviera. Stanley and Jefferson Pyke had stayed at the three hotels in question.

The next post brought a letter from the Lincoln police. It appeared that the three young people, about whom inquiries had been made, had lived in the district at the time mentioned. Dr Considine was a well-known practitioner in the town until his death in 1912, but little was known of his daughter Phyllis, save the mere fact of her existence. Stanley and Jefferson Pyke had lived with a relative in the suburbs and had attended a private school kept by a Dr Oates. The relations between the girl and boys were not known, but it was probable that they had met, as they were in the same social set. More could probably be learned by further inquiries.

This seemed to French sufficient to corroborate the

statements of Jefferson Pyke and Mrs Berlyn, and he advised the Lincoln police not to trouble further in the matter.

He had scarcely written his note when a cable from the Argentine police was handed to him. Jefferson Pyke was well known as the owner of an estancia in the Rosario district. He was believed to be comfortably off, though not wealthy. He answered the description given in the wire from Scotland Yard and had left for England on the boat mentioned.

With the exception of the fact that Jefferson was away from his rooms at the time of the crime, all this was disappointing to French. So far he had learned little to help in the building up of his case. On the contrary, the tendency was in Jefferson Pyke's favour. He did not appear to be of the stuff of which murderers are made. Nor, from the purser's description, did it seem likely that he was hatching a crime while on the *Flintshire*. On the other hand, there was no knowing what even the mildest man might do under the stress of passion.

But what really worried French was the fact that he had made no progress towards the tracing of his suspects' present whereabouts. In vain he urged his men on to more intensive efforts. Nowhere could they learn anything to help.

But he realised that there was nothing for it but patience. The business was necessarily slow, as it meant individual inquiries from everyone concerned. French did not dare to advertise, lest Pyke should see the notice and take still further precautions against discovery.

The third day passed, and the fourth, French growing more restless and nervy every hour. He now began to consider publicity; broadcast descriptions, advertisements in the papers, even the offer of a reward for secret information.

Finally, he decided that, if by the following evening no news had come in, he would put these agencies in operation.

But the men of the C.I.D. are marvellously efficient and persistent. On returning from lunch on the fifth day French learned to his infinite satisfaction that a taximan whose information might prove valuable had been found and was on his way to the Yard. Ten minutes later an intelligent looking man in a driver's uniform was shown in.

'Good afternoon,' said French. 'You have something to tell me? Just let me have your name and address and then go ahead.'

William Service explained that he was the driver of a taxi in the employment of Metropolitan Transport, Ltd. On Monday night, the night in question, he had driven a fare to Euston for the 12.25 a.m. express. On leaving the station, he was returning to his garage through Russell Square, when near the end of Kepple Street he was hailed by a man from the sidewalk. He had not wished to take another fare, but the man had offered him an extra five shillings to do so, and he had then agreed. The man was of medium height and build and dressed in a fawn coat and soft hat. Service could not describe his features, the brim of his hat being pulled low to meet his upturned collar. He was carrying a largish suitcase.

He desired Service to drive to The Boltons, which, as the inspector probably knew, was an oval with a church not far from Chelsea. (the inspector knew it and recognised with delight that it was just beside Park Walk.) There he was to pick up a lady and to drive them both to a house in Victory Place, not far from the Elephant and Castle. The lady had been waiting. As far as he could see, she answered the inspector's description. He had driven both parties to the address mentioned. It was a big house of working-class flats.

'Good! You've told your story well,' French approved. 'Now, I want you to drive me to the place. I shall be ready in a moment.'

The last lap! A kind of cold excitement took possession of French. It had been a long and troublesome case, but it was over now. Another fine feather in his cap; another step to that somewhat overdue chief-inspectorship for which he had been so long hoping. A few minutes, an hour at most, and the thing would be an accomplished fact.

Hastily calling his two assistants, Carter and Harvey, he set off with them for Victory Place. 'It's a big thing, this,' he explained. 'There must be no mistake about it. If we let these people slip through our fingers we needn't go back to the Yard.'

They drove to the end of the block containing the house, and Carter and Harvey remaining in the taxi, French went alone to reconnoitre. He rang at a door in the basement and asked the woman who opened if she could direct him to the caretaker.

'My husband's the caretaker, sir,' she answered, 'but he's out at present. Is it anything I can do?'

'Probably you can,' said French with his most winning smile. 'I'm looking for the lady and gentleman who came in on last Monday night. They arrived by a late train and weren't here till after midnight.'

'Oh, yes. Mr and Mrs Perrin?'

'That's right. Which flat have they taken?'

'Number 19. That's the top one on the right of the stairs.'

'Thank you. Do you know if they are in at present?'

'Mrs Perrin is out. I saw her go about half an hour ago. So far as I know, Mr Perrin is in.'

'Thanks. I'll just go up and see.'

French returned to the taxi.

'The woman is out, but Pyke is supposed to be upstairs in No. 19 flat. You, Harvey, will stay in the entrance hall and watch the stairs and lift. Take him without fail, if we miss him above. If the woman appears, don't show up, but let her go in. Carter, you come upstairs with me.'

Harvey strolled to the door and became immersed in the list of flat holders while French and Carter began to climb the stairs. There were two flats on each storey, to right and left of the flights. When they reached the first landing French pointed to a fire escape notice. They followed the pointing hand to the back of the house along a passage between the two flats, and silently pushing open a door fitted with panic fastenings, saw an iron staircase leading down outside of the wall from the top storey to a paved yard.

'You'll have to stay and watch that, Carter. I can manage the blighter upstairs.'

For a moment, French wished he had brought another man. Then he thought of how many times he had carried out arrests single-handed. There was no difficulty. A whistle would bring his two men at top speed, and if by some incredibly unlikely accident he let Pyke slip through his hands, one or other of them would certainly take him on his way down.

He silently mounted the stairs to the tenth storey. No. 19 was the top flat, but the stairs led on to a door on to the roof. French knocked at No. 19. There was no answer. In a moment he knocked again, then after waiting a few seconds, he tried the door.

It was unlocked and French pushed it open and looked in. Through a tiny hall he could see into a living-room, small and poorly furnished, and with a kitchenette in the rear.

Other partially open doors led from the hall into bedrooms. So far as he could see, the place was deserted.

Softly closing the outer door, he passed into the living-room, and standing in its centre, looked round. Opposite him was the fireplace with a gas fire turned low. In the right wall was the window and against the left stood a table with a chair at each end. Two wicker arm-chairs were drawn up to the fireplace and to the right of the door was a dresser containing crockery. Some books lay on the floor in a corner, but the centre of the room was clear of furniture.

French could see everything in the room with one exception. At the side of the fireplace was a closed cupboard. Possibly this might contain something useful.

He had stepped across the room and put his hand on the cupboard door knob when the feel of a presence, rather than an actual sound, caused him to swing suddenly round. A man had entered and was watching him.

French stared in his turn. This was not Pyke. This was a smaller man and hollow of cheek, dark in colouring and with a pair of keen eyes uncovered by glasses. A friend of Pyke's, no doubt.

But this man was vaguely familiar. That he had seen him at no distant time French felt certain. Then the man moved slightly and French noticed the marks of pince-nez on his nose. As he did so he remembered where he had seen, not him, but his photograph, and he stared spellbound in speechless amazement.

For a moment neither moved, then French recovered himself. With a step forward he cried: 'Stanley Pyke, I arrest you on a charge of—'

He stopped. Had he gone mad? Wasn't the dead man

Stanley Pyke? How could he be charged with murdering himself?

French felt his brain reel. But he grew more and more convinced that the man was indeed Stanley Pyke. Therefore the victim must have been, of course, Berlyn! How the whole thing had happened French could not form an idea, but he saw that this could be straightened out later. For the moment, his course was clear. He must arrest this man.

Though these thoughts flashed through French's mind at lightning speed, in his extremity of surprise he remained for a moment speechless, his eyes fixed on the other's face. Then a slight movement of the man's right arm attracted his attention and he glanced downwards. Pyke had taken an automatic pistol from his coat pocket and was holding it steadily pointed at French's heart.

'No, Mr French,' he said quietly, and the voice was the voice of the man he had believed was Jefferson. 'I don't think so. You've not got me, but I've got you. Put up your hands.'

As he slowly obeyed, French saw that he was in imminent danger of his life. Pyke's features were set in an expression of ruthless determination and there was murder in his eyes. He went on speaking in quiet, grim tones.

'It's true that I may not get away with it, but I'm going to have a try. You won't, anyway. I suppose you have men posted below?'

'I've men coming up the stairs after me,' French lied.

'That so? They're not hurrying. I shall have plenty of time before they get to the top. I'm going to shoot you now, Mr Joseph French. The upper part of this building is deserted; no one across the way and only a couple of old women on the floor below. They're all out at work. I shall be across the roof and down the next stairs before your men are half-way up these. I may carry it off and I may not, but I'll not be taken alive.'

'And Mrs Berlyn?'

Pyke's eyes flashed.

'They'll not get her, either. I know where she is and I'll pick her up. Say your prayers, Mr French. You've only got seconds to live.'

He slowly raised the pistol from the level of his side pocket to that of his eyes, keeping it first directed to French's heart and then to his head. In those few moments French tasted the bitterness of death. He knew instinctively that the man meant to carry out his threat and he was powerless to prevent him. Covered by Pyke's steady gaze as well as by his pistol no sudden spring would help him. They were only about five feet apart, but the man would fire before he could reach across half the distance. Carter and Harvey were at the bottom of a hundred feet of stairs. They wouldn't even hear the shot. A numbing fear crept into French's heart while thoughts of his wife and visions of scenes in his past life floated before his mind's eye. And all the time he was desperately, despairingly racking his brains to find a way of escape.

An instinctive urge that he must gain time at all costs took possession of him. Then, as he was trying to evolve some further bluff, an idea shot into his mind which suggested a glimmering of hope. It was a terribly faint glimmering; the chances were a thousand to one against him. Almost a forlorn hope, but it was all he could think of.

Neither man had moved during the interview. French had swung round from the cupboard and was still facing the door through which the other had entered. Pyke, on his part, had his back to the door and was facing the cupboard.

French instantly began to act a part. First, he wished to show fear. Here he had not to act; the emotion was only too genuine. Indeed, had he let himself go he would have been paralysed with terror. Therefore, as he spoke his eyes were agonised, his features distorted, and his voice thick and trembling.

'Don't be a fool, Pyke. You can do better than that. I've sense enough to know when I'm beaten. My life's of more value to me than success in a case. You want your liberty and I want my life. I see a way in which we can each get what we want.'

Pyke did not relax his attitude.

'I believe you're a damned liar,' he said, only with a stronger adjective. 'However, shove ahead with your plan. Any tricks or movements and you're a dead man.'

'If you were once clear of me,' French went on, evincing the most transparent evidences of terror, 'you could walk out over the roof, or even past my men, and they'd never suspect you. They're here to look for a quite different man. And the mere fact that you walked quietly downstairs after I had gone up to look for Jefferson would show that you were not the man I was after. That all right, so far?'

'Well?'

French allowed his eyes to roam over the room, but without making any change in his expression. After the briefest pause, he went on:

'Now, to get away from me is the difficulty, for while I should be willing to give you my oath not to interfere, I don't suppose you would accept it. Well, this is my plan.'

Calling all his histrionic powers to his aid, French again glanced round the room, suddenly staying his gaze on the door. Then, with the whole strength of his will, he pretended to himself that he saw Carter entering. On this he fixed his mind, with the result that his eyes took on the appearance of definitely looking at something, while an expression of the utmost thankfulness and relief showed on his features. But he was quick to add the idea that Pyke must not follow what was in his mind, and he at once looked away and back to Pyke's face. With a fine effect of recovering a line of thought which had been disturbed, he continued, now trying to give the impression of faked fear.

'I propose that I withdraw to the kitchenette and there gag myself and tie myself up to your satisfaction. You, of course, would keep me covered all the time and it would be quite impossible for me to play you any trick. Or, if you preferred it, I could do the tying up in this room.'

Again he glanced at the door as if he could not keep his eyes off it. This time he slowly shifted the point at which he was looking to just behind Pyke, while he allowed relief and satisfaction to grow on his face. Once more he hurriedly withdrew his gaze and looked at Pyke.

'I noticed a clothes line in the kitchenette which would do,' he went on, but now absent-mindedly and giving quick, as if involuntary, glances behind Pyke. 'If you agree, I'll back in there and get it down. If I attempt to play you false you can shoot.'

He paused, and looking directly behind Pyke, allowed a slight triumphant smile to appear on his lips.

Pyke had obviously followed the direction of his glances and he had been getting more and more uneasy. At French's smile he could stand it no longer. For the tenth of a second he glanced behind him. And at that moment French, standing braced and ready, sprang. Like lightning he dropped his head while his left fist struck the other's right wrist upwards.

Instantly Pyke fired and a hot iron seemed to sear the crown of French's head. But he was not disabled. Seizing Pyke's right wrist with his left hand he drove with his right for the man's chin.

But Pyke ducked and he missed. Then the two men, clinching with their free hands, began a voiceless struggle for their lives. Pyke's desperate efforts were to turn the pistol inwards, French's to prevent him. Locked together, they swayed backwards and forwards. Then French tripped over a chair and they swung with a crash against the table. It gave way, and staggering across its wreckage, they fell. French found himself underneath and redoubled his efforts, but he was hampered by the blood from his wound, which ran down and blinded one of his eyes. Fortunately he was the stronger man, and in spite of his handicap slowly his strength and weight began to tell. Gradually he forced Pyke's arm round until the other had to roll over on his back to save its dislocation.

Both men were now gasping and sobbing from want of breath. But French, with a superhuman effort, dropped Pyke's left arm, and seizing his collar, twisted it tight. Pyke laid out with his free arm, but he was weakening, and French, spent and giddy, but thankful, felt he could hold on in spite of the blows and that the affair was now only a matter of time.

And then, lying grimly clinging to the choking man's collar, he felt a real thrill of delight as he saw the door slowly open, just as he had pictured it. Carter at last! It was over.

But it was not Carter who appeared. There, gazing down on them with amazement printed on her features, was Mrs Berlyn.

It did not take her long to appreciate the situation and with a muffled scream she threw herself on the heaving mass.

'Give me the pistol, Stanley,' she cried softly. 'I'll settle him.'

But Pyke was beyond coherent thought. Half-insensible, he still kept his hand locked and she could not release the fingers. French, seeing the end, put all his remaining strength into a shrill cry of 'Help,' before he felt the woman's fingers tighten round his throat.

Letting go of the now unconscious Pyke, he tried desperately to loosen their clinging grip. But he was too weak. Choking, he struggled impotently, while gradually it grew darker and he sank slowly into a roaring abyss of nothingness.

20

Conclusion

When French struggled back into consciousness he found himself lying on the floor of that upper room with Sergeant Carter bending solicitously over him.

'He's coming to,' he heard him say as if from a great distance. 'He'll be none the worse in a few minutes.'

'I'm all right,' French whispered faintly.

'What about—'

'Both safe as a house,' Carter answered. 'I thought you were taking too long over the job and was coming up the fire escape when I heard you shout. I whistled down the stairs for Harvey and ran on. Lucky, I got up in time. But it was a near thing, Mr French; just as near a thing as I should like to see. Don't you be in any hurry, you've all the day before you. Take a nip of this brandy that Harvey has brought.'

The stimulant made French once again feel his own man and he sat up to find that his assailants had been safely handcuffed. Mrs Berlyn sat in one of the wicker arm-chairs, deadly pale and with an expression of murderous hate in her eyes. Pyke was still unconscious and the others at once turned their attention to him, with the result that presently he too revived. The taxi was waiting and before many minutes had passed both prisoners were lodged in the cells.

When French sat down in his own room to think over this unexpected development he very soon saw that he had made a terrible error in his handling of the case. Never before had he blundered so inexcusably! The clue to the truth was there in his hand and he had missed it. Though, even now, he could not understand all that had happened, he saw enough to appreciate his mistake, to locate the point at which he had strayed from the right path.

He had accepted the identification of the remains; but on whose testimony? On that of the criminals, Mrs Berlyn and the man whom he had thought was Jefferson Pyke. Of course, at the time at which he interviewed them he had no idea of their connection with the crime and, therefore, no reason to doubt their statements, but his error came in just here; that by the time he began to suspect them the identification was so firmly fixed in his mind that he overlooked the fact that it depended on them. If he had remembered that supremely important point, he would have questioned the dead man's identity. This would have led him to investigate, even more closely than he had, the movements of the Pykes, and, no doubt, he would have thus discovered the impersonation which had been carried out.

The first question, then, which demanded solution was: If the man whom he had thought was Jefferson Pyke was really his cousin, where was Jefferson himself?

Like a man in a dream French went back to Kepple Street. Was Mrs Welsh *absolutely* sure that the Mr Pyke who had engaged her rooms on the 22nd July was the same man who had occupied them ever since? Mrs Welsh, when at last she had been made to understand the question, was absolutely sure.

If she were right, Stanley's impersonation of Jefferson must have begun on that 22nd of July. They had both been at the Houston in the morning. By the evening Jefferson, the real Jefferson, apparently had vanished.

Then suddenly French remembered the episode of the broken basin. It had not occurred to him before, but now he wondered if there was not more here than met the eye. The accident was unlikely. Had the basin been deliberately broken to help on some trick?

He went back to the Houston and once again interviewed the reception clerk. But she could add nothing to her former statement. Then he re-examined the chambermaid. From her, at last, he obtained a new fact, an apparently trifling fact, but what a difference it made in his conclusion!

The girl had stated that the gentleman who broke the basin had told her that he had overslept himself and had asked her to see that his friend in No. 351 was awake. She had gone and found that the friend was already up. Now, French learned that by 'up' she had meant that the man was up and dressed and had left his room.

At this a light shone into French's mind. He retired to a corner of the smoking-room, and after half an hour's hard thinking he reached a detailed solution.

He saw that it would be possible for Stanley to arrive at the hotel and engage two rooms, ostensibly for himself and his cousin. He would go to his own room after explaining that his cousin would arrive later in the day. After impressing his personality on the staff he would go out, make up as Jefferson, return with more luggage and occupy the second room which had been engaged. He would sleep in Jefferson's room and in the morning ring early for shaving water, get up, dress, take his luggage down, pay his bill, and leave the hotel. Then, hurrying back, he would slip into his own room unobserved, go to bed and ring again for hot water, giving the maid the message about his friend. Lest the incident should be forgotten in the event of future inquiries, he would smash the basin, thus impressing his identity on all concerned.

That was what Stanley had done, French was now pretty sure, and he despatched wires to the French and Italian police asking if the same trick had been carried out in Paris and at Grasse and San Remo. After some time, there were replies. It had been carried out in Paris, but not at the other two places. At the latter there was no doubt that both men had been present.

Jefferson Pyke had therefore disappeared at some point between Grasse and Paris, and French soon saw that there was nothing for it but to go to the Riviera and himself inquire into the men's movements. Accordingly, after consultation with his chief, he obtained a letter to the French police, and travelling to Marseilles, began work. Slowly and painfully he traced the two from Marseilles to San Remo, to Monte Carlo, to Grasse, and finally to Nice. And there, in the pleasure city on the shores of the Mediterranean, he came on the explanation he sought.

For at Nice, Jefferson Pyke had died. At first, knowing what he did, French had suspected foul play. But in this he found he was mistaken. Jefferson had been taken ill at his hotel and had at once been moved to a hospital. There he had been operated on for appendicitis. French saw the doctor who had had charge of the case and learned the details. There had been complications and the operation could not save him.

French was deeply chagrined at his failure to learn so essential a fact at an earlier stage in his investigation. He swore great oaths to his gods that never, *never* again should he fail to follow up to the very end every clue which presented itself, whether he thought it likely to prove valuable or not.

With identity of murderer and victim established, a comparatively short further inquiry sufficed to clear up the details of the affair which were still in doubt. And dreadful reading they made.

It seemed that soon after Phyllis Considine came to Ashburton as the bride of Charles Berlyn she found she had made a terrible mistake in her marriage. The feeling which she had imagined was love died away and she saw herself tied for life to a man whom she disliked. A mutual coldness inevitably, resulted, which rapidly widened as the husband also found himself disillusioned. On Phyllis's side less than a year sufficed to turn it into a bitter hatred.

Under these miserable circumstances she began to look elsewhere for companionship, and Stanley Pyke, who found himself strongly attracted to his former playmate, was only too ready to fill the breach. They saw a good deal of each other and the inevitable happened. Before long, both were deeply in love.

Though they were careful to act discreetly when under observation, they were not careful enough, and Berlyn became aware of what was going on. He at once remonstrated with his wife, finally telling her in no ambiguous terms that, if given cause, he would not hesitate to divorce her. If this had been all Phyllis would, no doubt, have eagerly seized so complete a solution of her difficulty, but both she and Pyke saw that it was by no means all. Berlyn, as joint owner of the business, would certainly have dismissed Pyke as well as cutting Phyllis out of his will. The couple would therefore have been without money or prospects. This she was not prepared for, and while admitting unwise behaviour, she denied that there was anything serious in her relations with Pyke and undertook that Berlyn should have no further cause of complaint. Then she began to meet Pyke secretly, and gradually the terrible solution which they afterwards adopted grew subconsciously in both their minds. If Berlyn should die the whole situation would be straightened out.

From that time the idea of murder was never far from the thoughts of either. But they could see no way in which the dreadful deed could be safely accomplished. Pyke, however, was sufficiently callous and far-seeing to suggest the flirtation with Domlio, partly as a proof that the lady's feeling for himself was a thing of the past, and partly lest a scapegoat should afterwards be wanted in connection with the murder.

Then came Jefferson's visit and the cousins' holiday and Jefferson's unexpected death. Pyke was about to give up the tour and come home, when it suddenly struck him that here was the solution for which he and Phyllis had been looking. He travelled up to Paris and there spent a few days in working out his plan.

The idea of diverting suspicion from the murder of Berlyn by staging the accident on the moor had already occurred to him. But this plan had the objection that it involved his own disappearance as well as Berlyn's. If, however, he disappeared, the whole fruits of the murder would be lost, as he was committing it simply to enable him to marry Phyllis. Jefferson's death showed him how he might escape this dilemma.

He would, in brief, murder Berlyn, stage the accident on the moor and disappear—as Stanley Pyke. He would immediately reappear—as Jefferson. By impersonating Jefferson he could marry Phyllis and get all his cousin's money as well.

In this scheme there was a risk of course, but the chances of anyone learning of Jefferson's death were, he thought, sufficiently remote to make the scheme practicable. As soon as he could without suspicion, he would go abroad, where Phyllis could presently follow him.

At first the plan seemed full of snags, but as he thought over it he saw ways of overcoming one difficulty after another until the whole ghastly affair grew coherent and feasible. When he returned to Ashburton the scheme was cut and dry and he had only to get Phyllis's approval and promise of help.

Jefferson, the real Jefferson, had already visited Ashburton, but he had only been seen closely by the landlady, Mrs Billing, the Berlyns and their servants, Domlio, and one or two others. Of these the only one Stanley need interview was Mrs Billing, and he felt sure he could deceive her. Sergeant Daw, with whom in his inquiries about the tragedy he would have most to do, had only seen Jefferson in the distance. Personation would therefore be possible.

The first thing necessary was to prove Jefferson still alive. Stanley found it easier than he had expected. From a theatrical supplies shop he bought shoes with false internal heels to increase his height, padded underclothes to give him the necessary girth, rubber discs to wear inside his cheeks to alter the shape of his face, and glasses. When in addition to these

261

he wore Jefferson's clothes and copied, as best he could, Jefferson's walk, speech and deportment, it was not surprising that the unsuspecting and unobservant persons at Ashburton should be taken in.

On his way home he carried out the tricks at the hotels, then taking the room in Kepple Street. For some hectic weeks he managed to live at Kepple Street as Jefferson and at Ashburton as Stanley. His continual absences from Ashburton, travelling for his firm, enabled him to put in the necessary appearances in Kepple Street, where he gave out that in the intervals he was making business trips in England and France.

He saw that, by a judicious interview with the clerk of the Tavistock Urban District Council, he could arrange for the evening journey across the moor. His first idea had been to dispose of Berlyn's body on the way back by throwing it into one of the small mires close to the road. But when he considered this in detail he realised that the difficulties were overwhelming, just as had been suggested to French by Sergeant Daw. He therefore devised the episode of the duplicator in order to provide a means for its removal from the district. He thought that if he could throw it into some estuary from which it would be carried out to sea, he would be safe. At first, he proposed doing so from the bridge at Teignmouth, then he saw that this would be too near home. If by some chance the body were discovered it might be connected with a local disappearance. The Burry Inlet, which also he knew, next occurred to him. This seemed to meet all his requirements and the date of a suitable tide became the foundation on which the rest of the plan was built.

In London he bought the second-hand typewriter and wrote the letters ordering the duplicator and crane-lorry on paper he had obtained from the L.M.S. hotels. These letters he handed to the tobacconist, Ganope, who for a consideration undertook to post them on the proper dates. Neither he nor Phyllis were therefore in London when they were sent out, though he called in person at the hotels for the replies. He similarly obtained the duplicate magneto. This he handed to Phyllis and she damaged it and ran it on the car until it gave up, then replacing the original.

On the fatal night every movement of each conspirator was carefully timed and cut-and-dry to the last detail. When near the works on the return journey Stanley called out to Berlyn to stop, saying that he had seen a man lying on the road. He jumped out and ran round the car, and on Berlyn following him he slipped behind his victim and sandbagged him. Hastily throwing the body into the car, he drove to the works' gate. There he was met by Phyllis, who two hours earlier, in the interval of her party, had already drugged Gurney's tea in the way French had surmised.

At the works, Phyllis helped Pyke to carry the body to the packing shed. After replacing Gurney's drugged tea with fresh, she put her bicycle in the tonneau of the car and drove out to the selected spot on the moor. She changed the magneto and made the two lines of footmarks by putting on shoes of Berlyn's, which she had brought for the purpose. Then, mounting her bicycle, she returned to the works. The bicycle and the magneto she hid in a clump of shrubs, waiting until Pyke came out to say that the ghastly job in the works was complete. She then went home, silently let herself in, replaced Berlyn's shoes in his room, changed her clothes, wakened the maid and called up Sergeant Daw.

In the meantime Stanley Pyke rode on the bicycle to Colonel Domlio's, dropped the clothes and other objects into the well and continued on his way to Plymouth. There he left the bicycle in a dark entry in the lower part of the town where he was sure it would speedily be found and annexed. He took the first train to London, returning to Ashburton in the character of Jefferson on receipt of Daw's wire about the tragedy.

Such was the plan, and had the conspirators been sure their actions would have remained unquestioned they would have stopped there. But both were afraid that in some unforeseen way suspicion might be aroused, and they took several other steps in the hope of turning such possible suspicion on to other persons.

First, they considered it necessary that, should the crate be discovered, the body therein should be taken as Stanley Pyke's. This would effectually prevent a doubt arising as to Jefferson's identity. Pyke therefore changed his own underclothes with those of the dead man and dropped his own suit down the well, while both he and Phyllis stated that the birth-mark on Berlyn's arm was really on Pyke's.

To carry on the same deception, Pyke decided to make up as Berlyn while disposing of the crate. In height and build he was, in his disguise, not unlike Berlyn. The chief difference between them was their colouring, both the Pykes being dark and Berlyn fair. Stanley, therefore, dyed his hair and lightened his complexion before going to Wales.

The episode of the blackmailing letter was designed with a similar object. Phyllis Berlyn had staged the farce of the twisted ankle. She had fallen into Domlio's arms in such a way that a photograph might have really been a profitable investment to a blackmailer. Pyke, had of course, forged the letter. The confederates hoped that the taking out of the car which they believed would result, together with the finding of the articles in the well, which they thought a competent detective might achieve, would throw the suspicion on Domlio.

With regard to money, Pyke had resolved on a bold stroke. French found that he had instructed a firm of solicitors in London to get in touch with Jefferson's lawyers in the Argentine for the purpose of arranging the sale of Jefferson's property there. He had forged Jefferson's signature to the necessary documents, and the matter was well advanced.

This piece of greed had prevented Stanley from leaving London and had caused him to rent the Victory Place flat as a refuge in case Kepple Street got too hot to hold him. Flight thither under such circumstances had been decided on, and therefore when danger threatened, only the time and method of reaching it remained to be settled.

As all Berlyn's property went to Phyllis under the deceased's will, she also would have been well off, so that when the two took up their abode in a rather out of the way part of Algeria, as they had intended, they would have been comparatively rich.

But thanks to Evan Morgan's desire for a fishing expedition on the last day of his holidays, together with Inspector French's steady pegging away at a puzzling and wearisome case, these evil hopes were frustrated. Some three weeks after the next assizes both Stanley Pyke and Phyllis Berlyn paid for their crime with their lives, leaving the ownership of Jefferson's money as a juicy morsel on which the lawyers of England and the Argentine could pile up fees to their hearts' content.

For French the case had not been an unmixed triumph. Though in the end he had taken the criminals and added to his reputation with his superiors, in his heart of hearts he knew that he had been saved by the skin of his teeth alone, and that he had had a lesson in the danger of neglecting to follow up unlikely clues to the very end which would last him for his life. But, on the whole, he was satisfied.